# IN KITHAIRON'S SHADOW

A Novel of Ancient Greece
and the Persian War

Jon Edward Martin

iUniverse, Inc.
New York  Lincoln  Shanghai

**In Kithairon's Shadow**

A Novel of Ancient Greece and the Persian War

iUniverse, Inc.

For information address:
iUniverse, Inc.
2021 Pine Lake Road, Suite 100
Lincoln, NE 68512
www.iuniverse.com

ISBN: 0-595-29906-7 (pbk)
ISBN: 0-595-66075-4 (cloth)

Printed in the United States of America

# Historical Note

In 480 BC the Persian Empire, under the rule of Xerxes I, embarked upon the invasion of Europe. His army was vast, its ranks of Egyptians, Bactrians, Medes, Scythians, Persians, Indians and scores of other nations drawn from across Asia. In late summer of that year a small holding force of Greek warriors, led by King Leonidas of Sparta and his bodyguard of 300 heavy infantrymen, fought and perished at the mountain pass of Thermopylae. Delayed briefly by this glorious stand, Xerxes' army swarmed into Greece, marching irresistibly toward Athens. A month later the largest sea battle of the ancient world took place in the Bay of Salamis, where through a combination of skill, subterfuge and luck the outnumbered Greek fleet defeated the Persians. Although reeling from this setback Xerxes' army still possessed the larger portion of Greece, and it would require one final confrontation to settle the fate of this tiny country, and the future of Western civilization.

*"I shall fight as long as I live, and not think it more important to be alive than to be free, and I shall not fail the taxiarch or the enomotarch, be he alive or dead, and I shall not retreat unless the commander leads away, and I will do whatever the generals command. Those who die, of the allied warriors, I shall bury on the spot and leave no one unburied…"*

—Oath taken by the allied Greeks before the battle of Plataea

# CHAPTER 1

▼

"They are all dead."

For a moment the slave's announcement suspended the banter. "Who are dead?" asked Myronides as he swirled the wine in his kylix.

"The Spartans. Thermopylai has fallen." This news struck them breathless; no army stood between the invaders and violet-crowned Athens.

"Impossible," said Praxis with a snort.

The evening's host, Myronides, rising from his divan, commanded the attention of all. For each of his banquets, or symposions as they are called, he would spare scant coin on his appearance: his beard trimmed as if by a sculptor to project the strength of his jaw and outline perfectly formed lips; his fine linen chiton dyed in rare Phoenician sea-purple; the garland upon his head fashioned from the choicest blossoms the agora had to offer. "Due in no small part to Themistokles, we cannot field an army. The bulk of our men are at sea," he said shaking his head. Presently Myronides called for the serving girl to fetch the orange pitcher, the one with the Thasian wine, for his symposion now traded the shallow saucer-like kylix cups for deep kothons. Their capacity in drink would make for looser tongues. He would know his guests' thoughts on the stratagem of Themistokles, this wooden wall, as he so quaintly names it—an attempt to connect a sacred presentiment to his insistence on war by sea. The scheme apparently failed at Artemesion, the seaward flank of Thermopylai. Where could it succeed? Wine soon unshackled the words of the diners while at the same time numbing them to the magnitude of the defeat. The host waved at the entertainers to disport them with music.

"Myronides. This flute-boy is much too quick for me. Have you another, more round one?" asked Lykidas as he rolled from his couch, hand out stretched fingering the empty air.

"Now I understand why you lie about here in Athens while your brothers contend at Olympia. All the fast boys are running in the games there," laughed Myronides, "but even the slowest here would prove too swift for your thick legs and swollen belly."

The others laughed with him, sipped their wine genteelly and talked of the fleet and its unpredicted retreat. Every one of the dining club derided Themistokles for his perceived bungling of the war thus far—and for his relinquishment of naval command to Sparta. Only here amongst the closest companions and out of earshot of the demos—the mob—did they speak plainly and in complaint of this man of the people.

"Friends, I ask this of you to ponder," said Myronides as he plucked a sliver of boarfish from the relish platter. "Does the fleet fight now to save Athens or Themistokles?" His question so softly posed boomed like a thunderclap with its implication, silencing all present in the andros to rumination. He dipped a long-fingered hand into the wash bowl, stroking the water like a musician thrumming a lyre, waiting for a response.

"If our savior Themistokles did not sail with the fleet, then where, I ask, would we meet the invader?" interjected Praxis. He drank slowly and thought carefully. His hard-etched face, framed by a raven beard, grew grave under his words; his garlanded head now seemed absurdly adorned.

"On the plains of Boiotia. I declare that is where we should have fought. Men of the hoplite class. Citizens who have a genuine stake in

Athens future. There we would prevail over the Persians as we did ten years ago at Marathon." Myronides words were thick with wine now. "Not improvidently leave our fate to so many out-of-work potters and shopkeepers—these newly elevated citizens of Athens," he added. The wine also fired his cheeks to rubicund, with abhorrence for fleet and the mob that peopled it. He needed but meager drink to bring him here.

"By Zeus! Must we hear of Marathon again?" pleaded Lykidas. "We, your mortal companions, are not so fortunate to revel in the glory of that day as you are, and remind us, as you do, of your part in it. And these shopkeepers have been citizens since the days of Kleisthenes," he said assuredly. "Simply put, you despise the navy because your son now serves aboard the Eleutheria as a marine."

"Despise might be too sharp a word," countered Myronides. "Distrust—that may be more apt, for I cannot rely on the fickleness of these sailors. How can a man be trusted when everything he owns can be carried on his back?"

"Because a man lives his life modestly does not make him a criminal," remonstrated Praxis.

"Empty purses cry to be filled, and by any means at hand." Myronides gestured for the pitcher. "We, on the other hand have more to risk than an oar, a cushion, and a fist full of obols. We are compelled to stand and fight."

"Athens is now a maritime city. We cannot hope to prevail without the fleet's protection," rejoindered Lykidas. He did indeed favor the fleet and the leadership of Themistokles, for if the fleet fought he did not, and like the Spartans he preferred this course of action.

Praxis, Lykidas and Myronides debated the merit of this expedition long past the threshold of gentlemanly discourse. Now they argued as politicians. The others—Skiron, Aischines and Aigisias—lounged in a haze of wine, entertained by the musicians and apart from the seriousness of their comrades.

From the darkened portal that led to the courtyard a lone figure slunk into the andros; the man stood wordless, waiting to be acknowledged by the host. In a pause of intensity—an intensity that dominated the atmosphere of the three talkers—Myronides flicked his gaze at the man in the doorway. "Well Krios! What is it now?" he bellowed impatiently, for he felt his argument had formed beyond assault and only a few more words would complete the logic needed to convince, at the very least, Lykidas.

"Master." The word barely slipped from Krios' mouth. "The warship Eleutheria has been captured."

Myronides, his knees weakened by these words stumbled rearwards until his legs slammed into the couch, plunging him to a seat.

*     *     *     *

For a week now Asfandiar and the heavy cavalry of the Great King Xerxes, Lord of Asia, loitered in Mallis waiting for the infantry to clear the pass that leads into central Greece. The very road to Athens—this arrogant little city that instigated rebellion and defied the suzerainty of Persia—now lay open. The battle, he had been told, was won the day prior, but the Great King sent not soldiers into the open pass but engineers, pioneers and laborers, armed with spade, pick and other implements of excavation. With their task seemingly completed Asfandiar's squadron now rode south to the pass the Greeks called the Hot Gates. His troop crossed several rivers, and as the road carried them very near the sea, to his spear-side, tucked into a cleft in the mountains, he spotted the stony citadel of Trachis, this not far from the cliffs that penned them. This dusty, rock-choked land evoked a certain uneasiness in him, for now he saw why his cavalry was kept apart from the battle; only infantry could contend in such a compressed and rugged tract.

The gold bands encircling his arms jingled in time with the horse's canter. He reined up. Now he curled his long beard up to his nose, to inhale the obliging perfume as an inoculation against the malodor of battle.

Ahead men were dragging tree branches and sowing fallen leaves like seeds across the dark hollows of freshly filled trenches. The smell of turned earth mingled with the lingering stench of battle; death hung invisible between the cliffs and the sea, drawing spirals of cawing gulls closer. Oddly the corpses of Greek warriors seemed as though they had been carefully arranged about the floor of the pass, positioned with design and not in the least exhibiting typical morbid randomness of the battlefield. Here and there the trousered form of a Mede, Bactrian, Sogdian or the like could be seen, but as he proceeded to the defile marked by the springs, most all the stripped bodies were Greeks.

An earth-bedaubed slave near a small hillock commenced to gather up broken sword grips and fractured pieces of what days before had been the massive bronze-covered shields of the Greeks, these all shattered. Not much use as trophies and surely worthless for battle, he continued tossing them into an old grain wagon. As he stalked about, he brushed aside arrows, thousands of which bristled from the hill as though it were a massive cache for the King's archers. Across the choked roadway lay other corpses too, ones of squared stone and timbers, part of a wall that once had spanned the pass. Asfandiar threaded his way amongst the detritus, coming to the base of the hillock and the scavenging slave.

There looming above him, bodiless and upon a tall cornel stake hung the vile Spartan Leonidas—or so read the parchment nailed beneath him—his long hair and beard snowy with age.

"Why a week?" asked Asfandiar to himself as he trotted through the sprawl of death, measuring the number of slain—several hundred Greeks and half again as many Persians. The rumor mongers said thousands of the Great King's men had perished. This scene spoke of a brief and violent struggle. "Why an entire week?"

\*     \*     \*     \*

Nikandros crouched in a pool of oil beside the leaking stone bowl, cursing. He had no more cork to patch the seeping joint, and pitch, well pitch would tinge the flavor most regrettably. He traced the fracture with his knobby, calloused fingers, then rose hesitatingly against the protest of his knees.

"I told you," reminded his father Pankratios in his usual growl, "to soak the lever first. It has been a dry summer."

Nikandros most always heeded his father's instruction, but there was so much to do, for his brother was away with the army, leaving him with only a single laborer and three sons. One of his boys, Theron, was recovering from a broken leg and in the care of his sister-in-law.

The lever was in fact dust dry, and it sundered on the first downstroke. Not only did it snap in two but Nikandros and the severed timber smashed into the stone mill-bowl, cracking it, while at the same time releasing a flood of pressings. His father would remind him of his hasty and thoughtless doings, most especially when it meant thinning his already meager income from oil.

His family's land had formerly produced the best olives in Tegea, with the slopes expertly groomed, robust and bountiful trees grew upon them, and of course these produced the utmost flavorful and sought-after oil. That is until Nikandros superintended the groves. Granted, in his younger days his father had hired a score or more for the harvest, and his wife assisted in managing the crop with him, but Nikandros' staff was much depleted; he could barely afford the price of a single farmhand and his wife had been dead since last autumn. Also, as the older Pankratios would often admonish, Nikandros did not honor Demeter as the goddess deserved, as he had throughout his life. Nikandros' yield apportioned but meager first fruit sacrifices to her, and in turn she withheld her blessings.

He continued to stare at the weeping seams of his oil-press, rubbing his uneven beard to the point of combustion, hoping the leak would seal by itself. From the road beyond his fenced yard he heard the braying of a mule; upon it rode his neighbor Diagoras.

"They've returned," Diagoras yelled to Pankratios, flicking his mule with a thumb stick, keeping the animal to its pace.

Nikandros' younger brother Athamos had been gone now a few days short of a month, part of the small Peloponnesian force that marched north following their Spartan allies to Thermopylai. So far from home and in a land of Hellenes where he had never tread, nor had his father or his father's father, his brother stood amongst strangers defending strangers. But loyally, as the small city-state of Tegea was to her large and powerful neighbor of Sparta to the south, she sent her sons and fathers to fight where the Spartans led.

"Come Nikandros," instructed his father, "We'll greet your brother properly and hear of the battle at the Hot Gates." He paused, staring. "Look at you!" he shouted, throwing up his hands.

"What?" Nikandros bowed back a bit, trying to inspect his appearance. He inhaled deeply. His face puckered, then he hopped on one leg while pulling the sole of his sandal into view. He hustled to the water trough, doused himself, then kicked off the sandals. Now wet and barefoot he looked like a wild man, a companion to the god Pan, his soaked chiton clinging to him, his tangled hair and beard a seeming invitation for a pair of homeless larks to nest.

Nikandros carried his youngest son Alketes upon his shoulders, thankful to be apart from the problem of the oil press and at the same time hoping that the farmhand Selagos would repair the olive mill while he departed for the town. By mid afternoon they sauntered by the Temple of Demeter, past the bouleterion where the council met and into the agora. Bands of young men stood ringed by townsfolk, and these offered cups of wine, flaps of bread and fist-sized hunks of cheese to the survivors. Beside each warrior stood a pair of gaunt attendants—either younger brothers, slaves or freemen unfit for combat—

all shouldering panoplies of armor slung litter-like from spears and wooden staves. So many of the men bore wounds.

Nikandros looked up at his son and spoke, "Do you see uncle?"

The boy shaded his eyes with a salute and scanned the chattering crowd in the agora. "Yes pappa. Over there," he shouted while stabbing the air with his fingers.

The elder Pankratios slid off the mule and hobbled away to where the boy pointed. Nikandros followed, correcting his course through the observations of his perched son and soon stood in front of his brother. Athamos, sitting upon a corner of the fountain trough, dipped his cloak into the water, then swabbed his face with it. His arms were hatched with blade wounds, both thighs bound in linen.

"My son!" the old man bellowed as he stepped forward, "the gods have preserved you. We feared the worst."

Athamos barely had the presence of thought to lift his face to respond. Nikandros lowered Alketes from his shoulders, depositing the boy gently on the fountain's edge next to his uncle. Then he slowly crouched, bringing his eyes to his brother's. He stared into them; they were hollow as in death, and it frightened him. "Brother, what happened at the Gates?" he whispered

Suddenly life flickered in his eyes. "Destruction," he answered.

\*        \*        \*        \*

Weeks before he watched from this very spot atop the north-facing slopes of his father's farm amongst the vines as the army of the allied Hellenes marched toward Lamia and the Hot Gates. Now instead men poured southward over the land, men not from Hellas but Asia. Eurydamos seemed to find small comfort that his polis of Thebes had supported the aims of the Great King, abandoned as it was by her sister cities once Thermopylai had fallen. The small contingent of hoplites that did fight at the pass, allied with the Spartans and others, ingloriously surrendered their arms to Xerxes' hordes on the final day of battle. These survivors now trudged along the road to the city, kicking up veils of dust as they moved along slowly and disheartened, for it was these few who had opposed collaboration with the Persians. They knew now a greater discomfort than the branded mark of the Great King upon their foreheads awaited them at the hands of their own countrymen. Eurydamos stared at this melancholy procession, spinning a twig of laurel between his lips.

"And you, my son, had wished to go with them," said Timagenides as he reined up beside him. "And what is that in your mouth! Are you a bumpkin farm-hand?"

Eurydamos said nothing, letting the sprig tumble from his mouth. His eyes locked upon the beaten column of warriors, as squadrons of Persians and Medes galloped by, swirling like water around a single rock centered in a fast-moving stream; their dust erased the marchers from sight. He admired their horsemanship, these Persians, for in fact only the Thessalians and his own countrymen from Thebes had mastered this art here in Hellas, and it was odd to see so many accomplished riders. He twisted the reins around his slender fingers, fingers that had never endured neither callous nor blister, fidgeting away his anger.

From his vantage Eurydamos could see far into the plain beyond; the wheat and barley harvest was in, spared from trampling by the barbarian horde, for to the very limits of his vision men, like swarms of black ants, smothered the land.

"We will all profit from this alliance, Eurydamos."

"Will we father? Will our mark show any less than theirs?" he said directing Timagenides' glance to the homecoming warriors.

*       *       *       *

The snap and thud of ax upon wood thundered a thousand fold across the Isthmos. Above flaming Helios appeared to pause mid course to assure all of his power; even for midsummer the heat seemed amplified somehow. Sunlight danced wildly upon the swells in the Gulf of Korinth and not even the whisper of a breeze lifted today from the face of the sea. This day was beyond bright.

Across the length of the breastworks and wall, contingents from each city worked their section, scrambling bands of motley men, hardly distinctive as a group, but certainly so as individuals, except for the Spartans. Distinguished by their uniform garb, long, eight-locked hair and clean shaven upper lips, they appeared as a massive crimson pennant, swathing the center of the works.

Amomphoretos labored amongst the other Spartiates on their section of the wall, assisted by his Helot battle-servant Prokles, and not in the least burdened by his task. Earth-filled baskets piled two men tall stretched between old stone towers and newly hewn log walls. Nearby the Mantineans whittled wicked looking points onto their timbers before planting them into the soil. The wall grew quickly.

"Another month," groaned Kallikrates as he heaved a bark-stripped log upon his shoulder. "I pray we have that long," he added walking over to a scaffold. From above two Helots snatched the log, struggling a bit with its weight, and then slipped one end into a prepared hole atop the earthworks.

"A year of months and this wall might be complete," exclaimed Amompharetos. "Battlements and towers will require stone, not earth to construct," he added, crumbling a handful of the dry soil with his fingers.

"Then why do they toil so deliberately?" asked Kallikrates as he poked his fingers in the direction of the other soldiers from the Peloponnese.

"Because the fools that they are reckon the spoils of Athens will satisfy Xerxes. They talk as though this wall will never look upon the barbarians."

Abruptly, as so often is the case with these warriors, their discourse stopped; they had expressed what they wished and disdained persiflage. On for an hour or more Amompharetos and his companion hewed and planted timbers. All around activity slowed, but not with the Spartans. The heat did not task them. Now the Korinthians tossed good-natured jibes at them.

"Look at them," bellowed a sweat-soaked man as he tugged at his chiton; it clung to him pulling at each movement of his arms. "They are not men, these Spartans."

"They are the infernal machines of Ares, or Enyalios, as they call their raging god of war," laughed another as he leaned on his spade. "They dare not tire until ordered so by their polemarch."

"Friend, so much of your strength is dispensed in a wagging tongue," quipped Kallikrates, displaying his ever-present grin. "Do you need my servant to knead your weary muscles? Or perhaps you would prefer a linen parasol to help shield you from the sun?"

The loudest of the Korinthians bounded up the partially con-structed barrier using it as his speaking platform. "I have always been told that you Lakedaimonians never stoop to such menial tasks. They tell me that the ax and spade are as foreign to you as are letters and learning."

"When it is the spade that wins battles that is our weapon. As far as learning is concerned we are well taught to speak of lofty things only with lofty thinkers. To you I can only offer silence." Amompharetos finished his riposte with a disarming grin, initiating a bout of laughter from all within earshot. Even the flummoxed Korinthian atop the berm chuckled.

Still carrying a bit of laughter with them the Korinthians dropped their tools and walked off to a grove where servants had gathered amongst the food wagons.

"Did you hear of Pantites?" questioned Amompharetos as he paused studying the gleaming edge of the ax. Now he ran his thumb across it.

"Yes," replied Kallikrates shaking the long, inky hair from his eyes. "Found swinging behind his mess hall."

"Better he had died at the Gates. Now only Aristodemos remains. And he marked as a Trembler." Amompharetos could not comprehend how these two had absurdly chosen life over a glorious death, for he, like so many in his regiment longed to have been selected to march to Thermopylai. He had pleaded his case with both his father and King Leonidas.

"But some say Pantites was not even there. Sent by Leonidas to Thessalia in the north," said Kallikrates.

"No matter, for he is with them now," said Amompharetos as he unleashed the ax; chunks of wood exploded from the cleft log.

Presently the hacking of ax and scrape of spade which had all morning sung loudly began to fade. Servants toting flagons of wine scurried about the place as hands shot dry cups beneath the spigots. Amompharetos, Kallikrates and their regiment of Equals, as these citizens of Sparta are dubbed, fell into small bands surrounding the nearest wine-servant. Next cool water was distributed, not for drinking but for dousing away the heat. Amompharetos slipped his right arm through the dropped sleeve of his exomis—a garment worn only by workmen or Spartan warriors because of its versatility of design and the freedom it afforded—tugging it back to fall comfortably across his dark, thick muscled chest. Then with cupped hands he tossed water upon his face. In the scorching sun of midday the lambent water quickly vanished.

"Look there," directed Kallikrates as he pointed to a graying officer that leaned on the handle of a spade.

Both men stared at their commander as he wobbled over the implement, his knees flexing then straightening. A Helot rushed to Kleombrotos' side and thrust a shoulder under his arm as support. Another servant raced to help and within moments the two had dragged him to the shade of some thick-topped oaks.

"The heat taxes even him," observed Kallikrates. Now he emptied his kothon with a hearty swig.

"I would prefer battle to this my friend. And so would Kleombrotos," commented Amompharetos. "But what follows next is in the hands of the fleet and the Athenian Themistokles."

# CHAPTER 2

▼

Myronides had little time to mourn the death of his son. The body of Autolykos was returned to him by his friend Phormos, transported by mule through Locris, Boiotia and Attika, arriving a week before the Persians, for he was slain on the first day of battle off the point of land called the Ovens. During this initial inglorious encounter with the Persian fleet three Allied triremes were taken. Two had been captured and the third, Autolykos' warship, was forced to beach after being mauled by a squadron of the enemy. It was here that his son perished. Myronides contempt for the fleet and its master Themistokles festered; hate smothered his grief.

Although he had more than enough money to hire a sculptor to chisel a stele—a grave marker—this practice of elaborately marking graves had fallen out of favor. Nonetheless, he had the cremated bones of his son buried beside his father's upon their land near Phyle, then hurried back to Athens, to his townhouse and his wife. From there his entire household—two laundrywomen, one cook, a hostler, the steward Krios along with his wife Thyia made for Phaleron Bay. Thousands crammed the broad streets and narrow lanes, panicked by the news of the advancing Persian hordes. Order had been abandoned along with the city. Only at the final points of embarkation did Myronides encounter any representatives of civil authority, and these were recently appointed from the more desperate elements—men elevated in position by the opportunities that the chaos of invasion presented.

"What are they doing husband?" asked Thyia, looking ahead over the press of refugees that jammed the creaking quays. Suddenly a flurry of hoots issued from the front of the queue, drowning out the caws of whirling sea birds high above.

"Searching baggage. The Goddess's ornaments were stolen from the temple." He leaned to peer over the shoulder of the man in front. "Seems they have found something."

Clubbed fists flailed high and struck the man. He folded to his knees in sobs, gathering in the unwrapped contents of his parcel, penning it all with his arms.

"Isn't that your friend Lykidas?" Thyia said bobbing her head from side to side, straining to see over the crowd.

"It is he, the fool," remarked Myronides disdainfully. "He knew the stricture imposed—bring only the necessities. He should have stashed those trinkets under his house, for now Themistokles will use them to fill the purses of his rowers." Myronides had so shrewdly instructed his servants to hide the family's valuables in amongst the dead, buried between his father and the newly dug grave of Autolykos. No one dare disturb the bones of the dead, not even barbarians.

Lykidas, finally free of his beating whimpered, clutching his loot as he sat upon the wooden-planked quay; spittle hung in globs from his hair. The embroidery on his food-stained chiton glittered as he pulled it straight. Myronides, Thyia and their bevy of servants shuffled by him, halting before the inspectors that loomed at the gangway to the freighter. Around them hundreds crowded the sandy shore, desperate to cross the bay to the safety of the island of Salamis. Thousands had fled already.

"Open that, will you," instructed the leather-capped weasel in command. He stood astride a trove of confiscated valuables waving his hand at the hide bag slung from poles shouldered by two slaves. In unison they slipped the staves from them, lowering gently the bulging leather sack to the dock. Then one of the armed men pulled it apart. Out poured a blue-crested bronze helm, polished greaves, and a leather and scale thorax trimmed in blue to match the helmet's crown.

"Ye should trade all that for an oar an' a cushion," snickered a crewman of the freighter as he yanked on the mast's rigging. "But could ya pull an oar with such fine and dainty fingers?"

"Haven't seen the army in years," added another.

Myronides' face flushed, but he held his tongue. He would not be their sport today. Lykidas had taken care of that. A sudden breeze snatched his brimmed linen hat, carrying it out into the bay. Quickly he threw his hand up to rake his hair forward to cover his gleaming, high forehead.

"Onboard with you," snapped the weasel, apparently dismayed that no contraband had fallen to the dock.

Myronides and Thyia worked through the full deck of fleeing Athenians, he fighting the sense of nausea that afflicted him now among the tightly packed rabble that he despised. From the stench around him he surmised these *citizens* hardly were intimate with a bath, and laundering clothes a task beyond them.

"Thank Poseidon the voyage to the island of Salamis will prove a short one," announced Myronides.

Upon reaching the balustrade at the stern of the vessel, and mercifully separate from the mob, Myronides sucked the air deep into him, hoping its salty redolence would quell his nausea. Piercing the chatter of the crowded deck, muffled sobs drew his attention to Thyia, her back to him as she fought to subdue convulsions of grief. He reached out while moving to consider her veiled face. Even through the misty fabric he kenned the uncommon tears streaking her alabaster cheeks.

"What dear Thyia?"

"Look husband," she said pointing skyward. Far beyond the harbor, in the direction of the Aereopagos Hill but further still, a dark pall of smoke hung, fed by scores of twirling columns of smoke. Myronides knew the flames of his home fed those thickening clouds.

\*        \*        \*        \*

Asfandiar's squadron of cavalry tore through Attika with orders from their commander Masistios—burn everything in Athens. But these orders, he thought, for the time being could be ignored while he sought shelter from the sun and the acrid haze that choked the afternoon air. From atop a modest knoll he could see the walls of the city and the templed hill that dominated its far precincts.

*Such a small, poor and insignificant place,* he thought. *Hardly worth the notice of the Great King.* In peace and in war he had traveled to Babylon, Susa, Ecbatana, to Egyptian Thebes, Sardis and Ephesus. By comparison the Royal attentions given to this land of rocky farms and puny towns seemed so incongruous to him.

Tired, hot and thirsty he slid from the horse, his high-booted feet landing hard into the dust of the farmhouse path. He stepped through the doorway lifting his peaked cap, then wiped his brow with his sleeve and continued on to the cool dark within. The lintel hung low, forcing him to duck as he entered.

Nothing in this place spoke of wealth. A black iron pot, several stools, and a plain table of oak were the only items of notice in the first room that he entered. He flung open the shutters for light. *What plunder!* Bending low, he snatched a ladle from the pot, burnt porridge encrusting the long since handled kitchen tool. He stared at the implement smiling, finally letting it drop from his fingers. It struck the earthen floor with a muffled thud sending several mice scampering.

He sat for awhile. Finger by finger he freed his hands of the gauntlets and these he paired then dropped upon a toppled stool, their gold-embroidered gryphons snarling up at him. More gold, he pondered, was on these gloves than in all of Hellas. Then, pulling a jar from the calfskin sack that hung from his shoulder, he pried open the lid and poured out a handful of figs. He nibbled his meal then washed it down with some date-wine from a flagon.

With appetite satisfied he wandered through the home, poking his head into one room then the next, until he came upon a small chamber empty of all but a few leather sacks. Asfandiar knelt, lifting one of the discarded bags from the dirt floor. It was large, nearly three cubits across, the distance from his knee to his neck, and it was shaped circular and graven with images of battle; he snapped back the scalloped flap to inspect the vacant interior.

"Brother, there you are." Tooraj stepped into the dark chamber, wiping the tears from his eyes as he took another bite from an onion. "What loot have you uncovered here?" he asked with a grin of sarcasm.

"Only another one of these," Asfandiar replied presenting the painted leather sack. "The same empty bags we find at every farmstead. The bags these Greeks use to store their shields."

*　　*　　*　　*

"Come, come my brother, there are not that many men under the sky!" argued Nikandros. "How could Xerxes feed them?" So like a farmer he framed his perceptions with thoughts of food and the land's capacity to produce it.

"I tell you truly Nikandros," said Athamos. "I stood in the pass and looked beyond. Upon every inch of ground, as far as these two eyes could see, stood a Persian. Beyond Trachis, north past the River Speirchios and into Lamia they marshaled." Athamos' eyes widened. "We killed them by the thousands, and still they came on. Brother, their numbers wore out our weapons."

"So now," Nikandros said with a sigh, "what do we do? Will it matter?" Still he talked of the battle as if it were a far off event whose ramifications would never infringe upon his farm and family. Thermopylai was so distant. Not so to Athamos. But the elder Pankratios—named for the sport his father won at the Isthmian Games the day he was born—sat in silence to this talk.

"Sparta will never knuckle under, Nikandros. They will fight to their very last man—and ours," his brother assured. "At Thermopylai they sent her best, King Leonidas. No finer man, no nobler a warrior has ever been born to a mortal woman. And he surrounded by three hundred Spartiate knights. In but a few days they were all dead." Athamos displayed the same lifeless look he bore on the day of his return. "Would have been far better had we drawn up at the Isthmos, as you will soon do." Athamos spoke of the scrawny stretch of land that joined the Peloponnese to central Greece, a feature of geography that formed a natural choke point for an invading army. It would be here that the surviving armies would stand.

Now Pankratios, a grin upon his face, waved to Selagos to fill his cup. "Shhh! Listen to me," he commanded with his coarse voice, a voice owed to many a smack in the throat as a youthful boxer. "This defense of the wall is folly, for Xerxes fleet need but sail by it and land his vast army where he pleases."

Athamos' grim demeanor grew to rival Hades while his brother Nikandros' mouth yawned in disbelief. "Then why do I march there!" he exclaimed. "I prefer to die here amongst my kin and upon my land if defeat is what the deathless gods ordain."

"Shhh," again the father of them both cautioned, waving a single crooked finger before Nikandros' face. "Our fleet prevents this. Pray to Zeus-Protector and the Earth-Shaker Poseidon that it continues to deny the sea to the barbarian."

Nikandros left his father and brother and walked out through the small kitchen-garden of pungent herbs and poorly tended onions that hugged the south wall of his home to the olive-press. Little Alketes sat in a puddle of oil slapping mud onto the cracked mill-bowl. "I've fixed it for you, father," he said with a great smile.

"Come here," Nikandros said as he lifted the boy from his oily seat. "Tomorrow I must make a journey, so let's go to visit brother."

Without thought Nikandros walked off with his son straightaway, not stopping to clean the boy up before seeing his dead wife's sister— the sister that for the past weeks had cared for his injured son.

Little Alketes sped down the road urging his father to hurry, for he had not seen his eldest brother Theron nor his aunt in nearly a week, and Niobe would always indulge him with honeyed-milk and let him strum the kithera while praising his skill. *I need no lessons*, he thought as he plucked at imaginary strings.

Within the hour they arrived at the sprawling farmhouse, a house larger several times over than his own. A slave greeted them at the door and guided them into the courtyard where they both sat in the shadow of a small plane tree. Niobe was well heard before she was seen.

"Nikandros," she caterwauled as she flew through an open doorway, her blue trimmed peplos gown flowing wildly. "And dear Alketes." She bent to reach for the child but quickly withdrew her clutching hands. "What is that?" she yelped. "Has he crawled into an amphora again?" She winced, stabbing her finger at the oil-soaked chiton of the boy. Suddenly Niobe turned, shouting to a servant, "Take him. Strigil him clean and put something dry on him." The servant snatched the boy's hand and tugged him out of the courtyard.

"Theron?"

"Why in better health than it seems young Alketes is," she said, looking down her nose. "Don't you bathe him?"

Nikandros knew from the senseless verbal bouts his own wife once had with Niobe that silence now was his best weapon. He rose from the bench and proceeded to the stairs at the far end of the courtyard. Niobe, angry at the lack of a challenge, hustled after him.

"Why are you here? You know he must rest," insisted the woman.

Nikandros paused now at the first step and turned to her. "I am leaving for the Isthmos tomorrow and wish to speak with my son." With a bound his short legs cleared several stairs, then some more, reaching the gallery quickly; she hurried behind. As he approached the door to his son's room he slowed, halting momentarily as if to listen for sounds within. From the lintel hung sprays of buckthorn and 'round the door was smudged with pitch—all remedies to avert evil. "What is all this?" he barked. "Is my boy in fear of dark daimons?" Carefully he creaked open the door and poked his head in. Frankincense choked him; he hacked in the thick smoky cloud, waving his hand to clear the haze from his face. A triple spouted oil lamp—an ornate Korinthian type—suspended from the ceiling floated three halos of light above his son.

"Father!" announced the boy as he blinked open his eyes, a grin widening across his face.

"How is it?" asked Nikandros. He bent to look at his son's leg still dressed in strips of immaculate linen.

From behind, the door swung open and struck the wall with a whack. Niobe gasping, stepped into the room. "He is doing well," she assured. "The iatros prescribed the incense, and I have funded several expensive devotions to Apollo and Asklepios."

"And which physician prescribed this?" he asked, waving his hand at the heavy, fragrant air. "The very same one who sells you the incense?" quizzed Nikandros. Now he looked upon his son again, his demeanor calmed and his words mollified. "Theron, tomorrow I leave for the Isthmos. Be thankful you are here unable to walk or they would have called you too."

"But father, I want to go," insisted the boy as this discussion seemed to reanimate his young body. "I wanted to go with uncle Athamos, but you wouldn't allow it."

"I would not agree to it because you were not needed," snapped Nikandros, his affable mood quickly fleeing. "The council decides who shall go and who shall stay. They have decided that tomorrow I will leave Tegea."

"But father, my leg is near-perfect," assured the boy. He glanced furtively, then wobbled a finger for his father to draw near. "Aunt Niobe will not let me up from here." He dropped back into the bed. "And why the Isthmos father?"

Now Nikandros turned his open palm to the boy and spoke. "Son, let us imagine that my hand is the Peloponnese," he said, "and far up here at my elbow is the pass of Thermopylai, where your uncle fought." He looked at his son. The boy nodded back clear-eyed so he continued. "My wrist here is the Isthmos, sealing off Pelop's Isle from the Persians."

Niobe, against her nature, watched in silence as the two conversed realizing her place was outside this discussion of men. Nikandros whispered to Theron, imploring his understanding and begging his promise to help his grandfather with the farm and his youngest brother Alketes, for Medios, the middle son would accompany him north.

"Niobe, forgive me for my short-temper, for I know you love your sister's children as I do." These words brought a silent grin to the woman's face. "Can I ask another favor of you before I take my leave?"

She nodded.

"Please watch over Alketes while I am away?" Presently her modest grin transformed to a smile that threatened to burst her milk-white face.

*             *             *             *

Eurydamos reclined upon a couch in the andros of Attaginos—a Boiotarch and man of much influence in Thebes, and a patron of the invaders—watching the Persian officers sip their wine and fill their mouths with Theban bread and relish. His father Timagenides brought him to this banquet, to introduce him to the future of Hellas as he put it, to cultivate him, and to make it known to all that Eurydamos, his son, was also a loyal friend to the Great King of Persia. Timagenides extended himself beyond respectability to these Asians, laughing in exaggeration at their jokes and agreeing too swiftly to their remarks. But so did all the other great men of Thebes. The most wealthy had transformed to beggars. The poor, fearing loss of nothing, kept their pride.

"Athens is an empty husk," boasted the Persian Artabazus as he snapped a fig from the platter beside him. "And where are the Spartans?"

"Hiding behind their wall at the Isthmos," laughed Attaginos, sending the garland atop his head into a quiver.

"They huddle behind a bolted door to a house that has no walls." Artabazus curled his beard around a finger. "But my friends, let us talk of our alliance and what we, your benefactors, shall share with you." His earrings wobbled as he spoke, glittering with orange from the lamps above.

"Your friendship is gift enough noble Artabazus," said Attaginos. "A friendship that all of Hellas should now embrace."

Eurydamos felt the heat rise in him at these words and hoped his face would not betray his thoughts. The gods knew he longed for release from this place; he would be more at ease with the branded survivors of Thermopylai than here at this symposion of dishonor.

"Young Eurydamos," bellowed Artabazus, "you appear uneasy. Does our discourse upset you?" The Persian pulled on a garland that hung around a servant-boy's neck, drawing him to within a hand's breadth of his face. He buried his nose in a blossom. The boy trembled.

Eurydamos, for a discomforting moment ignored the question, swirling the wine in his kylix as he looked off, at bare walls it seemed. Artabazus' smile melted from his face.

"Son!" Timagenides eyes flared. "Answer our guest."

His father's words delivered him from his trance. "Why no sir," answered the young man. "I beg your indulgence. My mind wanders." He stared in disgust at the rouge on the Persian's face, and the lines of kohl around his eyes. *He looks like a whore*, he thought.

"Timagenides. We are always in need of good horsemen and I understand that Eurydamos here is an excellent one. I suggest he ride with us," announced the Persian. Sly Artabazus would insure the full compliance of the Theban nobles by employing theirs sons in his army—far better than hostages for they could fight for him, and die for him if needs be.

Timagenides' face dispatched its pleasant grin; Eurydamos answered the invitation with a restrained scowl. The Persian laughed, setting his earrings to a bounce. "Then it is settled. When we depart Thebes your son will come with us, as will all the sons of this most hospitable city."

*         *         *         *

"Commander, they are defending their temple," announced the trooper. He and two other men spun their horses around Asfandiar nervously.

"Show me," said Asfandiar, and with a vault propelled himself onto his war-steed. Now he kicked his mount hard, working to keep pace with the three; they sped by the Royal Colonnade, through the Agora, dodging knots of infantry that scavenged the stalls and vending booths, soon galloping onto an avenue lined with white-washed townhouses. Ahead loomed the templed hill of the High City. All around the wide street officers fought to keep order amongst the foot soldiers; this unexpected act of resistance upon the hill above had confused some and caused the death of others. Asfandiar forced his horse through the press of men to the gated end of the esplanade.

"My lord," said a flustered infantryman, "we have tried to assault the hill but it is too steep and the gateway and the road up are too well guarded." He paused, looked up at Asfandiar then tossed his hands in the air. "There, up there. They just roll blocks of stone down up us." He pointed to a large structure, partially constructed from which the defenders replenished their supplies of missiles. The air stunk of wood-smoke; the smoldering stubs of a wooden wall caught his sight. "And the entrance has been barricaded with furniture and wooden planks."

Asfandiar jumped from his horse. Before him rose a wide, stepped ramp leading up the hill to the columned gatehouse. Several slain Persian infantrymen littered the walkway. He glance up then turned to survey adjacent hill, calculating the interval between the two. "Is that one clear?" The officers nodded. Leaving his horse, he ran along the street until he came upon the pathway leading up the second hill. The steps, cut into the living rock and polished by countless footsteps, gleamed in the midday sun. His slid with his first defiant step, bringing him to a knee. Carefully he ascended.

"Has anyone tried speaking with them?" he asked the captain of bowmen, who had scampered after him. The man answered not but pointed with his bow at the bloodied bodies upon the road. "Call up your men," Asfandiar commanded. "Have them send my greetings to these fanatics on the hill. I will ride 'round it."

Asfandiar savored his tour of the hill, calculating the angle of rise and height of each section of the rocky fortress that held the High City aloft. Above him, silhouetted by the cloudless sky, he spied the figures that took notice of him. Now he came upon clusters of houses that spread from the base of the hill, and passing these he peered up at an ever-steepening curtain of stone. From the woods of plane and olive the hoot of an owl, soft and prophetic, wafted to him. He ignored the omen and rode on. By mid-afternoon he had circumscribed the hill.

"Come here," he ordered the captain of archers. "Split your hazara-bam in two equal parts. Five-hundred are to climb the hill behind us and use it as a firing platform, while the others will feign advances up this road. Do you understand me?" His voice carried a cold and deadly sternness; the man nodded. "Tooraj. Lead the Median infantry around the hill, past those houses, to the steepest portion. There a scout waits for you." More officers pushed their way to hear Asfandiar's commands. His horse pranced skittishly in the throng of men. "No one guards the hill on the far side." He flicked his glance up at the bobbing figures of men atop the High City. His commands were sententious, ringing with clarity. This time archers would pin the defenders to one side of the hill while his mountain troops scaled the cliff-face deemed unassailable by the Greeks.

The archers, expertly grouped into teams, raced up the stone-stepped incline, volleyed then withdrew, replaced perfunctorily by another team of missile men. Every so often they would pause as the barrage clouds launched from the adjacent hill screamed through the air, these arrows rippling with flames. Soon the barricade roared in conflagration. Thin clutches of javelins sputtered from above; squared boulders tumbled down the road scattering the archers; cheers boomed from the defenders on high. For better than an hour this pattern repeated until the triumphant shouts above transformed to shrieks. The walls of the High City, which had been speckled with black figures of men, went empty. Combat roared from high up. Men jumped from the walls, plunging into the wooded slope.

"Now we go," shouted Asfandiar. At his words the brigade of archers charged up the roadway. No javelins or stones greeted their advance now. Quickly they were up the ramp, through smoldering barricades at the gatehouse and onto the High City. The last free patch of soil in Athens now fell to the Persians.

He rode up and amongst the swarm of victors, studying the temples and their slain defenders. To his right lay the partially constructed columns of a long stone building; left of him, surrounded by a head-high wall rose another structure, this complete with an orange-tiled roof and wrapped in fluted columns. Dead Greeks—mostly old men—lay scattered between the two structures and from the earth grew myriads of fletched arrow shafts, giving the appearance of a farmer's field on the day before the harvest. None of his men dared enter these sacred buildings without orders; most stood at the walls looking out to the bay and hundreds of warships that choked it.

By sunset, in a most orderly manner, the gods' possessions were evacuated from the temples by details of slaves. Throughout the evening, burdened with fatigue, Asfandiar sat staring at the temple to this city's goddess, its protectress Athena as the Greeks call her. He did not leave this place until the word was passed to fire it all. It hardly felt like a victory; many years had passed since their defeat at Marathon, and Darios—now supplanted by his son Xerxes—schemed to exact retribution from the Greeks by Athens' destruction. Here and now the plan culminated. But here and now it all rang hollow to him.

Urged by his brother Tooraj, he quit the High City and rode out past the Agora where companies of light infantry assembled—three thousand—all trading spears for torches, detailed to set the city alight. He sat atop his horse, watching flickering snakes slither through the narrow streets. Asfandiar's eyes caught shimmers of light dancing off the upper stories of the townhouses while the squads of incendiaries continued to file away from the marketplace. Suddenly the air crackled with fire while sparks swirled high into the dead night. The breathless air of summer would not whisk away the sulphurous haze that began to thicken about him so he paused not, following the statued road out of Athens; he turned only once, looking back upon a night sky lapped by flame.

# CHAPTER 3

▼

From the high hill on Salamis, Myronides watched Eos in her saffron robes smother the night; a crease of light slipped over the far shore of Attika striking the polished masts of Greek triremes as they rocked gently in the south bay, hidden from the Persian fleet by the tail of land known as Kynosura. To his left—to the north of the city—the squadrons of Athenian and Korinthian warships waited also, every eye of every sailor aimed to the south, straining to spot the glint of sun off the oars of the approaching Persian fleet. Suddenly the slap of oars—Greek oars—could be heard lashing the mild swells of the northern bay. The Korinthians were moving.

Across the water flutes echoed the cadence as the rowers drew and dipped their oars, launching the Korinthians into the wide channel and full view of the enemy fleet. Myronides, bewildered by this movement stood entranced, resembling the war-god Ares in his gleaming, blue-crested helmet and polished thorax armor.

Strangely, once dead-centered in the channel, the Korinthians paused and hoisted sail, a maneuver meant for flight and not combat. Motionless, their warships bobbed low in the rolling waves—suspended—waiting.

Now to his right Myronides saw what the Korinthians most undoubtedly viewed from their position in the channel. From behind the shadow of Kynosura salpinxes trumpeted, then gliding atop the waves scores of Persian warships surged into view. Myronides grinned. The Persians, seeing only what appeared to them to be the last of the withdrawing Greek fleet, shot up the channel leaving behind broad waters, abandoning all caution. Caught in the funnel-like straight their perimeter vessels crammed inwards, either slipping rearward to avoid collision, or slowing to safely ease into tighter formation. What began as a swell of warships now advanced in a trickle. The narrows here choked the enemy formation and thinned its apex, but still they pressed on after the fleeing Korinthians. Below in their lair of southern bay, the Megarians and Aiginetans lurked, hidden in the rocky shadows.

More trumpet blasts, but this time Myronides' sight was directed north again to the remaining Greeks who had been stationed with the Korinthians. They now rowed out into the channel exposing their sterns, as if in flight.

Voices. From the water he heard the paean where ten thousand men rose up in song to announce the coming battle and call on Kastor and Zeus. Voices stilled, but the constant rhythm of the flute skimmed ever on above the waves. Then from the leading squadron a new song poured forth. "Advance ye sons of Hellas, from slavery save your land, save your homes, your children save!" The verse they repeated, stirring the very waters with its clarion roar.

The town of Salamis stuck out thumb-like between the two bays looming high above the narrows, affording godlike vantage to all the hoplites that stood waiting to repel any landing of the Persians: to the right the Megarians and the ships from Aigina; to his left the rest of the Greeks; directly before him in the narrows of the channel his eyes followed the frantic advance of the barbarian warships as they sped deeper into the trap.

Upon a signal by salphinx, and with hurried precision, the Korinthians emptied their sails of the breeze; their crewmen, within minutes, had stowed the rigging and spun their triremes to face the oncoming enemy. So too did the Athenians and other Greeks. Still, the ships in south bay huddled.

Myronides twisted the spear in his boney hand as he watched the enemy triremes push through the slender waterway, while around him the others of his taxi stood in silence. Even the verbose Aeschylos watched, body and tongue frozen as though he posed for a sculptor.

Myronides smiled now, measuring the tactics of his countrymen; once through the funnel of the narrows the Persian captains could not maneuver to bring their greater numbers to bear without exposing the oared broadsides to the enemy. From the north, the Greek wooden wall heaved into them, surging ahead with their bronze-beaked warships hungry to bury them deep into enemy hulls. Ant-like, marines scurried forward on the assaulting vessels ready to board or repel. One, then another, and in violent succession more Greek triremes slammed into the high-built ships of the enemy. Hulls cracked open like eggshells under the thrust of speeding rams. Some of the enemy, even in tight quarters, worked to angle their triremes to avoid these deadly collisions, but the Greeks, failing a broadside hit, steered their triremes to grind along the sides, scraping off entire banks of oars with their bronze-sheathed rams, sending enemy vessels into futile turns.

Held up now by the charging Greeks, the foremost vessels of the Persians became further entangled by the compression of their own advancing middle and rear squadrons. With the head of the beast fully in the trap the Aiginetans and Megarians exploded from their covertures; they rowed hard and the enemy saw them, but the Persians could only watch as the Greeks descended upon them, snarled as they were in the congestion of the lean waterway. Like death cries in the slaughterhouse unearthly squeals of bronze on wood issued from the melee as the Greeks slammed their submerged rams relentlessly into the overwhelmed vessels of the enemy left. Ships slid sideways now through the waves, being driven by the impact of the attack. For hours he watched.

Without warning someone tugged on him. He stumbled rearwards. "Aristides!" It had not occurred to him till this very moment that his friend, who had been exiled from Athens, would have returned under the general amnesty granted. Political rivalries were set aside. All good men were needed now.

Fully armored, with his helm tipped back upon his head to reveal his face, Aristides was not here to chat. "Come. We are to land on the island of Psyttaleia." He thrust his spear out, stabbing at the spoon-shaped lump of rock and scrub that sat in the middle of the channel. "The Persians have marines there."

In his supreme confidence the Great King of Asia commanded that Persian troops take possession of the slim island, not for any tactical reason, for the place was of no value; he ordered it seized and held so if any of the Greek oarsmen survived the inevitable sinking of their vessels, and by good fortune swam to the island for refuge, his men would dispatch them without mercy. Now his agents of slaughter, by the current course of battle, found themselves isolated.

"By Ares and Poseidon look," shouted Myronides. Below, in the narrows, the Persian fleet collapsed inward like so many hundreds of fish snared in the fisherman's net. Pressure from the encircling Greeks drove them; the allied warships, from their prowl on the edges, would strike and withdraw. The Persian ships could only contract their formation in desperation with no room to maneuver, and no clear commands to deliver them from their doom.

"Hurry. We now join in," bellowed Aristides.

Myronides slipped his hoplon onto his back using the loosened grip cord in the shield's interior as carry-straps, then followed in column as the others in his taxi descended the steep path from the outlook through the rows of shacks to the stony beach at the foot of the hill. He had wished his son Autolykos would be at his side in battle; this thought he had always carried with him whenever he fell into formation with his taxi.

They tromped to the rustle of leather and the clang of bronze, descending quickly to the awaiting slips, ferries and light freighters that would speed them on their short cruise to the island. Upon reaching the beach Myronides' eyes fell upon the heaps of bobbing wreckage that drifted into the bay. Men hung in the waves face down. Splintered oars and thick planks that had once spanned the cedar ribbing of Phoenician triremes clogged the shoreline of the inlet. With a sickening rhythm the tossing swells slapped this flotsam upon the hollow boats, drumming morbidly. They hurried aboard—most cheerfully—anxious to unleash their martial prowess on these invaders who they had only watched and retreated from until this day.

Now with midday well past, the squadron of the troop ships heaved away from the shore, out towards the gaping mouth of the bay. What slight wind Myronides felt day long upon him blew from the north, but it abruptly shifted, fanning them now from their backs—from the southwest—and this raked up the sea in the channel tossing white-tips amongst the tangle of enemy ships.

Myronides heard the screams—mostly in tongues he could not recognize, but some in Greek and these flashed thoughts of his son to him. A man shoved him aside—clutching a bundle of javelins—and shouldered his way across the heaving deck to the rail. From beyond his view Myronides heard cries in the water. The javelineer raised a loaded arm high above his head then with a stroke launched the missile. Cheers exploded from the men on the rail. Suddenly others snatched javelins from his bundle and commenced to fire them. More screams, but now from closer proximity.

"I got that one," announced the javelineer.

"No," shouted the man next to him. "I got him. Right through the neck with my shot."

Myronides shoved his way to the rail and peered out into the boiling waves. Several men floated, each sprouting at least a single javelin, some two and three, as clouds of scarlet dyed the water around them. He recoiled from it; death in war he had seen, but not this—not murder. *This is the honor of the fleet,* he thought.

The island grew in surges with each oar-stroke. Upon the beach he saw men scrambling, forming up a battle line preparing to repel them;

the great combat of ships left his thoughts as he measured the enemy ahead. Around him men drank. A few shook—from the wine or fear he could not tell. Across the swells to his right several penteconters sliced forward; the first to beach would suffer. Now he heard arrows drumming into the hull, but still no man bent to shield himself. The gray rock shore filled his eyes, and clambering over the beach the barbarians marshaled to deny them. The defenders, at first glance appeared not as men, but as faceless figures set to a pother, and still somehow not living, but as the interval slipped away, he distinguished individuals. From the mob of defenders he eyed a tall, trousered man, his corselet of purple glimmered in the hot light of day. Oddly, the man returned the glance.

Suddenly Myronides heard the hollow groan of his ship's keel as it buried into the shoreline, and before fully gripped by the beach hoplites leapt from the rails. Persians rushed to strike at them before they could form. Beside him a penteconter ground onto shore and this followed by other smaller craft, all unloading their furious cargo. Myronides yanked his helmet down to cover his face. The roar of combat became instantly muffled now that his head was surrounded by thick bronze; his world he viewed through narrow slits. Mindlessly following the others, for his vision reached only as far as his arms, he swung over the rail, soaring from the ship to land upon the stony beach, seventy pounds of weapons and armor driving him hard. He slipped while fighting to shoulder his hoplon, the wet gravel offering little purchase. Others, rallied by the cries of the taxiarch, coalesced into battle-ranks then shoved forward, hacking down the swirling knots of enemy infantry with spear and sword.

The Greeks landed with three times over more warriors than stood against them, and the barbarians, brave as they were and struggling fiercely with their wicker shields were no match against iron spears; their short lances and thin blades cracked and splintered against the brazen aspides of the Athenians. Myronides and his company rolled over the defenders on the shore and up the sloped beach in pursuit of the fleeing survivors.

Carried forward by this tide of slaughter, he came upon a Mede bereft of sword and shield, clutching a gash in his thigh while blood pulsed through his fingers; wordless the man pleaded with his eyes for mercy. Myronides reared back, staring through the hollow blackness of his helmet and without compunction buried the butt-spike of his spear in him. Quickly he twisted the weapon and with a crackle of bone pulled it free, releasing a gush of air and crimson.

The Athenians washed over the defenders in a murderous wave; when they ebbed not a single Persian stood on the island of Psyttaleia. Small bands of hoplites roamed the heaps of the slain, testing every enemy body with a spear point or sword; any sound, from a reboant moan to a fleeting sigh drew a blade. In the channel the barbarian fleet fared no better; the narrows were clogged with dead ships and dead men. For this day at least, the Persian would advance no further.

\*      \*      \*      \*

On the seaward slopes of Mount Aigaleos, the Lord of Asia, the Great King, Xerxes son of Darios sat on his marble throne venting reprobations amidst dozens of scribes—lettered courtiers who, at the outset documented the particulars of this victory and single out the most praiseworthy, but now scribbled furiously the names of the various captains and steer-boardmen who would be executed.

"Masistios," he boomed, "bring the Phoenician captains to me at once." Xerxes buried his head in his hands while all around stared wide-eyed, awaiting this temporary quiescence to give way to the tempest of rage the monarch would inevitably unleash. He spread his fingers, peering through them, down at the narrow waters and muttered, "My fleet, my fleet."

Masistios bowed and backed away from the Great King then turned to Asfandiar. "Come."

"Lord Masistios what has happened?"

"Are you blind, man? Those splintered wrecks there," he paused thrusting a finger downward towards the cauldron of battle, "belong to us."

"I can see. I also see that we still out number the Greeks, both at sea and on land."

"At sea modestly if at all. On land, yes we outnumber them, but scant good are these numbers if they hide behind the wall at the Isthmos. Without the fleet—a victorious fleet—we cannot hope to land behind their wall."

Upon reaching their tethered horses the two men mounted quickly and skidded down the trail and onto the road that would take them to Phaleron and the battered remnants of the fleet. Across the water, where the Greeks now lit fires along the shore, the last glow of the sun slipped away. The evening was warm and pleasant. Above, streaks of clouds scudded across the darkening sky as crickets, encouraged by the silence, commenced to sing. Momentarily the war faded.

"And now, Lord Masistios?"

The tall cavalryman laughed a bit. "Now the war is ours to fight. A land war once more."

They rode alone for a quarter hour or so until from behind thundered a horseman, a Royal courier no doubt, for he tore along the dark road impelled by duty or fear. Dust hung in his wake, obscuring the rider as he sped on. Silence returned.

"Asfandiar, this battle today changes everything." Masistios reined his horse, stopping before a shrine—a small, columned building of painted marble that stood sentinel beside the road. From his head he lifted his peaked hat, letting the cool evening air caress him while he stared through the trees across the water to the shore of Salamis, now bright with fires of celebration. He heard voices—and laughter—in the tongue of the Greeks. "They rejoice. And well they should."

*     *     *     *

Cheers rang out across the Isthmos. Becharmed by the tidings from Salamis, men danced about laughing, quickly tossing aside their shovels and axes to partake in the revelry. The Spartans paused for a moment to view with a detached curiosity the sudden change in behavior of their comrades. Amompharetos plunged the spade deep into the soil and with his heel pried loose a chunk of sun-hardened earth. "They are hardly defeated," he grunted.

"What?"

"I said the Persians are hardly defeated, Kallikrates. Why do they rejoice so?" said Amompharetos, pointing to the displays of jubilation among the allies along the wall.

"Good news, perhaps. We have had so little. But we are safe. Xerxes dare not venture past the Isthmos now."

"Momentarily. But as soon as he replenishes his losses he will attack us. That is certain."

"You speak like Kleombrotos. He urged for regiments to be sent to Thermopylai. He argues now that we should be attacking across the Isthmos while the Strangers are in disarray."

"He is right, you know. This war is not over and most certainly the Persians are not done with us." Amompharetos heaved another shovelful of dirt into the basket beside him, his long locks swirling in the gaining breeze.

"By the Holy Twins, you do sound like him. If your father could hear this talk he—."

"My father! Men like my father would drive our allies into the Persian's arms. To him everyone outside of Lakonia speaks crooked words, hardly worth saving. I think he rejoiced at the burning of Athens." He fired the empty spade into the earth and looked up. "Men look to us to lead, not hide behind this." Amompharetos stabbed his finger at the earth and timber barricade.

"The influence of Kleombrotos is rising, in spite of this recent victory. I think he can sway the ephors, excepting your father of course," said Kallikrates, muffling a laugh.

"At least he understands that our fight lies to the north, outside of Lakonia and not in our valley along the Eurotas. If we deliver Athens, we deliver Sparta."

Now the slap of leather on stone could be heard—footfalls of hundreds of shod feet upon the paved slipway, or Diolkos, rumbled loudly. When not in use hauling ships from the port of Lechaion on Gulf of Korinth to Kenchriai on the Saronic Gulf, it makes for a convenient highway.

A regiment of armored infantry—hoplites—marched toward the warriors already laboring along the embankment. The pair of Spartans paused their work to watch the arriving soldiers. "They appear like they're going to market," said Kallikrates. Both he and the other Spartans looked somewhat disdainfully upon the presentation of march displayed. No columns formed; men strolled in clusters, pulling on the reins of mules. Children toted wicker baskets and bedrolls. Only the shields and long spears slung upon the baggage animals offered any indication that the party was of warriors. "Tegeans!" Amompharetos spit the word out. "And not a soul among them is singing."

Within the mob of hoplites walked Nikandros, wearing his broad-brimmed linen hat, yanking on the lead of his mule, which bore his panoply of armor and weapons. Also tucked in with these implements of warfare were found tools more common to him—spade, hoe and ax. "Father, are they Spartans?" asked Medios, as he looked at the single band of toiling warriors.

"Yes son. See, they shave their upper, that is how you can tell."

Medios unknowingly rubbed his face, measuring a beard that was years off. To him they looked very strange. He continued to stare.

Ahead Nikandros spotted the waving arm of his commander Chileos, marked out by the chiton of his favored color green. He directed them off the Diolkos and into trampled meadow that seemed to have at one time been camp grounds: brown rectangles of parched grasses that once hid beneath tents checkered the open area; dusty footpaths laced it.

Medios reached down the front of his chiton, fingering a string that hung around his neck, finally retrieving a syrinx flute. "Mother's flute," he announced, smiling as he put it to his lips. He piped a simple tune. Nikandros smiled.

Amompharetos watched his shadow fade, and strangely so, for it was near midmorning and there were no clouds in the azure sky of late summer. He shaded his eyes and squinted, searching out the sun and found it being swallowed by a black disc. All along the earthworks the shouts of revelry ceased, as the wind raked up a stinging dust. Medios dropped the syrinx from his mouth. Now in silence thousands of men craned their necks, locking vision upon the heavenly spectacle, until the disc smothered the face of Helios.

"What evil does this portend?" whispered Kallikrates as he looked up. "For Kleombrotos performs the sacrifices now, at this very moment."

"This bodes evil I fear. Worse yet, my father will use this to dissuade the Gerousia from ordering the army north. It is an ill omen." Indeed, some men wailed while others cried out in prayer, but most simply stood wordless—their eyes transfixed upon the night-dark heavens.

# CHAPTER 4

▼

As in the spring Persian horse clogged the road through Boiotia, but now so differently, for instead of riding to Athens the invaders streamed north toward Thessalia, exiting Attika, fleeing their conquered territories. Eurydamos looked out once more from the very same hill he had first caught sight of the Persians months previous, twirling a laurel twig between his smiling lips. This was the last of them he hoped, as he watched the rearguard cavalry trot by, churning the rain-soaked highway to a muddy track. Daylong an icy wind swept the rain. Pulling his cloak tight he brushed the rainwater from his horse's neck and smiled.

"Master Eurydamos," yelled the slave Nestorides. "Your father summons you. He waits for you at the Kadmea."

The sky roared now, but Eurydamos merely hunched his shoulders and steered his horse to the down slope, trotting it leisurely to follow the departing servant. Wheat and barley had been planted and the rain was welcome by all but the withdrawing Persians. This weather paused activity. As he rode through the scattering of mud-brick dwellings that fronted the agora, he saw few people out; some stood in open doorways watching the shower. Only the clang of iron upon iron could be heard over the downpour. Here, as he passed the orange glow of the forge, Eurydamos bent low to catch the smith muscling a slab of red-hot metal into shape with his hammer. "Making plows, Stenthelias?" he inquired as their eyes met. He slowed the horse's gait, still bending to see into the forge.

"Plows, why no master Eurydamos. These be spear points." He pounded the glowing bar sending sparks in arced sprays. A small boy stepped from behind a woodpile toting several logs, and smiled upon seeing Eurydamos.

"Heed your father, Leukides," he said, then wrapped his heels into the horse's ribs, initiating a gallop. Soon the block-work wall of the Kadmea emerged from the gloom, its open gate beckoning. He could see Nestorides standing within, marking the spot for him to dismount. The servant reached up and grabbed the reins while Eurydamos slid free. "The twig!", he cautioned. Eurydamos spit it out then quickly stepped to cover and the open doorway.

"My boy," announced Timagenides, looking up from the ring of conversation he stood within. Seven other men, all Boiotarchs—the leaders of this compartment of Hellas—hovered in the armory, and upon the walls shadows danced amongst the gleaming shields and rows of neatly stacked spears. "We are finished here, are we not?"

"Then I will see you tonight Timagenides?" said Attaginos while tugging slightly on the man's shoulder. "And bring your son," he added, while grinning at Eurydamos.

"We both will attend," he assured, then ushered his son deeper into the arsenal.

"Father, why are you here?" Eurydamos looked about. The armory was steeped in the smell of oil, ash wood and burnished iron.

"Inventory of war, son. The Persians have ridden north. If they fail to return in the spring, as they have promised, I fear we will be facing not only our ancient enemy of Athens but the Spartans as well. We must prepare."

"Surely they will return. Would the Persians abandon their allies?" Eurydamos despised the Persians but knew in his heart this to be a new hatred, not nearly as deep as the long rooted animosity between

Thebes and Athens, for that had been cultivated over the centuries and its roots grew deep and firm. The Athenians would exact a heavy payment from his city if it fell to them and the Spartans.

"Xerxes has left this war to his cousin. Mardonios, through pride and stubbornness will not heed our counsel. He means to defeat both the Spartans and Athenians in battle."

"And what is our counsel father?" asked Eurydamos.

"Trade silver for spears my son, and fracture this alliance. With Athens separated from the prospects of Spartan aid they will sue for peace. Likewise the other cities of the Peloponnese, if properly induced, will slip from the League of Korinth." Timagenides spoke emphatically, so sure was he of this scheme. "It is an unnatural alliance," he added in terse monotone.

"Sparta will never treat with the Great King," insisted Eurydamos.

"Maybe so, but they'll never leave their valley if they must defend it against a sea-borne invasion, an invasion removed now by the presence of an Athenian fleet." Timagenides smiled. "That is all we work for. To keep them at home."

*     *     *     *

"Spartans!" cried the captain of Immortals—men comprising the bodyguard of Xerxes that ringed the grand pavilion. This body of superb infantry drew its name from the fact that their numbers, despite casualties, would never dwindle below ten thousand. Asfandiar looked up to see a pair of riders being led to station near the entrance of the Royal Quarters. He stared at the scarlet-cloaked men who wore no fine garments nor were tended to by servants, guards or slaves. Upon their heads were simple felt hats, and in place of a spear each carried a short staff. Long braided hair fell across broad shoulders in eight uniform locks; their expressions were grim indeed. Upon dismounting the two swirled their triboun cloaks free of their bodies revealing short swords slung beneath their left arms. These they surrendered to Hydarnes, commander of the Immortals, then both slipped into the pavilion.

"Brother, what brings our enemy here?" asked Tooraj.

"Possibly the Thebans are correct. They may hate Athens more than us," he said. "Come to seal an alliance, perchance? These Greeks are a strange lot. In the midst of invasion they quarrel amongst themselves. For their well-being they should submit to the Great King."

The two brothers lingered about the Royal Quarters, anxious to learn of the intent of so strange a pair of visitors. Asfandiar, every so often, strolled by the Spartan envoys' tethered horses, shaking his head in disdain at their lack of size and nobility of breeding, while Tooraj nibbled on an onion watching nothing in particular. Within the hour the Spartans emerged. Hydarnes, with a clap of his gloved hands, ordered a servant forward, who presented the pair their swords before they remounted their horses. No words were exchanged; they departed wearing the same cloaks and grim faces they displayed on their arrival. Asfandiar stepped forward, dipped his head and touched his brow, then in a couched voice addressed Hydarnes. "What do they seek?"

"Ha!" popped Hydarnes. "They are an arrogant people. Their council dispatched that pair to demand an apology from the Great King."

"Apology?"

"Yes, for slaying their king."

\*　　　\*　　　\*　　　\*

Upon the island of Salamis Aristides, where through the beneficence of a friend now quartered, had called a symposion of his lochagoi, the commanders of one hundred within his taxi. The thirty men crowded into the small andros of his borrowed home, where most stood, for the several couches that were available remained empty. Myronides approached his taxiarch. "Aristides, do we now return to Athens?"

"Soon, but the concerns of the others turn toward the Persian fleet. Themistokles lobbied to destroy the floating bridges at the Hellespont, and then he argued to pursue the remains of their navy. Thank the gods that Eurybiades convinced him otherwise. It is a prudent law of the Spartans not to force a fleeing enemy into desperation."

"Gossip says that Athens and Attika are free of Persian troops. Is this true?" asked Myronides. He tipped his kylix empty and motioned for the wine-servant.

"True enough, but we first want to dispatch scouts to the mountain passes to be certain. Then we will be allowed back to the city—to measure the destruction and institute a plan of rebuilding."

"They dallied long enough to prevent our planting of crops," added Myronides.

"And will the Spartans march their army north to protect us?"

"This they did not say, but Themistokles has been invited to Sparta. Let us see if he can persuade them. But first our generals, along with the commanders of our allies, will convene at the Isthmos. Seems the prizes for valor are to be awarded for the battle."

"Is it not premature to be distributing awards, my friend?"

"These small things are what hold the alliance together," said Aristides, smiling. "But your are right Myronides. We have only delayed our fate by this victory. But we have delivered southern Greece from invasion." He plucked a barley cake from a stacked platter and snapped a corner off, which he flicked into his mouth. A sip of wine. "Athens, without the Spartan army, beckons invasion. I pray our brethren to the south appreciate what service we have rendered and reciprocate."

The mood of the gathering sobered after Aristides conveyed his information as to the intentions of the allies—this winter no army would leave the Peloponnese to protect Athens from re-invasion. The Spartans and her allies would continue to strengthen the wall across the Isthmos. Myronides felt a chasm open in him into which his very spirit plummeted. Was Athens lost, now to become a minor precinct of the vast Persian Empire? Would he never debate upon the Pnyx Hill, to gaze across to the gleaming High City, or look down to ponder the dealings of the Agora. Would he never set eyes upon his father and son again, or the wealth of his family that reposed between them?

$$*\qquad*\qquad*\qquad*$$

"And what was Xerxes' response?" quizzed Posidonios in the presence of his messmates. They ate in traditional Spartan-style, seated upright and not reclined upon couches as other Hellenes do. A servant walked amongst the diners carrying a caddichos bowl atop his head, pausing before each member of the phidition, or dining hall. Amompharetos twirled the small pebble of bread, studying this vote he held between his fingers. He cast it into the bowl. The servant moved on.

"Xerxes did not speak directly to us you understand. An interpreter conveyed his words," he explained. "We plainly stated our grievance as directed by the oracle."

"Yes, yes and what did he say?" asked Posidonios.

"He turned to another nobleman and said, 'Mardonios here will deliver your payment in the spring.' Then he dismissed us, laughing."

The servant, upon completing his rounds halted before Tolmidas, the kreodaites or senior of the phidition, and presented him the bowl.

"Now we will see if Amnestos is to be admitted." One by one he emptied the bowl of the small balls of bread. Twelve perfectly round spheres sat atop the table indicating, so far, approbation. Number thirteen. It too was undeformed. Tolmidas reached for the final vote. His hand delayed a bit in withdrawing the bread, until he plucked the final, still round affirmative vote from the bowl. "Amnestos is accepted," he announced with a smile.

Amompharetos glared at the round gobs of bread atop the table in disbelief. The door creaked open and in stepped a thin, brown-haired youth sporting a tempered grin, eyes cast down. He moved to the center of the small room. "Welcome to our mess-table," bellowed Tolmidas. Beginning with Tolmidas and continuing throughout the gathering, young Amnestos thanked each member briefly. Each Spartiate smiled in acknowledgment, excepting Amompharetos. He brushed past the boy disdaining any greeting.

Outside darkness had come early, for the overcast skies held scant light, especially in autumn. Leisurely, the men of the phidition strolled out and made for their homes. Amompharetos lingered within.

"Why did you do that?" he asked Tolmidas sharply. The older man smiled through his snowy beard at the question.

"Do what, my dear Amompharetos?"

"Admit him!"

"Why I cast but a single vote. We all admitted him." Tolmidas had the guilty smirk of a thief who possessed the perfect alibi.

"You cast two votes here tonight. And stole mine." Amompharetos thought better of his anger and exhaled releasing most of it. "Why did you alter my vote?"

"His father died at the Gates. That is reason enough to admit him," countered Tolmidas.

"Not here. Not with us. Already a hebontes, yet he has no Inspirer." Amompharetos referred to the mentor or advisor each Spartan youth relied on for guidance in his early life.

"You would make an excellent one." Tolmidas grin now widened his face.

"What! My battalion is enough for me. N-no," stammered Amompharetos. He paused, then stared at his senior. "No!"

"His father and I were close, you know."

Two servants now entered and commenced to sweep the creaking floor of the mess hall. A third swirled a cloth with pride atop a table, till it gleamed. Both Spartiates exited, pulling their cloaks tight to carry the warmth of the phidition with them into the darkness. They stepped down from the raised doorway to the path that led to the Hyakinthia Way—the road that wound southward toward Amyklai.

"Before he departed for Thermopylai Eurytos exacted a pledge from me," intimated Tolmidas, "and now, I in turn, ask one of you."

"He is ruled by his temper. How many times has he—?"

"But you are right," interrupted Tolmidas. "Who better to correct this deficiency?" The older man smiled broadly. Amompharetos returned a glare. Still smiling, Tolmidas continued. "Mark these words. He will prove a worthy Spartiate in time." Tolmidas stopped when he noticed Amompharetos turning down a different path. "I thought we would walk together."

"Goodnight." He faded into the darkness quickly in the cold, wet night, relieved when Tolmidas' footsteps faded also. The path belonged to him alone. Sparta is not a city as other Hellenes are accustomed to. There are no walls. No great collections of tightly packed townhouses, or majestic precincts of awesome civic buildings as in Athens. Four of its six villages are bounded in the triangle of land formed by the river Eurotas to the east, the Knakion to the southwest, and a spur of the Taygetos mountains to the west. Centered tall in this triple bounded expanse stood the acropolis, its citadel looming over the villages of the ancient tribes of Konosoura, Limnai, Mesoa and Pitane. Beyond the Plane Tree Ground, where the mock battles of the Agoge take place, one can find the community of Therapne, and further south Amyklai. But Amompharetos would have but a short stroll to his house, for his phidition split the distance between the agora and Pitane—a mere quarter hour's walk.

Gripped in ruminations, he stopped outside his small house, considering the warm light that slipped through the shuttered windows. He turned away and continued on the road. He found himself sloshing carelessly along the puddled route, upset with the admission of the boy—so much so, that he walked by the theatron, skirting the precincts of the temple of the Diouskuri, past the tomb of the poet Alkman until he found himself staring at the moat that surrounded the Plane Tree Ground.

With a smile of recollection he crossed the Herakles bridge to stand upon the ground of his boyhood triumphs. Although cloaked in the dark of late evening, he easily reformed this most familiar terrain in his mind; in boyish but brutal combat his face had become acquainted intimately with every patch of grass, every sharp stone and each stumble-inducing root. Tough lessons were learned here. Ones that he hoped had imparted some sense to young Amnestos. He walked toward the only other bridge that spanned the moat—the bridge of Lykourgos—but stopped before it. He would not cross. This was the bridge of his enemies. His boua had always defended the bridge of Herakles, and he would not now offend his patron hero by exiting by the other.

Soaked by his maundering he turned and began to retrace his steps back toward home. Soon, and quite by accident, he found himself before his father's house. Light still shone through the covered windows. Several dogs, Kastorian hounds as he well knew, commenced to bark as he turned off the main thoroughfare and down the narrow path. Ahead he watched as a shutter creaked slightly, revealing a crevice of lamplight, followed by the squeal of the door on its hinge pins.

"Amompharetos," announced a figure in the glowing doorway. "Get out of the rain," commanded his mother, "your father will be home shortly. He will be happy to see you." She beamed while studying him. A servant-girl offered an arm to take his wet triboun cloak, which she promptly placed upon a peg near the hearth.

"He dines late tonight, does he not?"

"He dines late often. All the ephors remain far into the night in discussions." She walked him to a seat by the fire and pushed him gently into it. The servant-girl returned with a kothon of hot wine, which he commenced to sip without pause. "And tonight they entertain an Athenian."

"An Athenian?" he said, lifting his lips from the warm cup. "Who is this Athenian?"

"Themistokles, they call him."

"Why mother, he is the Athenian navarch and their warleader. A very important Athenian," he added. The warm wine and hearth quickly restored animation to him; he rose and stretched, then paced about the room.

His mother Timandra watched him and grinned. "What brings you here besides a visit to your mother?"

"The war commands me to attend," he said. "I would know what our intentions are."

"My dear, you will not argue with him again, will you? He does what he thinks best for Sparta." Her eyes smiled at him peacefully.

Powerless to her words, he sat and began to reconsider his thoughts. For an hour or more they talked of other things. She asked for his wife, daughter and son. He spoke to her of his father's kleroi and the yield this past year, for she managed the details of their farms, leaving his father free to exercise his duty as citizen and ephor. Now he stood and reached for his cloak and tugged it close, preparing to leave.

"Tell father I will come tomorrow," he said turning to the door, when suddenly it swung open. In the portal stood the drenched figure of Poliadas.

"Well son," he said matter-of-factly while shaking the rain from his cloak, "what brings you here on such a night?"

Signaling caution, his mother caught his eye before he answered. "I came to pay a visit, that is all sir."

"Oh come now son. I know you, and you would not be here if it were not to rethink my decisions."

"Not so father," returned Amompharetos. "Mother and I were discussing the barley."

Now his father looked back over his shoulder while draping the rain-heavy cloak upon a wall-peg. "Barley?" he said shaking his head. "And is this also mismanaged?"

"Why no sir. Mother has this well tended to." He smiled at her. She glared. "I understand you entertained an honored guest tonight."

"Yes. Our good friend Themistokles."

"Our good friend?" said Amompharetos.

Poliadas moved to his seat by the fire and while doing so called for the servant-girl to fetch him some wine. Attending to his command she quickly ladled a cup full from a bowl atop the hearth. To this she sprinkled a bit of goat cheese and a few pearls of barley, touching off a grin on her master's face which Poliadas quickly suppressed. He sipped the posset, still not answering his son. Timandra, his wife, brought him a dry cloak, lovingly draped it over his shoulders then slipped out of the room. Amompharetos stood silent, mindful of his father's habits, and patient in his manner.

Finally, after draining his cup, Poliadas spoke. "Do you know what this Athenian has done for us?"

"Throttled the fleet of the Great King?" answered the son.

Poliadas lifted the cup above his head. Amompharetos snatched it from his father's hand and promptly refilled it. Poliadas sipped again. "Oh he has vanquished the Strangers' war fleet, but he has also delivered southern Greece from invasion. When the navy of the Athenians' sails, it preserves the lives of our soldiers."

"Preserves our soldiers?" said Amompharetos, somewhat puzzled.

"Why yes. As long as the Athenians persist in making this war one of sea and not land."

"You and the other ephors would relinquish leadership to the Athenians?" countered his son. Again he felt the blood rising and fought to suppress it. "The barbarians roost in Hellas, not upon its waters. They must be defeated upon its land."

"Now you are a strategist, my son?" he asked mockingly. "As for the Athenians, they may call themselves leaders, if that is what they wish, just so long as they keep the Persians north of the Isthmos." The father turned away from the warmth of the hearth to look upon his son. "I understand you admitted Amnestos this evening?" he coolly added as an after thought.

Amompharetos eyes widened. He did not answer. Again his father seemed to know his thoughts and deeds before they occurred, and it left Amompharetos wondering.

"I heard this from Kallikrates on my way here. The boy will be trouble," he added, in his familiar, pedantic tone.

"For once father we agree. But Tolmidas thinks otherwise."

"Although I do no agree with him that should be enough for you. Tolmidas has the gift to see the real man. Few are left that do, for Kleombrotos is dead."

"Dead," repeated Amompharetos, broadening the word in disbelief.

"Fever. He died this evening."

"Father, when we were at the Isthmos he fell ill, upon the very day of the eclipse."

"And you question *why* we do not march north? The deathless gods have sent this warning to us," lectured Tolmidas.

His father had invoked the gods, and now the argument was unwinnable. With no further words Amompharetos dipped his head in respect, rose and departed.

✳     ✳     ✳     ✳

"There Medios! The bridge!" shouted Nikandros over the crackles of thunder and pounding rain. Ahead, barely visible through the deluge that raged from above was the small wooden bridge spanning the boundary stream between the territories of Mantinea and Tegea. "We should be home by sunset."

"How can you tell, father?" asked Medios.

"Why son, by the stream. We will be in Tegea soon."

"No father, I meant how can you tell when it will be sunset? It has been dark all day long." The boy wore a troubled look, and was perplexed by the confusion in the heavy sky above.

"Oh it will get darker," assured Nikandros.

Avalanches of rain continued to roar from the boiling black clouds. They walked not on a road but what now was transformed to a fast flowing stream, that by its force of current propelled them toward the bridge and the confused water it spanned.

"Hurry before it's washed away," he shouted over the roar of the storm. Breaking into a trot he snapped hard on the reins of the mule while his son flicked the beast in its haunches with a thumb-stick. They hustled toward the bridge, all the while the stream rushed furiously beneath it. A wave burst over its low timbers, momentarily obliterating it from view. On either end the banks of shoreline that anchored it were turning soupy. Another swell smacked the timbers. Now the bridge began to slide.

"Run!" screamed Nikandros, sending the mule and his son into a sprint for the twisting bridge. Waves peeled over its surface. It wobbled in the grip of the tossing stream. Nikandros' feet slid as he jumped onto it, fighting to keep the mule in tow and his son within sight. Suddenly, and with a deep groan, the bridge shuddered free of the bank and careened downstream, propelling the three while it spun. The animal brayed in terror; both man and boy hunched over, struggling for balance, wide-eyed. As though snatched by the hand of some unseen god, the disintegrating bridge crashed amongst a knot of boulders; the upstream side began to lift under the power of the surging water until it flipped to the vertical, sending them into the chaos of the stream.

Panic saved the mule. It pulled free of Nikandros' grip and scrambled through the stormy water, over boulders and to the shore where it halted, shivering. Nikandros had wedged his bent knees between two stout rocks and frantically groped for his son; he was not behind him, nor in front. The man's eyes flitted wildly, searching. Above the roar of the torrent he heard a voice.

On the shore slightly above him, knelt his son waving, smiling, and stripped bare. Nikandros carefully edged his way toward the shoreline, bracing against the power of the current and unsure footing of the boulders in the streambed. Medios thrust out a hand and pulled him up.

Nikandros sat, his chest heaving for air, for several minutes beside his son. Neither spoke. Eventually he turned to look upon him and smiled. "We prayed to the wrong gods," he laughed, "for we did not need protection from the Persians, but from our own rivers."

The rain mattered little. The two sat, drenched but thankful for their deliverance and proximity to home. Nikandros pulled a cloak from a panniered basket atop the mule and draped it over his son. The boy's hair stuck in slick strands to his face; Nikandros brushed it clear of his son's eyes and looked at the life within.

"The gods are surely with you," he said embracing him.

Medios' grin faded as he felt for the familiar string that secured his flute. He looked to his father, his eyes bearing pain and disbelief. Nikandros need say no words, for he felt the same pain. They packed up and patched together what they could manage to find, but the stream still held claim to the flute.

Selagos spotted the pair as they approached the farmhouse. Hardly paying heed to the storm, he pulled an old blanket over his head and hurried out to usher them, splashing through the walkway, Theron following close behind, trying to mask his limp. In the doorway stood Pankratios. "Get in here," he shouted as he leaned out into the rain.

The pair, too spent to run, shuffled to the open door. Nikandros fell into a stool near the hearth, while his father ushered the boy to a seat at the table where a bowl of steaming porridge sat alone atop it. He instructed the lad to rid himself of his cloak and dropped a thick, dry blanket atop his shoulders, which Medios pulled snug about him. He shivered.

"Get that food into you boy," commanded Pankratios. "And you my son. Why did you continue on in this weather?"

Nikandros did not answer him but continued to turn his hands over the glowing coals, savoring the warmth of the hearth. Theron, in silence, brought him some wine. Suddenly the door opened, swung hard by the gale, a hand halting it before it slammed against the wall. "The mule's barned and fed master Nikandros," informed Selagos. "I will be off now."

"Get some rest. Tomorrow we will be planting the corn." Nikandros reached for the cup.

"Master, the corn is already planted. Between each and every olive grove. Done four days ago."

"And how did you manage that?" Nikandros sipped the wine, waiting for Selagos to respond. But the man stared at Pankratios, his eyes pleading for assistance.

"I hired men," said Nikandros' father. "But do not worry, I also paid for them."

"And how will I repay you?"

"By keeping my grandson safe—and dry," he said in his usual, raspy tone. "Now accept the good news for what it is."

The two talked of family matters and finances: the condition of Nikandros' brother Athamos; little Alketes; payment for loyal Selagos. All were well tended to and Nikandros' mind was put at ease. The Persian tide was stemmed and at little cost to him, his family, his polis, and further, he would turn a modest profit with this year's olive harvest.

# CHAPTER 5

▼

"What is he doing here?" asked Praxis. A burly man with perfectly curled hair and a trim beard walked up before the Assembly of citizens. By Athenian convention his dress was gaudy and proud. He and Myronides followed the man with a glance. "I do not trust this Macedonian even if he be a king."

"Alexandros is a friend to our city, and we would benefit to hear his words," said Myronides, "although I would think he works to rid his country of the Persians and the burden of hospitality forced upon him."

King Alexandros stepped up to the marble platform and removed his platter-like causia hat, looking out upon the gathering; the beat of carpenters' hammers and hum of slow-drawn saws ceased.

"Men of Athens," he boomed. "I bring you a message from the Great King Xerxes." He paused, for the mere mention of the Persian monarch ignited a grumble of discontent throughout the assembly. "Xerxes is willing to forget all the injuries that Athens has done to him. You may have your land back—and more. You make take any other territory that you wish for your own, and retain your liberty. All this if you are willing to make terms with him."

Again they grumbled. Heads turned from side to side in conversation. Alexandros raised his arms, gesturing for silence.

"These words I convey to you from Xerxes' commander Mardonios. He asks: 'Why are you so mad to take arms against the king? You have seen the army, its size and what it can do. We may re-enter Athens at our leisure. Come to terms, now that Xerxes is inclined that way.'

"So much for what Mardonios has instructed me to say. Now let me speak for myself. You good Athenians know of my love for your city and must know also that I would not be here relaying the wishes of the Persian king if I did not think it in your best interest. But the fact is Xerxes' power is insuperable, and his arm is long. Do therefore agree to his terms, for surely it is no small thing that the Great King has singled you out from all the people of Hellas to become his friends."

The Macedonian quit the podium, leaving the Assembly to digest his words.

In focused silence Myronides listened to the envoys from Sparta as they whispered worried commentary. From the speaker's perch the Spartans were summoned to address the Assembly, for it was in fact their original purpose in coming to Salamis and only by coincidence— or clever arrangement by the Athenians—did they happen to be present for Alexandros' speech.

"Look who attends," said Praxis, watching the two Lakonians shoulder their way to the speaker's platform of marble. "Spartans. And I would gather they are a bit uneased by Alexandros." He grinned and so did Myronides, for now they might finally see Spartan troops.

The taller of the two envoys stepped forward and spoke. "The Spartans have sent us here to entreat you not to abandon your current policy, and to listen not to Persian proposals. Do not betray Hellas. And do remember that it was by your actions that this war began." The Spartan paused looking for confirmation from the faces of the Assembly that his words were well taken. He continued. "We in Sparta are not indifferent to your hardships—your loss of two harvests plus the destruction of your homes and property. In compensation we offer, in the name of Sparta and her allies, to provide for all the women, children and elders for as long as the war lasts."

The pair of envoys stepped from the platform, and unlike Alexandros, continued on past the array of magistrates and out of the proximity of the council and assembly. Myronides moved with Praxis toward his friend Lykidas, who now spoke with Alexandros.

"King Alexandros, come and dine with me tonight. I wish to hear more of this proposal of the Great King," said Lykidas. Alexandros nodded, then walked off before Myronides or Praxis could extend a greeting.

"And my friend Lykidas, how will you entertain such a man? Does your councilorship provide you with privilege I am unaware of?" inquired Myronides. He scrutinized him in silence now. With the war most all his friends had grown thinner, but Lykidas' belly stretched his chiton like the wind in a trireme's sail.

"Myronides, you are also welcome to attend. And in fact I have come into a small bit of wealth quite unexpectedly, and would share it with my friends. Please come tonight." Lykidas was someone who hardly guarded his words.

Myronides and Praxis shook their heads at this. Praxis spoke for them both. "We cannot dine with such a man, this agent of Persia. How can you Lykidas, a man of the council, do such?"

"I dine with him to educate myself of our enemy. And of our options, for it would be a malversation indeed if I did not learn all I can from him while he is here among us."

"Lykidas, I pray these are your true intentions, for you play a perilous game. This government of the demos hardly trusts any of the aristocracy. Do not confirm their suspicions."

True were his words. At this very time Themistokles and the commoners held sway in the council, fashioning policy and smothering the influence of the noble families. Ruled by the incantations of fiery orators, the demos little pondered their actions, but flitted to and fro like a flock of sparrows, eager to follow the impulses of their leader.

Lykidas, smiling, bade farewell to his two friends and left them to converse with others of the council. Praxis grabbed the arm of

Myronides and leaned to his ear. "He cannot resist any temptation, especially one of the flesh. An offer of delicate food or of a young boy will have him very pliable indeed," hissed Praxis.

"Remember this Praxis, he is more of an Athenian than most in this crowd. His line goes back to the days of Erechtheos. He would not betray us."

*          *          *          *

Chileos, in his bright green chiton and pleated chalmys half-cloak surveyed the milling farmers and craftsmen that comprised the assembly of Tegea. Above, the overcast skies revealed no hint of the sun, but at least for today the winter rains had abated—the chilled winds had not. Nikandros huddled with the members of his ancient tribe according to law and custom, rocking from foot to foot, cloak pulled tight, waiting for Chlieos to speak. Athamos and his father Pankratios stood with him.

"Men of Tegea," began Chileos, "I bring you news. The Persians have offered to make a separate peace with the Athenians."

Now the assembly rumbled with scattered conversations. With the turn of a few words, the Tegeans stared at a bleak future. Athamos and the veterans of Thermopylai knew full well what the loss of the Athenians would mean to their survival. The invaders, unimpeded at sea could land where they will.

A voice blurted out, "What of Sparta?" A second, then a third echoed the question.

"Sparta will not change her policy toward the barbarian, for this you can be assured. But it is the Athenians, which concern her now," quickly answered Chileos.

Nikandros stood tall and shouted, "Will Athens abandon her fellow Hellenes? And what then, will happen to us?" Again many others repeated the question.

"We will abide by Sparta's policy and fight. As far as Athens goes, their council has not announced their intentions, but if we of the Peloponnese do not move to defend them, Athens—like Thebes to the north—would have little choice but to side with Xerxes."

"But what of Sparta? Will they march north?" boomed a desperate voice. Nikandros looked to his father's eyes for an answer. The old man shot him an empty stare.

"I go to Sparta on the morrow to meet with the ephors and then I will speak to the Apella—their assembly. They are a deliberate folk, as we all know, and do not entertain lightly ventures outside of Lakonia." Chileos moved off the high step and down amongst the crowd of men, coming by chance to the elder Pankratios.

"Chileos. What else do you hear from abroad?" he asked.

"I dared not say this before the assembly, but Persian agents ply their silver in all the cities of Hellas now, working to unsettle the alliance. The Spartans must act, and quickly." The man shouldered past the three, slipping into the swirl of men beyond.

"Without Leonidas, they will not march from their valley," said Athamos. "He was the only voice of sense in Sparta, excepting of course his brother Kleombrotos, and now he is dead also."

"We must hope the new regent has the foresight of his uncle Leonidas," added Pankratios.

*       *       *       *

Never in the history of Sparta had a foreigner been afforded such honors. The Athenian Themistokles departed the city, escorted by the three hundred knights—young Spartiate warriors, the most accomplished of the hebontes, selected as the king's bodyguard. Amomphare-tos rode with them, not as one of the royal hippeis, but a battalion commander adding to the prestige of this party.

Themistokles traveled in a gilded racing chariot—gift from the people of Sparta for his leadership in the naval war against Persia. Poliadas rode beside his son, and they chatted of weather and crops—anything but war policy. Passing a small shrine to the twin patron gods of Sparta, Kastor and Polydeukes, the boundary stones came into view. Soon they would part company with the Athenian, leaving him and his attendants to pass into the territory of their allies the Skiritai.

Themistokles pulled back on the reins. His quadruple team of horses pranced a bit, then halted. "I thank you Poliadas, for your hospitality and friendship," said Themistokles. "Remember. Our navy will be there for you. Can I assure our council that likewise your army will be there for Athens?"

"No single man can answer that question," responded Poliadas. "I am but one of many who speaks for our citizens. I will make clear to them your concerns."

"I pray Sparta marches, for if not others may gain influence in Athens, leaving me unable to guarantee our alliance," warned Themistokles. "I have come here at great risk to my position at home. Your failure to support Athens will become my failure."

*      *      *      *

"Father, why do you spirit money to the cities?" asked Eurydamos. "Already Xerxes has dispatched agents sowing talents of silver throughout Hellas." Since the Persians had withdrawn beyond their territory, at every meal all discussions eventually returned to the purchase of allies, for Thebes had faint chance of standing alone against a vengeful Greece. Eurydamos' father was beyond doubt that money would easily accomplish what the Persian army, up until now could not do—fracture the alliance.

"Xerxes has indeed expended much wealth and many promises on certain men to the south. Men that he deems receptive to his aims. Son, I do what is prudent." Timagenides studied the wine in his kylix. Tonight only he and Eurydamos dined in the andros—a most untypical night. "My money and influence now are more important to Xerxes than is a son to ride in his cavalry."

"You buy my release from his service?"

"To free you from riding as escort to this fleeing Persian, why yes." His father knew too well the price of most men, for whether in war or trade he always prepared the ground of contest to his favor.

"Xerxes retreats through Thrace now, returning headlong to his restless empire. We are secondary in his plans."

The sea battle of Salamis, although not liberating Hellas from the vast land army of Persia, did indeed entice the cities of coastal Asia to reconsider their submission to the Great King; they saw the fallibility of the Empire and Xerxes' absence encouraged them. The Great King hurried back to restore order.

# CHAPTER 6

▼

"Good citizen did I hear it truly?" inquired a motley-clothed potter to Myronides as he exited the bouleterion, or council chamber. The man hung about the doorway sucking phlegm from his throat then spit it in gobs on the post beam of the entrance. He loitered here, hoping to learn of the vote tally for the ten new strategoi that Athens elected annually, one from each of its ten tribes. They would be the generals to lead the city in the war against Xerxes.

"Hear what, man?" Myronides answered, turning away from the odorous fellow and his irksome talk.

"About Themistokles. Is he out?"

Myronides could hardly contain the grin that worked to undermine his stern manner. Another look at the potter rid him of any cheer.

"Themistokles no longer commands the fleet; Xanthippos has been elected navarch." Myronides repeated this several times, only to himself, so pleased was he with the composition of the sentence and the many years it took to come to fruition.

The air outside, although cool and damp, was a welcome change from the choked atmosphere of the small council-room of Salamis. Here the displaced government of Athens met in borrowed chambers for their deliberations. Here too the voice of the aristocracy grew loud—loud enough it seems to have nudged the architect of the battle of Salamis from his command. Aristides and the landed men of bronze—the hoplites—steered policy now.

From within, Myronides heard the name of his friend Lykidas announced, for he would now address the council. Full of clear air and clearer thought, Myronides slipped back through the crowded doorway, staring up at the stepped rows of full seats that climbed three of the four walls of the building to hear the words of his friend.

"Fellow Athenians," began Lykidas, "we have selected our generals—all excellent choices for which I commend you. Now more importantly we must choose our battles and our true adversaries." Presently the muffled remnants of conversation ceased; the council-room was gripped in a cool silence.

"Some here would have us ignore the words of King Alexandros, a friend of Athens. A noble man who thinks of his fellow Hellenes. A noble man who, with words of common sense, has revealed Xerxes' affinity for our city."

Rumblings erupted here and there. Lykidas, unshaken, went on. "And what do you propose, Lykidas?" challenged someone from amongst the tiers of seats.

"I propose reason. Why do we continue to provoke Xerxes? He has guaranteed our autonomy. Further, he has offered us what additional land in Hellas we desire. All we need do is—."

"Bow to him!" shouted a man in workman's attire—drab garments made duller by the rage in the man's face.

"Not bow to him. Let him think we are his subjects. For in return he grants us prosperity," countered Lykidas, daubing the sweat from his brow with the tail of his himation cloak.

"And what would my son think of your plan?" yelled another.

"Your son? And who is he," asked Lykidas haughtily.

"My son is a zugites, a rower. He now rests in Poseidon's realm along with many other good Athenians, in the waters off this island. What would they say to this proposal?"

Now the air grew thick with growls of anger. Myronides had never witnessed ire of this sort, although he had been told by his father of the days of the tyrant Hippias and what rage that man evoked from the people. Now from outside, men not of the council pushed their way in and added to the cries of outrage that were discharged at Lykidas. He rocked nervously from side to side, toweling his sweaty face with his cloak. Not a soul came to his defense—not even Myronides.

More men shoved their way in, causing the others on the floor of council-room to surge forward. No longer individuals, but combined into some sort of thought-robbed fury, the mob—like a wave—rolled up the seats and snatched Lykidas, then the whirlwind retreated to the agora, carrying him in their collective grasp, arms reaching high then falling swiftly to strike. Myronides heard the pleadings of his friend above the storm of the mob; Lykidas cried for reason; he begged them to stop; ultimately he wailed in pain. The crowd boiled around him but not for long. It was over quickly. Death quenched their rage.

Myronides staggered from the council-room. Outside he saw the disfigured corpse of his friend come into view as the crowd melted away. The few that lingered cursed and spat upon the body, shouting warnings to others that would deal with the barbarians. Myronides approached circumspectly then stood over Lykidas, quite alone.

*       *       *       *

A year previous, the vast nations of Asia flooded southward, over-whelmed the valiant defenders of Thermopylai and continued on to Athens. And like a sea-tide this past winter they ebbed by the same route to quarter in the north amongst their allies in Thessalia and Macedonia. But now with the coming of spring, the invaders flowed south once more onto the broad plains of Boiotia. All around wheat rippled in the breeze. Farmers, deep in the fields, paid little heed to the thunder of Persian horse; the first harvest was little more than a month off, and distractions would cost them now. Asfandiar let his horse wander, for the beast sought relief from its thirst; it paused beside a trickle of a brook. The animal dipped its neck and began to drink, while he watched thousands of cavalry trot past.

"Brother," shouted Tooraj. He galloped from the columns of horse to greet Asfandiar. "Mardonios means to push straight on to Athens."

"The Athenians have refused the Great King?" he asked. The horse snorted while pulling away from the brook, now satisfied.

"Seems so. And there is no army to contest us either. Athens is ours once more," said Tooraj. His horse nudged forward seeking the water.

"These Greeks are an odd people. The Spartans refuse to fight, and the Athenians refuse to submit, while both it would seem, have scant choice." Asfandiar looked out upon the vast sea of men that washed into the plain and smiled. "This time brother, we will fight on land. And this time the contest will be settled."

Both men urged their horses forward to join in the long columns that moved deeper into Boiotia. Thebes, the city of their allies, they would reach by sunset. Within the week they would feast in Athens.

$$*\qquad *\qquad *\qquad *$$

Krios ambled through the toppled stone and brick that in days past made up his master's townhouse. Once in several steps he would spy a sliver of a broken pot, a rusted knife or some such remnant of this once fine abode, pick it up and reform the object in his mind, allowing this to bring him back to more pleasant days. Beyond the Agora, to the south and toward the gate to the Sacred Way the air shook, filled with the rapping of hammers and the rip of saws; Athens had begun to rise again.

The Persians had left few buildings untouched. Every structure of wood had been reduced to sooty ruin. Stone buildings—civic structures—had been toppled. Even the Fountain House, and the Temple of Hephaistos, high on the Aereopagos Hill, had been swept away. Much rebuilding must take place. Most anxious of all to commence the reconstruction were the tradesmen. Now he heard feet upon loose stone.

"Krios! Are you in there?" yelled Myronides. He leaned, shading his eyes from the sparkling sun of an Attic spring, searching. "Ah, there you are. The architect is here and wishes to walk the property."

Krios dropped the small wooden figure of a hoplite warrior that had once belonged to Autolykos and stepped from the old storeroom into the rubbled courtyard. There stood Diognetos, wax tablet in hand, studying the old layout of the house.

"The andros must be larger," instructed Myronides, pointing with his boney finger to the debris of his former hall. "And the fountain should be placed center of the courtyard, not so close to the doorway as it is now."

The oikodomos scratched figures with his stylus in silence, then deliberately paced the length of the wall. He added more to his tablet. After several strolls amidst the ruin, he sat upon a convenient block of stone, staring long at his work. Finally, he stood. "I will call upon you later with a price for this work."

"Later?" he said, somewhat puzzled.

"Why yes Myronides. The materials needed for your home are not yet available. You know the harbor has only recently reopened, and few dare venture out into the countryside to cut wood or stone."

"But what of them?" he asked indignantly. "What of the tradesmen and shopkeepers who are rebuilding this very day?"

"My dear friend. They hardly require the fine materials you do to nail together their shacks. And they surely do not turn away from scavenging. You would hardly want the bricolage they patch together." The architect stepped high over a fallen figure of Athena, its extended arm reaching skyward from its crib of charred timber and mud brick. "What is needed for this," he said tapping the stylus upon his tablet, "will come from many parts of Hellas. Difficult to assemble so much on short notice. And you know the civic projects have priority on all materials." He looked nowhere, and appeared to be calculating figures silently. "I will see you on Salamis, Myronides."

Now he stepped out into street where scores of laborers, both slave and freeman hired by the city, toiled with steady purpose. Teams of three men each filled baskets with the litter of fallen buildings, while others guided horse drawn wagons to collect the refuse. Even with Helios strong in the sky, unfettered by a single cloud, the work continued. In the shadows of a partial wall rested his tethered horse, dozing it seemed, for it stood motionless until he smacked it gently upon the neck, before vaulting onto its back. If he hurried he could reach his farm near Phyle by sunset.

"For you, master." Krios handed him the small clay fire pot, which he promptly slid into the single leather satchel slung across the horse's neck. "For cooking."

The going was slow through the ruined streets. The flurry of civic workmen added to the congestion. Nonetheless Myronides rode to the edge of the sparsely treed Agora, up the main thoroughfare and toward the outer wall, determined to survey his estate. Here, at the Double Gate, a squad of armed men stood watch. They nodded as Myronides trotted by, asked no questions, nor offered any conversation.

Soon he was free of the city, riding on an empty road. Odd thing. The Persians had left no shop, temple, or government building untouched within the city, but here outside its walls damage appeared less regular; a roadside shrine to Demeter lay smashed while a farmhouse nearby stood intact. The destruction of the city was a command of policy, while wreckage in the countryside had the aspect of randomness.

He saw only three others. A cart driven by a slave with two children passed by, heading for the city; none of the three spoke—even to each other—but stared empty-eyed as their cart rumbled by. Land once thick with wheat and olive trees now spread before him naked. Of course green was upon the fields, but not of the type nurtured by man, for nature had reclaimed these slopes and fields.

Light began slipping away when he sighted the boundary stone of his farm. Chilly air rushed past him. Crickets chirped in the gloomy evening as he turned up the path to the house. From here its outline rose as it should, and this did indeed lift his heart. The tall tower of his estate still thrust skyward from the back of the farmhouse. Even the stables were intact. As he rode on, the structure began to fill his sight: the door, although open, was still hung by its pivots to wall; the shuttered windows denied the night; herbs in the kitchen garden cowered, choked by weeds. Seeing this, he rode past the house and into the field beyond, heading for a gentle-sloped hill that dominated his farm. At its crest grew a cluster of a dozen or so oak. Myronides slid from his horse and walked to the trees, and there between two of the most ancient he stopped to look upon the graves of his father and son. The ground was blanketed by wild grass, an accidental flower sprouting here and there. His treasure was safe.

"My son," he spoke softly to the narrow marble slab, it bare of any design, but for the single name of Autolykos. "I hope your grandfather is good company." Slowly, he knelt upon the earth and gazed without focus. He thought of his father, the man who was struck down by Persian arrows ten years past at Marathon; with wounds destined to dispatch him to Hades Hall, he clung to life dearly, to return to this farm, where one stifling afternoon, weeks after the battle, he closed his eyes forever. The Persians had killed him, but they hardly stirred more hatred in Myronides than the demos. He blamed them and their fickleness for the devastation of his city and family. As the last light of sunset melted in the wide, dimming sky, he spoke his final words to them both.

Myronides rode quickly down hill and into the fenced yard of the farmhouse, memory guiding him through the inky shadows. With his horse stabled he creaked open the door and entered. The smell was foreign to him, a musty dampness—the smell of abandonment. Once inside he groped for the oil lamp that sat on the shelf above the hearth. In a most comforting way it slipped into his hand. He continued to sweep the shelf with his fingers, searching out the slender light stick; he plunged the tip into the smoldering embers of the firepot until it ignited, then transferred the nascent flame to the oil lamp.

Not long afterwards a small fire crackled in the hearth, the lamps were lit, and Myronides, holding the brightest of these, surveyed the interior of each room, scattering the mice that had begun their nocturnal romp. Back in the storeroom he saw the same emptiness of almost a year ago. Fatigue halted his search. Once again before the hearth and warmed by the fire, he looked about for the chair—his father's favorite—and found it nudging a tipped stool. Upon it lay a pair of jeweled black gauntlets, stitched with the likeness of golden gryphons. He studied them.

"Persian," he muttered, turning the gloves over. Urged by curiosity, he pushed the fingers of his right hand into a glove, finding it over-loose. *A large man*, he thought.

From outside he now heard voices. Hellenes, for he understood them. He jumped up and cracked the door open, just enough to peer out into the night. Four men, each armed with spears—these he saw easily for their tapering blades were silhouetted against the sky— moved too quickly to be armored infantry. Suddenly one of them turned and looked directly at him. "You!" he shouted. "You better leave now. They be Persians coming through the pass."

*     *     *     *

He enjoyed it. The long march actually relaxed him, although the others could hardly appreciate his delight in trotting fifteen miles in entire panoplia. Shield and spear did not burden them; it was the suffocating helmet that did. This bucket of bronze the infantry of other cities dread to wear. They fight to keep it from imprisoning their heads, even while marshaling for battle. These others are smart. They lower it only moments before the charge. Appointed just days previous,

Amompharetos and his regiment had been tearing down the road to Gythion for two hours wearing theirs.

Still in the fore, he stepped aside to allow the three columns of hoplites to pass by; this he did several times during the march to survey them, winnowing out in his mind the ones that struggled from the ones that flourished. Kallikrates bounded past him grinning. A few of the younger ones just out of the Agoge, the twenty-year-old hebontes, bowed their heads in fatigue but pressed on. They all had their round, deep hopla slung tortoise-like upon their backs; the scarlet lambdas beamed bright upon the bronze facings of their shields.

"Put the bucket on," boomed a voice from the chugging column. Amompharetos turned to seek the one voice in this thunder of march and saw Posidonios—a huge man—whacking the youngster Amnestos with the shaft of his spear; the boy had pulled his helmet off and was carrying it in his hand.

"Amnestos," he yelled from his roadside perch. "Over here!"

The boy slipped from the road, shuffling toward him with his head still helmetless, eyes in the dirt he approached.

"Everyone marches with it on." He snatched the helmet from the lad. His face puckered in disgust, as he tossed it back."Is it all out of you?"

The boy, eyes still down, nodded.

"Take it over to that stream and wash it out," he said while rubbing a fistful of road dust in his palms. "Then run your ass off to catch up with them."

Amnestos sprinted as fast as his weary legs would allow. Arriving at the stream's edge, he scooped and dumped water quickly from the helmet, but did not sip a single drop, for no permission had been granted to refresh himself, and none would be for the veterans had not yet received their water ration; that would not be till they paused at Gythion. Within moments he sprinted off, stumbling once or twice in the meadow and stirring up the grasshoppers that clicked and clattered above the grass, finally catching up to his platoon. Posidonios whacked him with the spear again, grinning.

Every other day for the past full month they had marched at the double-quick. Little time had been spent at the Plane Tree Ground in gymnastics; speed marches and formation evolutions occupied the regiments. This was the focus of their training, and these drills, in particular, consistently preceded war. After weeks of criss-crossing the Eurotas valley on training rations, they would welcome battle.

At midmorning they chugged past Amyklai, still clinging to the Gythion Road, but by now the pace had slowed under the strengthening gaze of Helios. A few hours later he saw the provender train and the midpoint of their trek, and could smell the salt air of the port. A hundred or so Helots milled about the array of wagons, waiting for the regiment to halt for their meal and a short respite. In order of company, the men peeled from the road and walked in column to the food wagons. Amompharetos, along with Kallikrates, stood by while each man in turn stepped forward to receive his ration of zomos broth, flatbread and slab of salted venison.

"Not for him," shouted Amompharetos as Amnestos reached for food. "He gets none today." The boy turned, his eyes pleading against the command. From behind, a shove sent him past the Helot doling out the food. "Get moving sweetheart," snapped Posidonios, giving him another push; quickly he snatched the lad's portion then stepped to speak with Amompharetos. "I didn't think he would make it," he laughed, ripping a piece of bread off with his teeth."

"He will be ready or he will die," said Kallikrates.

"But why Bull, did you force that egg potion on him?" said Amompharetos, addressing Posidonios by his Agoge nickname. "And they say our pig's blood broth turns the stomach." He shook his head while he grinned.

"Well the lad wanted to know what I ate to strengthen myself when I was a hebon, fresh out of the Agoge." All the young men who had completed the Upbringing—the military training begun at aged seven, and lasting until their twentieth birthday—anxiously inquired of the veterans any particle of advice, no matter how minute—or bizarre— that would enhance their constitution. Bull's elixir consisted of eggs and vinegar, although he conveniently omitted the havoc wreaked upon a youthful stomach by such a sulphurous diet.

"And why only eggs? Why not the entire hen? Why I recall when you ate that chicken, feathers and all. Hardly a civilized act," said Amompharetos grinning.

The trio walked over to the shade of a swooning willow and sat to finish their meal. Beyond them, down a small path stood a shrine to Enyalios, the Spartan god of war, and this Amompharetos fixed his eyes upon as he ate in silence. The other two laughed, for Bull tried entertaining them with amusing tales of the Argives and how they had promised Xerxes to *rout the Spartans* if they dared leave their valley to fight. Argos, a city north of Sparta, declared itself neutral during the war thus far, and at the same time secretly courted Xerxes, promising assistance to the Great King. But unlike the other Medizers, such as the Thebans, Macedonians and the like, the Argives were hemmed in by loyal Hellenes, and uncomfortably close to Sparta and its indomitable army.

Now Amompharetos stood and stretched a bit, arching his back, then strolled the path to the shrine. The likeness of the war-god was fierce: shield held upon the shoulder; spear raised overhead, ready to strike; its helmet pushed back upon his head to reveal a snarl of combat upon his lips. All around, scattered upon the stepped altar were figurines of warriors, votive offerings, deposited here in thanks and also to facilitate new prayers. Amompharetos reached into a pouch and pulled free a leaden image of a hoplite and placed it upon the altar. "I pray to you dread Enyalios, fickle god of war, to fill our spirits," he chanted. "Sparta must fight."

From behind him he heard someone approach. Amnestos shuffled down the path. He had removed his bronze breastplate and helmet, but retained spear and shield—a regulation of campaign that even in his washed-out state he would never fail to follow. With a mere glance Amompharetos froze him in the path. The lad lowered his eyes and spoke. "Sir, I do not mean to disturb you. I bring a token for the god."

"I was on my way," Amompharetos said as he walked back toward his companions. He paused to look back and watched the boy as he placed the votive upon the altar next to his gift. Amnestos began to talk, but in words meant only for Enyalios. He waited there, mid way up the path for him to finish.

Done with his prayer he walked back toward the lounging soldiers, not lifting his eyes from the ground upon which he tread until he came astride his commander. "Pardon me sir," he nervously offered. "I did not see you."

"And how could you? You are a warrior now and must stop watching ants. Gaze at the world of men." His commander's voice retreated. "Was that for your father?"

"Yes sir," answered Amnestos, looking up. "Thanks to the god that allowed him to fight." His father Eurytos perished during the final morning at the Hot Gates. Leonidas had released him from duty and had, in fact, ordered him home along with Aristodemos; both suffered from ophthalmitis, a swelling shut of the eyes by the thick dry dust raised in march and combat. Aristodemos obeyed his king—Eurytos could not. He commanded a Helot attendant to gear him for war then lead him to the battle lines, where sightless he fought and died with the last of the Spartans. The boy parted company with his commander.

"What did he want?" said Bull.

"The lad?" answered Amompharetos in a most detached manner.

"Who else? Enyalios himself?"

"I talk to the gods quite often, but unlike you, they never seem to answer," said Amompharetos

Kallikrates grinned. He always grinned. He grinned when he ate. He grinned when he slept. He even grinned when he fought, but this was a most different grin, one that was most disturbing, for it was gleeful. "Tomorrow the Hyakinthia commences. You must get us home early commander."

# CHAPTER 7

▼

Myronides, along with the other Athenian ambassador Xanthippos, stated his case emphatically to the ephors. "Spartans, we do not seek to coerce, but only state facts. Athens is once again in ruin. Two harvests lost. We cannot forfeit another." Myronides paused, studying the faces of the five Spartan overseers, but they revealed no more life than the statue of Apollo that greeted them outside the chamber. "We cannot hope to expel the barbarian without you. And we will not settle for a dishonorable peace with Xerxes. You know this. But neither we will continue to live as vagabonds. If you will not help us, we will be forced to sail to new lands, leaving ours to the Persian. I think they will make ungracious neighbors."

Still the ephors said nothing. They exhibited scant concern over his words and this puzzled Myronides. He rose, sighed, and shook his head in frustration.

"We thank you Myronides. And thanks to you also, Xanthippos," said Poliadas curtly, seemingly unmoved by the discussion. "Please attend a dinner tonight in your honor." The two Athenians, stunned wordless, left the room by escort and stepped out onto the sunlit steps where a breeze greeted them. Myronides, impelled by reflex, palmed his steely hair forward, working against nature. From the street below a man climbed up to greet them.

"Did you convince them?" he asked. "Oh I beg your indulgence," the stranger added apologetically. "I am Chileos, from Tegea. I ask because I wiled away most of yesterday, jawing at those five stone faces."

Myronides, grim until now smiled. "How, my friend, can you tell if they have even heard you?"

"Oh do not let their silence disarm you. They hear what you say, and more." He squeezed his lips tight and shook his head. "Farewell," he said slipping by them and through the doorway, "for I must try once again."

*    *    *    *

"Lord Asfandiar, we found him hiding in the rubble," announced the Median infantryman. He prodded the kneeling man with his falchion, but the Greek would not look up. "A slave, I am sure," added the brightly trousered warrior as he pressed the blade into the flesh of his throat.

"I speak your tongue," assured Asfandiar. "What were you doing? Spying perhaps?" Again the Median poked him with the sword, eliciting a wince, and a trickle of blood. "Tell me and you shall live."

The man craned his neck to look up. "My name is Krios, lord. I am no spy, but a poor slave who works to repair his master's house." Again he cast down his eyes.

"Your master is the Great King," shouted the Median in broken Greek as he prodded him with the blade.

Asfandiar slid from his horse, then tugged the gauntlets from his hands while studying his truckling captive. He did not care for these new gloves; although richly crafted with gold threaded gryphons and of the most supple goatskin, they did not fit as comfortably as his old ones.

"Let him stand," commanded Asfandiar. Slowly the old Greek unfolded his body from its cower. "You may go. But there is one task I would charge you with."

Krios' eyes widened with question. "Anything, my lord," he answered while touching his brow.

"Greek, open your eyes and look about you."

Far from being closed, Krios' eyes gleamed like two white saucers.

"Count the myriads of Asia that again pour through your tiny city's streets. Beyond the wall many thousands more assemble, girded for battle. Like the tide of the sea, there is nothing you Greeks can do to keep us from your land. Go back to your master and tell him what you have seen. Tell all of your countrymen of the power of the Great King."

Krios stared unblinking. He watched while companies of light infantry bearing torches streamed toward the Kerameikos and the newly resurrected shops, single room manufactories and dwellings. Soon his nostrils burned with smoke; it hung like a hot fog, for the wind had ceased. Anything that would ignite, be it of men or the gods, was set alight by the Persians.

"Get him to the harbor," said Asfandiar. With a spin he was upon his horse once more and galloping through the Agora.

\*     \*     \*     \*

The day was perfect. To the north west the peaks of Taygetos snagged the few clouds that tried to slip over but everywhere else the sky was unblemished. Amompharetos entered the theatron of Amyklai with his wife Polydora, eyes scanning the crowd for friends and suitable seats. Someone tugged his shoulder.

"Amompharetos. It is good to see you again, my friend," said the Tegean.

"Chileos," he announced with a smile. The two embraced, then the Spartan stood back revealing his wife. "You have met Polydora. Several years back I think and at this very festival."

"Why yes," added Chileos. He dipped his head to the lady. "And how is your daughter? And I understand you also have a new son."

"Both are in good health and growing," said Polydora. "Why don't you join us, sir," she offered. "I see several seats over there."

The three moved deeper into the row, saying their *good mornings* as they edged past others already seated. Some knew the Tegean while others did not and were presently acquainted with him by Amompharetos. Below them, centered in the first row of the theatron was a bank of empty seats—these reserved for the Gerousia and ephors. Now this body of men, the power in Sparta, entered through a portal to the right of the orkestra. Twenty-eight elders, all men over age sixty, comprised the Gerousia and held these posts for life. The five ephors—the Spartan appellation for magistrate—were newly elected each year. It was through their voices that Sparta addressed the world.

"There is your father," said Chileos, pointing to the procession of men. "I spoke with him for much of the afternoon yesterday. And that was after spending hours pleading with the council of ephors entire." Somewhat covertly he indicated the pair of Athenian ambassadors that sat in places of honor in the first row of seats. "They spoke prior to me."

Now in walked a score of young boys—the grade of rhobidas—all aged fourteen. It was the youngest of the paidiskoi of the Agoge that always began the ceremonies. They began a song of mourning and praise to the god Hyakinthos; the tale of his death, accidentally struck by a discus thrown by the god Apollo. This, his festival, also marked the death of spring.

"And what did the ephors say to you?" asked Amompharetos.

"I spoke, it seemed endlessly to them, detailing the predicament of Hellas and the lonely position we would find ourselves in shortly if we continued our procrastinations."

"And what did they say?"

"They invited me to dine with them," responded Chileos with a laugh. "And nothing more."

"This may bode well for us. The army has been intensifying its drill. And with each march we are attended in full commissariat. Wagons loaded, servants in campaign numbers. Pioneers, carpenters and armorers too. Hardly routine." Amompharetos and his Pitanate Regiment, along with four other lochoi, had continued field exercises in campaign compliment for several months. Never before had they maintained so grueling a regimen. In the past word of five Spartan regiments of Peers on the march would have carried to the corners of Hellas, seemingly upon wings, but now all grew dull to the news. He wondered if it were a ruse to mislead Argive and Persian spies. Or was it to prepare for the defense of the Isthmos?

For most of the morning choirs of boys, accompanied by flute and kithera, entertained the crowded theatron until, just before midday, the festival paused. The agora here in Amyklai had been prepared for a great outdoor feast and now everyone filed out to the garlanded avenue that would lead them there. Chileos walked with Amompharetos and his wife. Ahead of them he spied Poliadas and the other ephors; they stood watching and waiting in the shade of the temple of Apollo. Poliadas waved to them discreetly.

"He must want to speak with you, Chileos," said Amompharetos, "for he avoids me."

And indeed Poliadas and his group took Chileos aside; they neither excluded nor included Amompharetos in the discussion, proceeding in their talk as though he was not present. Poliadas greeted the Tegean, asked him how he enjoyed the festival and what he thought of the voices of the choirs. They talked of the peculiarly warm spring and how this would accelerate the growing season, at least south of the Isthmos. Then suddenly, and divorced from the current talk Poliadas asked, "Are your men ready to march?"

Chileos, taken aback by this request stammered a bit. "W-where?"

"Nowhere just yet my good friend Chileos, for as everyone knows we have two more days of the Hyakinthia to celebrate." Poliadas smiled. Chileos assured him that Tegea would indeed be ready. "Good. Then let us forget about this talk and enjoy our meal," said Poliadas.

It was as if a hand had reached deep into Amompharetos' belly and pulled out every bit of tissue; it felt desperately empty. Ten years past, he sped north—part of the expedition assembled to assist the Athenians at Marathon, arriving a full day after their glorious victory over the Persians. Sparta's reliability was questioned, and for many years he assured himself that never again would his city fail in its obligation to lead. But again a mere five men afflicted with aboulia, paralyzed Sparta with their indecision, inviting disaster.

*By the gods, they had not even determined where they would fight*, he thought. These maneuvers of the army were a ruse. His father would not sanction helping Athens. Sparta would hunker behind the wall at the Isthmos.

*        *        *        *

Theron slid the box from above the hearth, lifted the lid and gazed proudly at the horsehair crest within. Carefully—almost solemnly—he released it from its cradle, shook it slightly, billowing the strands of hair, then held it out before him.

"Father, do you have the pins," he asked, turning the crest while smiling.

Nikandros plucked up two narrow bronze rods, both slightly longer than his thumb and handed them to his son. Theron slipped the crest onto his helmet, wriggling it to align the holes in it with the matched fittings, then secured it with the pins.

"Here son, you'll need a bit of oil." He passed the small flask to him along with a wad of linen. Nikandros continued to work the olive oil into the bronze breastplate that he clamped between his knees.

"Theron. Your sword." His grandfather withdrew the long, leaf-shaped blade from its scabbard and stared at it admiringly. "Look closely my boy and you can see Argive blood still on the blade."

Pankratios had fought alongside the Spartans when their king Kleomenes defeated the Argives and secured peace in the Peloponnese. Many surmised the battle was prompted by Argos' collaboration with the Persians and King Darios; others supposed Kleomenes ambition had impelled him to fight. Fought at a place called Sepeia, the Spartans garnered victory. With the battle lost, the surviving Argives fled to a sacred grove, hoping to escape the pursuing Kleomenes by sheltering in the protection of the god, but the Spartan king would not be denied, and ordered Helots to set the grove alight, immolating the Argives. Some say it was this sacrilege that precipitated his madness and death, a punishment from the gods for defiling their sacred precinct. Others said it was Kleomenes' propensity for drink that stole his mind, pushing him to a grisly suicide. No matter, for after the battle of Sepeia the Argives never crossed beyond the boundary stones of their territory.

Upon the floor of the house were laid out two open bedrolls; Pankratios knelt, placing a small cup, bowl and oil lamp on each. "Nikandros, I will put the hand mill in the large basket," he said. Now he pushed himself from the cold floor, standing so very slowly, for his old back fought quick movement. Small as the hand mill was, it still proved weighty, but they would need the scooped-out stone to grind the pulse that would sustain them while on campaign. He plucked a pair of knives that hung above the table and tossed them, one onto each pile.

"Why will Chileos and the magistrates not allow anyone to leave the city?" asked Theron.

"Because the Spartans have told them so," answered the grandfather. "They want no word of this to make its way to the Persians."

"But when do we march?" asked the boy impatiently.

"When we are told." The old man heaved the loaded wickerwork basket onto the table and then fell, tired, into a stool. "Probably not for a few days at least. The Spartans celebrate their festival.

"The corn harvest is near," said Nikandros. "And the barley. It is the same in Lakedaimon. They will never leave now. Not so early in the season."

# CHAPTER 8

▼

"Spartans!" The messenger's eye grew white and wide. He trembled, whether from exhaustion or fear one could not tell.

"Lord Asfandiar, the Spartans are nearing Megara, but half a day's ride from here."

Both the man and his horse panted for breath. Asfandiar smiled and looked at him calmly and without a word conveyed the requirement for composure. The messenger gulped some air, then resumed.

"Our scouts counted at least a thousand advancing to the hills beyond the city."

"Ah well, a thousand you say? Are you sure?" Asfandiar had heard panic mixed in soldiers' words before and also knew how to dispel it. "Did *you* see any Spartans?"

"Well, no my lord, I did not. But I did speak with several who did."

Asfandiar thought, *we would know this if it were true. The Argives, friends of the Great King, had assured us they would stop the Spartans from exiting north into Attika. At the very least they would inform us of such a move. No, this must be some drink-induced specter. Bored sentries, swigging wine. That is all.*

From a ridge marked by the tower of a small farmhouse he spotted a single rider bob into view. The figure waved to him, and then broke into a gallop. Still quite a distance off he yelled to his brother. Tooraj waved again. Finally he pulled up near Asfandiar and the lugubrious messenger, greeting them both with a salute to his brow.

"Brother, I have come from Masistios," he said, then nodded acknowledging the other man. "He summons you."

The two set their horses to a sprint, up the road and to the grand pavilion of their commander. The landscape was in motion. Here platoons of archers, javelineers, sutlers and provender men hurried about, criss-crossing the hastily laid out encampment. Flaming pennants fluttered in the gentle south wind that carried the aroma of wood-smoke.

"Smells like Athens." Tooraj laughed.

They reined up near the tent, and seemingly from nowhere, a pair of grooms appeared to lead their horses to station near a distended basket of grain. Masistios, announced by the snap of the tent flap, stepped out into the sharp light of morning.

"Welcome," he waving them forward. "Come in." Masistios was indeed tall. His broad shoulders filled the entrance to the tent and again he bent to clear the opening. The two brothers, tall men themselves, walked straight in.

"Asfandiar sit," he commanded. "I have a small task for you both."

Now he snapped his fingers and a servant appeared shouldering a large silver pitcher. Another trailed him carrying three exquisitely crafted fine-stemmed goblets. Soon wine gurgled into the cups. Several more attendants entered the room bearing platters of steaming meat, cakes and bread.

"Eat and drink, for I will talk." He waited, watching as the servants offered food to Asfandiar and Tooraj; they reclined on plush silver-footed couches, sampling the meal but clearly attending to their commander.

Masistios walked about as he spoke while two servants chased after him with different articles of dress, hurrying to fit him when he paused."Our friends the Argives, have just sent word that the Spartans are marching north," He halted his talk when a servant came forward with a tray full of jewelry. One by one he slid the rings he wore from his fingers, wriggled his gloves on, then carefully selected new rings, eight in all, from the tray. "Yes I know, they had promised to stop them. But when did you ever meet a Greek who kept a promise. Some of our other friends tell us that a small group of them are already on the outskirts of Megara. I want you to lead four squadrons of cavalry. Catch them while they are isolated."

"Then the rumors are true. A rider had just come in from the frontier. He talked of a thousand of them."

Masistios sipped. "They will be in open country. Easy prey for your horsemen. We must remind these Greeks who is their master."

"What is their purpose?" asked Asfandiar, "In rushing ahead?"

"To secure the northern mountain passes out of Attika. To pen us in. I would think they prefer to fight here and not to the north in Boiotia where the terrain would suit our cavalry."

"When do we leave Lord Masistios?" Asfandiar rolled the stem of his goblet between his palms.

"When you have finished your wine," he answered buoyantly. "Attack quickly. Dispatch this vanguard, then meet us in Boiotia. Show these arrogant Spartans what is in store for them if they march further north."

Too quickly their wine cups sat empty upon the table. Masistios bade farewell to them, exiting the tent with the brothers into the heat of midday. When they had mounted their horses and were about to leave Masistios, as he would always do before battle, invoked a blessing from Ahura Mazda for success.

The brothers departed and within the hour sat in conference with the other officers of their squadrons. Most were happy at the prospects of battle. None of them had ridden north this past winter with Artabazus, deprived of participation in the attack on Potidaia. A winter of grazing in Thessalia followed by another trek to devastate Athens provided little plunder and less adventure. Finally it seemed as if the Greeks would fight, and this suited Asfandiar and his brother. By autumn they would be riding home.

\*        \*        \*        \*

Myronides stood up near the bow of the ship amongst the men, straining to pick out any movement on the far shore of Attika. The second day of the Hyakinthia in Sparta, the day he awoke to the unexpected news that the Spartan army had commenced its march north, he raced back to Salamis, nearly killing his horse with an unrelenting pace. He brought good news; the allies were to assemble at the sacred town of Eleusis, northwest of Athens. Now a day after returning he sailed across the narrows, along with his taxi of three thousand hoplites under the command of Aristides. Krios was at his side; he had slung about his shoulder a large bedroll and around the back of his neck hung a grass-rope that held two baskets of provisions.

"Krios, you may yet again meet your Persian benefactor," said Myronides. "If he is fortunate to be taken alive."

The slave said nothing. Silently he thanked the gods for his deliverance from the barbarians and his safe return to his true master.

Above the trees on the far shore to his left Myronides saw the dust of riders drifting skyward. It was the road to Megara—the road exiting the Isthmos. Strange, for he expected his taxi to be the first armed Hellenes to step into Attika. The Spartans were at least another day out, having initially to rendezvous with their allies near Tegea. *No matter,* he thought. *They soon would land.*

He looked about now, out into the swells, and saw as many boats as on the day of the great battle, but these were laden with armed men, ready to reclaim their city and their homes. Shouts rose up as the lead vessels ground ashore. At first it sounded like a far off storm, a rumble, but voices clear and jubilant broke the afternoon quiet. The goddess Echo returned their cheers from the shore.

He looked on as a small unit of cavalry, not quite a squadron, rallied around a bellowing officer then took off from the beach at Phaleron heading inland following the Athens Road. They would be the first.

He wished to be amongst them, to climb to the High City and catch sight of the fleeing barbarians. He stood better than half a day from his wish.

Now his transport groaned upon the beach, its false-keel burying into the soft sand. So unlike the attack on Psyttaleia, no one rushed to disembark but waited in good order for their turn to exit, knowing battle waited more than a few days away. Myronides trotted down the bowing gangplank and onto the beach, pausing for a moment to delight in his return. From behind he heard the bray of a mule and looked back over his shoulder to see Krios tugging reins; three spears were strapped to one side of the mule and on the other hung his aspis with the symbol of Athena—the owl—freshly painted upon it. Between the weapons and atop the mule was bound a large sack containing his helmet, greaves and thorax.

They assembled on the beaches by lochus—the Athenian unit of one hundred—and then marched the road into Athens, passing toppled stone foundations in this once thickly settled precinct. Straight ahead he saw the High City, and off to the left the Aereopagos Hill; in his mind he tried to place where his house once stood framed by the two but further north beyond the Eridanos Stream. When they reached the foot of the High City the column took the large gravel street—the Sacred Way—to the left of it toward the Agora.

The city didn't look as bad as it did to him just two months prior when he walked it for the first time since the Persians fired it. A spring of clearing rubble had left most of the main thoroughfares passable, but any repairs had been obliterated by the return of the barbarians. With every breath he tasted the potent smell of charred wood.

Presently the Agora began filling up with the men of Athens. As he pressed forward deeper into the marketplace Myronides watched a few units march off toward the gates and outer walls, while the remainder stood in assembly waiting. Now he could see Aristides climb atop a single column drum, one that had once belonged to the Fountain House. The fine tiled roof of the building was gone, and the chiseled lion-head spouts that once gushed water into the stone drawing basin had been hacked away, but water still flowed. A shout, then the jabbering of a thousand men ceased.

"Men of Athens!" exclaimed Aristides. "This is indeed a momentous day, for we stand once again in our great city." He paused and looked, singling out it seemed, every man for a moment, one after another. "I see some doubt on your faces. Does the destruction about us dishearten you? It should not. These are but lifeless bits of stone, the ashes of dead trees, and the dust of what was old and unimportant. You, my fellows, are Athens, and I see in you a bright future." The crowd roared with approval. Aristides smiled and nodded, allowing the thunder of their voices to fill the Agora, for each cheer seemingly resuscitated the city.

He continued. "Out there," he said pointing to the north, "is the Persian, waiting with our enemies from Thebes to settle this. And within a day our great ally, Sparta, shall join us." Once more cheers exploded. For more than a year they longed to hear those words.

"Tonight we sleep in Athens. Tomorrow we march out to meet our friends. And when we return—and return we shall—it will be to a free and secure Athens." Even Myronides yelled approval at his commander's words, for so unlike Aristides was this display of rhetorika, and so unlike Myronides was he stirred to respond in kind.

After Aristides finished, another man, Leon, announced the orders for the army. He detailed the units of guards, which consisted of the oldest and the very youngest, then assigned sections of the city for the remaining men to occupy. Myronides instructed Krios to go onto the section near the Hangman's Gate—his assigned area of bivouac—and prepare his dinner. He would follow shortly, but for now decided on a walk to the High City. He would see the Persians if he could from this vantage.

He took the broad avenue away from the wreck of the Council-House, passing the black stumps of plane trees that once grew on this side of the Agora. To his left, not a single recognizable house or shop could be distinguished amongst the mounds of toppled brick-work. Even the hastily erected sellers' booths that merchants had scrambled to build after the first occupation had been gutted by sys-tematic arson.

He gazed up at the High City—the Akropolis. The stone and brick wall that once ringed its base had been dismantled, so he cut across the rubble-strewn ground to intercept the walkway further up slope. The steps caught his eye for never had he seen these anything but sparkling clean. Now tufts of weeds pushed through the joints of the masonry. Oddly, of all the sights he beheld thus far, this neglected span of stairs troubled him the most.

Upon the hilltop the damage proved worse than he had guessed. The barbarian had defiled every structure, showing not the least bit of respect for his city's gods. Not a single statue remained, all the bronzes looted from each holy place. The new temple of Athena, the one that had begun construction just a year prior to the invasion, had each block and drum knocked from its walls, spilling about bright heaps of marble. The sight enraged him, then set him to tears. He did not cry at the sight of his extinct home or even at the return of his son's body. But now he cried. He dropped to a seat upon the crumbled step that once led to the altar of Athena Polias, raked his hands over his face, then cradling his head between them, he sobbed. He wept till darkness swallowed the High City.

A man, who he had never met, approached, bearing a torch of wood and pitch. The light flickered wildly upon his face. "Are you injured, friend?"

Myronides, now tired and emptied of his grief stood. He snatched the torch from the man and bounded to the top of the altar. "Persian!" he yelled to the darkness. "We are here." He whipped the sputtering branch from side screaming out at the gathering night.

\*     \*     \*     \*

The sun had slipped below the trees beckoning the dark—a welcome dark for the remnants of the four squadrons of Persian cavalry wished to see no more of this day. Asfandiar turned back to look upon the body of his brother; it hung like a pannier over the back of horse, bobbing and swaying with each step. He winced a bit as he spun slowly back to peer ahead up the road; the purpled bruise on his jaw ached with the barest movement. By now his makeshift tourniquet had stanched the wound in his thigh, but his bloody trousers clung cold to his flesh. Most others also rode with bound wounds. Some had weakened during the retreat from Megara and rolled off their horses, dead into the sunbaked limestone of the road.

How could this happen?" he mumbled to himself.

Early that afternoon Asfandiar, at the head of his four squadrons of heavy cavalry, galloped south on the road to Megara, expecting to set an ambuscade for an advanced unit of Spartan hoplites. There were no Spartans. There was nothing but a silent road that twisted between two steep hills in the wood, and it was here that the Greeks struck. Felled trees, formed into an abattis, blocked their route forward. Light-armed warriors—men with little more than spears and rocks—poured into them from the hilltops while archers fired inexorably into the rear of the column. Their horses spun in wild estrapades, churning up the dust that fed the confusion. Attackers tumbled down the slopes, working in groups of two or three, singling out targets on horseback. One or two would jab at the mount while another wrestled the rider to the ground. Spears quickly finished both man and animal.

Asfandiar tried to rally his men, exhorting them to form up and charge the archers in their rear, but when he saw his brother, bristling with arrows, drop from his horse, he rode to assist him, neglecting his duty as commander. More perished in this leaderless tumult. Mercifully the assaults faded with the sun and by dusk the Persians stumbled back into Attika.

The clinking of their gold fused oddly with the muffled patter of hoof beats upon the road as they retreated further north; Asfandiar's orders were not to take the short route into Boiotia, over the Kithairon Pass, but continue deep into Attika, to link up with the Persian rear-guard.

"What is that Lord Asfandiar?" asked an officer that rode beside him. The pair turned to look off toward Athens, and there high on the Akropolis, they spotted a solitary tongue of fire flitting back and forth.

"A torch. Seems the Athenians have reclaimed their city," he answered, as he watched the flicker of torchlight dance atop the High City of Athens. The column moved on.

*     *     *     *

"By now I would have expected the Argives to appear." Bull stood beside his friend Amompharetos; both watched as the regiment fell into its place in the circular camp upon the border of Lakedaimon. Arms were stacked and centered; in from the perimeter rode several groups of horseman, sentinels for the army during the day they relinquished this duty to the men of Skiritis. "Pausanias must perform the sacrifices here," he added, "Or we do not cross." He pointed with his kothon to the stream beyond, hidden by the onset of dark, but still heard.

"Since when does Pausanias wait for omens?" asked Amompharetos.

Pausanias, though not a king, stood in for the young Pleiostarchos—son of the slain hero Leonidas—as prodikos or regent. The dual kingship of Sparta, established long ago in the haze of the past, was unique among the Hellenes. Derived from two separate and competing families, the Agiads and the Eurypontids, these kings wielded supreme authority in the field; at home they merely added their two votes to the

Council of Twenty-Eight, although they did in fact, possess a certain measure of persuasion well beyond this mere vote.

Pausanias did indeed wait for no omen, but out of respect to the gods and the customs of his land performed the rites as an actor might perform in a play. He stood with Tisamenos the seer, the bearers of the sacred fire, the five polemarchs of the five regiments, and the two state envoys to Delphi—the Pythii—while the goat was brought forward. Pausanias dunked his hands into the bronze bowl of water and rubbed them dry with a square of unblemished linen. Following him Tisamenos also dipped his hands, then sprinkled water atop the beast's head. It shook and peered up at the sky—a good sign. Pausanias wrapped his forearm about the neck of the bleating goat and dropped it to the earth, pinning its rear legs with his knee. Smoothly he slid the blade of his short-bladed sword across the animal's throat. It wriggled. It shook. Cold death rushed in to replace the blood that coursed from the wound.

"Look, he smiles now as if he can see the omens for himself," said Kallikrates. He studied Pausanias. The regent again dunked his red-stained hands in the bowl then shook them dry while Tisamenos worked on the carcass. A short while later he approached Pausanias cradling his hands. Pausanias looked as kingly as any Amompharetos had seen before—in fact surely more so, for even the exiled Demaratos or the concomitant monarch Leotychidas possessed hardly the noble bearing and manner that he exhibited. Only Leonidas had stood as regal.

Now he turned to the three and grinned, acknowledging them as he approached.

Amompharetos stepped forward to greet him.

"The omens?"

"Aren't you going to offer me some wine before you begin your interrogations?" His eyes twinkled, revealing a combination of intellect and humor.

Amompharetos pointed to a servant then called for wine. He hurried away and shortly returned with a pitcher and kothon, and handed the cup to Pausanias.

"Come fellows and let us make good use of your fire," said the regent. He sipped a bit of the wine, then strolled to the far side of the brazier to an empty stool. "So you wish to know of the omens?" He paused and sipped again. "The omens are exquisitely perfect." The three grinned at his remarks, but so very quickly did this look of humor flee Amompharetos' face that it spoke to them all. "What is it Amompharetos? Do you think I manipulate the intentions of the gods?"

"Why no. But you speak as though they work to your commands," he answered.

"Hardly—for I, like you, am a pious soul and follow the way ordained by the gods. I just see this path more clearly than others." Pausanias looked at their faces over the rim of his kothon as he drank. "And you three. You should be more than pleased we march, for that is what you have been preaching for almost a year since the death of my uncle Leonidas."

"It is he who preaches," corrected Bull as he stabbed his finger at Amompharetos. "His father will attest to this. We who are his friends simply listen."

Now they all laughed at the big man's words. Serious talk fled the warriors, and for an hour or more they spoke of childhood adventures, confessed their infatuations and of course insulted the Argives. Reminded of the hour by the changing of the Skiritai sentries, the regent got up from his stool, placing his empty cup upon it in his stead. "Enough, gentlemen. I have duties beyond storytelling, you know." Pausanias melted into the dark beyond.

Prompted by the departure of their commander, the three stood, shaking off the chill of inactivity. Kallikrates shuffled off to a cluster of bushes and began watering them. Bull bid a goodnight and headed for his skene, the open-sided tent of the Spartan army. Amompharetos, however, knew the comfort of slumber still eluded him, so he strolled the camp, peering into each skene he passed, checking on his men. Most snored blissfully. Finally he came upon the tent of his comrades. Within all were sleeping—even Bull. The fire-lit canopy silhouetted a single kneeling figure.

"You need sleep, Amnestos."

"Amompharetos, I cannot sleep," he answered, his eyes reflecting the flittering orange of the campfire.

"Then come out and at least be warm."

Catlike the two moved through the tent. Near its open wall Amnestos stumbled to the ground. Bull's thick hand shackled his ankle. "And where are you going?"

"With my commander," he answered in a whisper.

"Shut up," mumbled a voice from the pile of bodies within.

Looking up through half open eyes and seeing Amompharetos, Bull uncurled his fingers then rolled over with a snort. They both moved out to the dying fire. Curled up on the ground slept a Helot. As soon as the two sat, he bounded up, rubbed his eyes, and commenced to flip charcoal into the brazier. For long moments neither spoke, but sat staring at the flames.

Finally Amompharetos broke the silence. "So why do you not sleep? You must be as tired as the rest of us. The pace proved lively today."

"I think of my father. His denies me rest," he answered.

"Eurytos?" Amompharetos seemed puzzled by the lad's words. "You should remember him with pride. None were braver."

"None braver," he repeated. "I hear this from everyone. Every day I am compared with my father. I look forward to the day when the enemy will finally measure me against him."

"Why Amnestos. You may lack many things, but courage is not amongst them," he countered. "Doubt rules your mind now as it sometimes does in youth."

"It is not a doubt spawned within me, but a doubt of others," said Amnestos. "Even you. You did not want me in your phidition."

"And where did you hear this?"

"From you."

"From me?" he answered shaking his head.

"You have a face that cannot disguise a lie. It betrays you now as it did on the night of the vote. You did not want a problem. You see me as one."

The youth's accusation numbed him. For moments his mind balked at forming words, normally a talent at he could call upon effortlessly. Erupting suddenly and without thought, he answered. "Yes you are a problem, but not because of your lack of courage. It is your anger that will be your undoing, and ours, if I allow it. I want clear heads around me in battle." He spoke as though addressing his messmates, not a solitary young man.

"There is a fire in me when I fight." Now he paused, for again he felt his blood rising in him and was ashamed by this.

"You feel it now, don't you?"

"Yes," he admitted with a sigh. "But having me standing guard with my shield all night will hardly quell it."

"Hardly," laughed Amompharetos," but it will surely strengthen your arm. And offer you a bit of thoughtful time."

The Helot sat cross-legged beside the fire, poking the embers with a stick to clear the ashes, and every so often would toss in another lump of charcoal. His eyes followed the blossoms of sparks skyward, paying scant heed to the conversation. The two men talked on, the elder launching inquires that provoked, while the younger Amnestos fought back his anger. The questions intensified; his rage, in time, did not. An hour or more passed and still Amompharetos hammered away at him. The boy at any time could have ended it, but his stamina was improving.

Now he stared at his commander while Amompharetos slid the xuele knife from its sheath, balancing the blade on his extended finger. It rocked slightly until coming to equipoise. "This is courage."

Now the youth's mouth opened. He shook his head. "What?"

"One end of the knife is fear, the other anger. Courage exists in a precarious balance somewhere between." He walked about keeping the knife motionless on his finger. "You have been schooled that fear has no place in the heart of a Spartan. Anger is deadlier, for it has killed more men than fear. Push your anger deep. It will always be there, but only you must know of it." Now he smiled. "This is good advice indeed. I live by it every day." Now he stood, stretching. "You have worn me out," he admitted finally. "I am going to sleep, as well you should."

The two stepped from the firelight. Again hugging the earth in slumber, the Helot did not see them leave.

*       *       *       *

"By the deathless gods!" yelled Theron. He snapped his hand away from the tent peg squeezing it to a fist, wincing. "That thumb has been hit more often than the peg." He fired the hammer-stone into the ground.

"Be thankful it is your shield hand you strike," commented his father Nikandros "With a thumb like that your spear would be useless."

The night was warm and the air still, even here at the Isthmos, for no breeze blew off the Gulf of Korinth. All day men from the Peloponnese streamed into the encampment: Epidaurians, Mykenians, Phlians, Orchomenians, Sikyonians, Korinthians and their colonists from Potidaia. These men were strewn about as though they were attending the Olympian Games or some such festival, chatting casually, some sleeping, many without tents or fire. The Spartans' circular camp projected the only sense of order across the Isthmos; each skene of fifteen men was pitched precisely in line with its neighbor, symmetrically forming the spokes of a huge wheel. Nikandros and the Tegeans' camp nudged the perimeter of it.

"Well pray to Aeolos that he sends no wind tonight and *that* might stand till morning," said Nikandros while looking at the tent his son had struggled to erect.

Nikandros and Theron walked toward the small fire that his younger son Medios and the servant Selagos tended. Medios cradled the battered and patched bronze helmet of his grandfather which now belonged to Theron. From a small aryballos flask he poured out oil onto a scrap of linen and commenced to rub the old helmet. Selagos hunched over a sandal, one of Nikandros', that had a broken strap. With a bronze needle and some dried sinew he worked to reunite the strap to the worn sole, but the dim light did little to ease his task. He leaned closer to the fire. Theron sat next to his brother, lifting his wooden aspis from the hard earth.

"That has as many patches and plugs as your helmet," said Nikandros.

His son tipped the shield upright and studied it in the faint glow of the fire. It was a symphony of repairs: the bowl had five strips of new oak doweled to its facing; the porpax armband wobbled when he slipped his arm into it; the rim was crisscrossed with splints that mended the fractures from sword hacks. Slowly he tipped it back upon the ground.

Theron now stared across the field to the Spartan camp, and there blooming from the earth in precise order were row upon row of standing shields, and these were all furnished with gleaming skins of bronze over wooden cores. Upon their facings and in perfect repetition was the lambda, ensign of their country.

"What is it son? You would prefer a shield such as the Spartans carry?" Nikandros pulled the aspis to him and hefted it upon his left arm and shoulder, then stood. "A Persian arrow will make no distinction," he said slapping his hand upon the shield's surface. "Yours is a shield that has always served well." He smiled and added, "And it will not call attention to you as some of the gentlemen of the other cities whose richly fashioned panoplies would announce their rank to the enemy."

"They look as warriors should—as I have always imagined them to look," said Theron sadly. He extended his hands to accept the ancient shield, then leaned it against his leg while plucking his spear free of the earth.

"Son, I am looking at a warrior now," said his father with a proud smile.

"Brother," announced Athamos as he stepped into the firelight, still hobbling a bit from his year old wounds.

Nikandros, being experienced and somewhat older than the other men in his platoon, had been appointed enomotarch. He did not seek this honor, but conjectured that his brother Athamos engineered the voting in his favor. By all rights Athamos himself should command the platoon for his duty at the Hot Gates. But he was the younger and deferred.

Never before had they all been together and so far from home. Gathered around the fire they spoke not as warriors but as sightseers might, describing the Diolkos slipway—the road used to convey seagoing vessels across the Isthmos from the Gulf of Korinth to the Saronic Gulf in the south—and commenting on the bright waters of the Gulf and the gleaming temples on the AkroKorinth. Now a breeze began to sweep up from the water, whisking away the mosquitoes that had been buzzing them since their evening meal. War to them was a diversion, a reason not to trail an ox and plow from dawn until dark.

Chileos, the leading strategos or general of Tegea, strolled the precincts of the encampment, stopping to talk with each group until he at last came to the fire of Nikandros and his family. "Ah Chileos," said Nikandros smiling. "Please join us." Now he turned toward his servant. "Selagos, some wine."

Chileos stepped toward the fire and greeted each in turn, finishing with the youngest. He accepted the wine from the servant and the stool offered to him by Medios. "I have just returned from council with Pausanias," he said looking around at the circle of faces. "His scouts say the Persians are running away."

"Running away?" said Athamos. "At the Gates they had more men than grains of sand on that beach," he added pointing towards the sea. "Why are they running away?"

"Xerxes has taken a good portion of those men back with him to Asia. The rest, it would seem, do not wish to face us." Chileos peered into his cup, swirling the wine a bit. "Our Spartan friends think they are falling back to Thebes. Too bad really. The Thriasian Plain would have been a splendid place for battle."

Nikandros knew of this plain and of the land of Attika, which surrounded Athens. Indeed it would have been a glorious place for the heavily armored men of Hellas to contest the barbarian—excellent infantry country, but less suitable for cavalry. Chileos went onto explain the plans of the army; with two days marching they, along with the Spartans and other Peloponnesians, would join the Athenians at Eleusis. Pausanias had shown the map to him and the catalogues of men. Over thirty-five thousand hoplites would gather there and this did not take into account at least that many light-armed warriors to be added to the total. The coming battle would not resemble Thermopylai, he reassured them, where only a few thousand Hellenes fought. Here all of Hellas would rally against the invader.

"Do not smile so broadly my friends," added Chileos, "for the Persian will double our great numbers. And he has vast hordes of cavalry."

"Then why does Mardonios retreat?" asked Athamos.

"He moves north into Boiotia to suit his cavalry."

\*      \*      \*      \*

The hour was late but still the council of Boiotia argued on into the night in the Kadmea. Eurydamos sat beside his father watching Attiginos as he delivered his oratory. "Father, why is he so fraught with concern?" whispered Eurydamos. "The Persians have not abandoned us."

Timagenides leaned toward his son. "Not yet, but if they do Thebes cannot stand against both the Athenians and Spartans. Messengers have brought word that the entire Peloponnese is assembling at Korinth and plans to pursue Mardonios."

"But father, you said they would never cross the Isthmos. Besides, how could they hope to match the Persian numbers?" Eurydamos in that moment realized what could be in store for them. "If Mardonios rides north into Thessalia we are doomed."

"And that is why Attiginos talks on," said Timagenides. "To convince the council and Mardonios to use Thebes as a base. It would be a small price to provide for the Great King's army if they keep our enemies at bay."

One of the Boiotarchs, Apollodorus captain of horse, argued against billeting the Persians for he said so large an army would exhaust this year's harvest leaving little for the people of the city. An absurd argument, but others listened and the council session limped on. Another put forth the motion of contacting Pausanias to sue for leniency now, anticipating his march into Boiotia.

"You forget Athens," countered Timagenides in a most frantic tone. "Must I remind even you that Athens would never allow the allies to spare us. Our only friend on their council was slain by a mob. We have chosen our lot and now we must make do." All knew his words hit the mark, for quiet dejection filled the chamber. "We fight along with Mardonios, and to this there can be no question. We are not the Persian's friend anymore than Sparta is Athens'. No, like them we ally ourselves with Xerxes because of a common enemy. This is the way of the world today, so let us not talk of anything but defending our homes."

"You hear it from Timagenides," shouted Attiginos. "We cannot wait for the Persians but should call up the army now."

None had the stamina to argue on; the council approved the muster, inked the katalogos and ordered its posting in the agora. Tomorrow the warriors of Thebes would assemble and march south to greet and escort their allies, the Persians.

# CHAPTER 9

▼

"Your Athenians will lead us through the pass." Pausanias stood amid the several dozen strategoi from the allied states as he directed his words at Aristides, general of Athens. "You have men that are familiar with this road. Your archers can cover the advance." With a poke of his index finger he indicated the road they would take over the mountains which separated Attika from Boiotia; the range stretched from west to east like a vast wall fashioned by a god, with only a few passes that the army could negotiate. The Persians, as he told them all, had taken one of the eastern roads, and this they did to avoid any advance scouts of the Hellenes.

But Pausanias' spies already hovered in the mountains. Some had watched as the Persians set camp, stripping every tree from the land around the village of Skolos to construct a massive stockade. They peered down from their lofty outlooks onto the plain that spread northwards and beheld the uncountable army of Mardonios stretched out for miles on the far bank of the Asopos River. Any approach would be across wide fields advantageous to the multitudes of barbarian cavalry that stared down from their prepared positions across the river.

Aristides nodded his approval and listened as the Spartan detailed the order of march over the pass. Every warrior would now be armed and ready; seventy pounds of armor in the heat of this summer day while climbing the steep slopes between Mount Kithairon and Mount Pastra would task them, but as Pausanias knew they might well march down from the heights directly into battle. For the Spartans it was all quite familiar.

By mid morning the meeting of strategoi ended. The eight Athenian generals left hurriedly, for they would be in the van. Myronides paused and looked up at the road, following its ascent into the hazy mountains.

"Gentlemen," said Aristides, "be sure to have your men fill their flasks. There will be no water until we are on the far side of the pass."

"Why does Mardonios allow us to cross?" asked Myronides. He continued to stare up at their proposed route, knowing that the climb coupled with the summer heat would tax them. Surely a small force of Persians left high in the passes would deal them much trouble.

"He invites us to," replied Aristides. "They say the Persians are waiting along the Asopos daring us to attack, I declare praying for us to do so, but our commander, as young as he is, appears very sensible in his planning."

"Then we should advance before Mardonios withdraws his invitation," said Myronides.

Now he trotted off to the company of a hundred kindred tribesmen that he commanded. Myronides had two slaves with him. Krios tended to his armor as hupaspites while another, Ateokles, prepared the packing of his bedroll and ration basket. All around men began donning their armor. Many wore the older types, inherited from their fathers, a bronze breastplate hammered to the form of a muscled chest, some with fine designs of warring gods framed by silvered vines of ivy etched into their surfaces. Myronides slid into a leather thorax, which Krios fastened around his chest and belly cylinder-like by laces under his left arm. Then he tugged each of the stiff shoulder flaps that sprouted from his back and curved them over, tying them down at Myronides' chest. The bright morning sun glinted off the bronze scales that encircled his abdomen. The bottom was trimmed with three rows of feathers, the long strips of bronze covered leather that hung like tatters to just below his crotch. He glanced at the men in their bronze chest plates. They would suffer in the climb.

Now he heard the blast of a horn issuing from the Spartan camp. He turned and watched the ground swell up in a wave of scarlet and polished bronze as the warriors rose as one. Every Spartiate wore a bronze cuirass and under each the distinctive blood-red chitons of the Lakedaimonians. Their helmets were exquisitely simple in adornment: all were of the closed face type with sweeping cheek pieces that hung to cover their collars, cut with eye-holes and a slit before their lips for breath. Crests matched the color of their clothing and only a very few had ones that spanned their helmets from ear to ear—the mark of a high officer or king; the rest had the more common fore to aft crest. Throughout the multitudes bronze and iron clattered, but in contrast the Spartans moved in silence to form into triple columns.

Myronides gestured to Krios for his scabbard; the slave now dropped this over his master's shoulder, letting it fall snug to his hip. Along with his two servants, he hustled to the road where his company of men waited, assembling just behind the three hundred archers that would form the agema. A breeze swept down from the slopes above carrying with it the scent of thyme. He breathed deeply. It reminded him of his wife and home for whenever she served boarfish Thyia would instruct the cook to apply the herb lavishly; it was a delicacy which deserved no skimping.

For a moment he envied the archers. They wore only flimsy wool chitons and in addition to their quiver of arrows and bow, carried a battle sword but had no shield or armor to encumber them; they would easily outpace the infantry.

Again Myronides spied movement from the Spartan camp, but now instead of hoplites he watched hundreds of Helots, armed as euzonoi or javilineers, stream away from them heading not north over the mountains but in parallel to them. He walked forward to locate his commander.

"Where do they go?" Myronides said looking at the departing Helots.

"To the Oaks Head road." Aristides smiled, cradling his triple-crested helmet in his left arm. "This young Pausanias has never been to Boiotia but knows the geography better than its natives. He has already sent word that our food will come to us over that road."

Indeed Pausanias selected the better of the two roads for the supply convoys; the Oak Heads was connected to Megara and the road south into the Peloponnese, convenient for carts, wagons and sumpter beasts to negotiate. The army would take the steep route, the one that would bring them onto the main road to Thebes, and into the cover of the foothills.

Even in the sizzle of this summer morning the bowmen trotted off briskly, churning up dust that hung dead and dry in the air. Within moments the rear ranks of the archers beckoned the infantry to follow at their pace, taunting their comrades to catch them, if they could.

The first two hours proved tolerable. Then as midday approached, Helios' embrace smothered them, slowing the advance until the path leveled near the head of the pass. Myronides leather thorax armor, which at the commencement of the march proved little burden, now became onerous, doubled in weight by perspiration. No pause was ordered; the loss of incline afforded the men a respite even while marching, so on they went. Myronides sucked a bit of water from his baked-clay flask, then satisfied let it fall free of his grip; it swayed on his hip in a scraping cadence to pace his stride. Others too refreshed themselves on this section of the road. He turned and looked back—a cloudy snake bespeckled with bronze and iron followed him, stretching for miles. Abruptly they halted.

"What's going on?" The infantryman's inquiry was joined by a dozen more. Here and there men eased to the dirt and sun-parched scrub, spears upright and wavering in their tired grips, forming a forest of branchless, iron-tipped trees. Before Myronides could kneel, Aristides called to him and the pair hustled to the van of the column.

"It is this road!" growled Olympiodoros, captain of archers.

"That goes to the quarry. It's this road," countered the other man while pointing to the path on the right.

"How can it be? The tracks are overgrown. This other one is well used. It must be the road." Sure enough the man jabbed at the earth with his bow, indicating the ruts formed by cartwheels.

Now Aristides stepped forward, studied the two routes and spoke. "Friends," he said, hardly meaning it. "That is the quarry road. Follow the one to the right," he commanded.

"But general," rebutted Olympiodoros, "that cannot be the road. Look at it. No one has been on that road for months."

"That maybe so, but unless the gods rearranged Mount Kithairon, that remains the road to Thebes. Follow it."

With not much more than a sideways glance the archers tromped ahead. The column resumed its ascent, straining against the incline, dust, and heat until a welcome breeze suddenly rushed over them from the north. But before Myronides could savor it, the rocky landscape fell away revealing the broad plain and the uncountable army of Persia.

$$* \quad * \quad * \quad *$$

Pausanias leaned upon his spear studying the boundless fields below. Amompharetos, along with the four other regimental commanders hovered nearby; they all scanned the enemy positions, calculating the number and constituent parts. Far off, the summit of Mount Parnassos poked the few clouds that scooted by. Closer loomed Mount Helikon. Amompharetos quickly summed up the terrain before him. As far as the foothills of the mountains would take them, the army would be protected from cavalry attack. Running parallel with the east-west range that they now stood upon was the road to Plataia and this they could cover. A few miles to the north lie the River Asopos where Persian tents, like ten thousand and more petals of wind tossed blossoms, festooned its northern bank. Amidst the gaiety of color loomed a stock-ade constructed of timbered walls each over a mile in length.

"The land in the foothills is filled with hummocks and holes," commented Amompharetos. "Difficult for cavalry."

"But if we advance further the fields are as flat as a platter," said Euryanax, commander of the Konosouran regiment. The six Spartiates stared. His words needed no embellishment. The plain pulled the mountains flat like the sea pulling upon the shore, stretching far off and featureless. It made them uneasy. Pausanias—at twenty-seven the youngest of them—locked his eyes upon the space between the river and the foothills to his left. Beyond the small village of Hysia he could see the shrine to the hero Androkrates, its red-tiled roof blazing in the sunlight. To his right the Shrine to Demeter indicated the portion of the road that veered east to Erythrai. The village hugged the foothills and would protect his army. Here also he could minimize the distance between the Persian and his army, tempting an attack.

"We will deploy to the east along the road as we descend. The Athenians are to move west toward Plataia." Pausanias now turned to Amompharetos, catching him in a scowl. "You do not agree?"

Somewhat surprised by his question, he did not answer quickly. He stroked his beard then spoke. "Why do we not move west to cover our supply road?" He reminded Pausanias of the Oak Heads Road, the path over the mountains that the dispatched Helots were sent to guard.

Pausanias grinned. "Our supplies will not arrive for several days more, but reinforcements will follow us by this road. And if we can induce Mardonios to attack us here, so much the better, for he will be advancing uphill into our shields."

"And if he does not attack, then what?" Amompharetos emptied his flask onto his head, quenching the dust. He blinked his eyes open to stare at his commander

\*　　\*　　\*　　\*

Asfandiar reclined upon the dining couch amid the sumptuous trappings typical to a noble Persian's campaign tent, eating his midday meal when a servant scurried in. "Spartans," said the man rushing his words.

He slammed his half-full cup upon the table and sprang to his feet, causing another servant to fumble for his calfskin boots. In an instant he knelt at his feet with them in hand.

"Where!" He stomped his booted foot hard upon the carpeted floor. The servant slid the second one on.

"The road to Athens," answered the messenger.

Asfandiar sat, extending both arms above his head to accept his scaled armor corselet that his body-servant draped onto him. Quickly he cinched the corselet tight, while other servants pushed ring over ring of gold upon his arms.

"Sword," he commanded, sending one other scurrying for the weapon. He snatched his peaked cap as he stepped through the doorway of his tent, his wine-bearer chasing after him with a brimful cup. Outside the sky was bright but his view restricted by the rampart of timbers that ringed the camp. A groom trotted forward leading his caparisoned mount. Asfandiar mounted quickly. He finished his draught then galloped off to the south gate, as he tossed away the empty cup.

Around him men buzzed. War-trumpets blared and he could see phantoms of dust rising outside of the stockade. The gates squealed open, inviting him out onto the plain beyond and, as he cleared them, he spotted a group of officers surrounding Masistios. The tall Persian and one other turned to acknowledge him while the rest stared south to the mountains. Beyond the river and past the bridge Asfandiar looked to the road in the foothills of Mount Kithairon saw two ribbons of bronze spangled dust slithering from the pass—one turning east, one west and each mimicking the contour of the mountains. From behind the thunder of a horse in full gallop called to them; both rider and mount outfitted in gold finery, reined to a halt.

"General," said the courier, almost breathless, "Lord Mardonios orders you to attack the Greeks on the road." The man gulped air, then continued, pointing with his lance, "where it crosses that field."

The entire group strained to follow the man as he pointed. Asfandiar spied the vulnerable terrain. Strange for they had expected to see the Greeks emerge from the mountains further west and under the protection of the Asopos Ridge near Plataia.

"Gentlemen, gather your squadrons." Masistios bowed his head in prayer, holding his voice within, allowing only a final whisper to escape his lips. Next he extended an empty hand to accept a goblet of wine. He sipped then handed it back to the servant who hurried off with it; Asfandiar watched smiling as the man cowered behind copse of bushes gulping the dregs.

A thousand horsemen thundered across the bridge then coalesced anxiously into a huge rectangle behind their commander. All along the river Persian infantry jostled into battle array. Asfandiar drew joy from this moment. He had crossed from Asia into Europe over a year ago, desirous to serve his king but had only been a spectator to the war so far. Now he would fight, as a noble of Persia should. He hefted his short lance, measuring its weight, taking satisfaction at its balance and familiarity. Next he reached for his bow; it was secure, slung about his shoulder, quiver full, and on his hip hung an akinakes sword in its silver plated scabbard. He shrugged his shoulders to feel it all. From ahead he heard the word: "Advance!"

The horsemen roared out into the undulating plain, maintaining a pace just short of a gallop. They closed upon the open section of road and noticed the Greeks waving and pointing at them with their weapons. A Greek officer stepped before his men barking commands, causing the disorganized throng to transform to an ordered wall of bronze. Now he heard shouts in foreign tongues, Greek he was sure, but the words were fired so quickly his mind could not process them. Ahead the front squadrons of horse began to disperse, selecting targets as they closed on the road.

Insanely a handful of the enemy charged out at the most prominent squadron of horsemen and managed to pull one rider to the ground. The Greek lines exploded in cheer. Swiftly the swarming cavalry cut down these few madmen.

The Greeks undertook desperately to reform their wall, but it was no good. Persian horse was amongst them now, and hitting them from all sides. The Greek infantry fought hard, but the Persians struck, sped off and struck again, eluding their long spears.

By chance Asfandiar focused now upon the man who had shouted orders to the rallying Greeks and thundered off towards him. This one stood apart, yelling at his men while pushing and tugging them into a ragged alignment. Asfandiar pulled up and loosed an arrow; it slipped beneath the Greek's helmet burying itself in his nape. In jerks, he bent forward while clutching his neck, finally slamming both knees into the trampled earth before collapsing.

Ahead of Asfandiar the road churned crazily; the enemy struggled to regain formation but clouds of arrows swept them into disarray. Now he targeted another Greek, nudged out of a group by the swirl of combat. He raised his bow and drew the string back to his chest and let the deadly missile fly; in an instant his victim flicked his shield up to catch the arrow in flight.

Masistios galloped toward the man, who now knelt bowed behind his shield, when suddenly, like a multitude of serpents spitting venom, the air hissed with arrows. Men around Masistios dropped from their mounts. He turned to his right and saw another barrage hurtling at them; more Persians crumbled from horseback. A troop of Greek archers had appeared on the flank; they fired in unison, raking the Persian horse with far-flung death, then surging forward, restrung their bows and launched once more. Masistios fought on, for the missiles bounded off his armored body, but this defiance only drew more notice to him. Now it seemed that every Greek archer took aim at him.

*     *     *     *

Amompharetos, leading the first pentekostys of his regiment, chugged along the front of the army, passing the other contingents, hastily making for the section of road where the Megarians battled with the Persian cavalry. He glanced across the plain northward to watch the Persian infantry; *they will not attack,* he thought. The Spartan heavy infantry closed now on the left flank of the Persian horse. His eye caught sight of a whirl of arrows launched at a singularly tall Persian. Reminiscent of Achilles, the missiles glanced off, effecting him not until several buried deep into his horse's flanks. The beast reared up, catapulting its rider from its back. Now the Athenian bowmen along with the battered Megarians swarmed over him, pumping their iron-tipped spears furiously.

"They seem to be out of practice," chuckled Bull through the slit in his helmet. "The Persian still lives." The Spartans began to roll forward in formation, presenting a wall of men eight deep by sixteen shields across as they approached the melee. Ahead the Persians launched a ferocious attack centered, it seemed, over the body of their fallen leader. Now Spartan shields began to slam into small pockets of Persian cavalry; some horses tumbled onto their sides, wailing in terror, while others rebounded away, unable to heed the commands of their riders to stand fast.

"That one on the ground must be their commander," shouted Amompharetos above the clamor. He heaved forward, stabbing at the flank of a turning horse with his spear; it snapped in two, its iron point burying deep in the thick, pulsing flesh.

The Megarians and Persians, intermixed as they now were, slowed the Spartan thrust by their confused combat. Into the thick of it, Athenian archers flung arrows at the enemy riders—men perched high on horses presenting unmistakable targets. The Spartans advanced rending the Persians from the tumble of allied infantry.

Finally the tide of enemy cavalry receded. The Spartans moved forward of the road and spread their bronze wall to cover the Megarians. Amompharetos, satisfied with their deployment, left the ranks and walked back to the men who crowded around the unhorsed Persian.

"Had to spear him in the eye, I did," said an Athenian as he wiped the spittle from his lips with the back of his hand. The man then reached down and tugged on the ravaged tunic of Masistios to reveal his scaled armor corselet. "We could not poke through that," he added.

"The armor is yours, my friend," said Amompharetos, "but his body belongs to the army." He looked around and spotted a young bowman. "Fetch a cart."

Shortly the archer returned leading several slaves and a two-wheeled cart. It took four of them to lift the body and place it in the cart; he was a large man, taller at least by a head than the tallest Hellene. They knew not his name but by the fight over his body indicated this noble Persian was of high rank. None of the Hellenes could guess that the man they had slain was second only to Mardonios of all the Persians.

*     *     *     *

They could hear the rumble of the oaken wheels as they knelt in battle formation fronting the road. Nikandros and his son Theron, sweltering in the afternoon heat, knew that someone down the line had fought the Persians, for an hour before he watched as a company of Spartans sped past them westward toward the Athenians. He peered down the ribbon of men that extended well beyond his sight, then leaned out again searching for the source of the noise; he saw a pair of men pulling a wagon, guarded by an infantryman, down the front of the entire army. From where he stood he knew it held a body, for from the rear of the cart dangled the legs of a man, and as it moved closer he spotted the high boots of a barbarian.

Chileos, the strategos, approached from his position on the right, curious as to the contents of the wagon, ordering the two men hauling the cart to a halt. Inside lay the huge body of a Persian, his face torn and encrusted in coagulated blood. The man was stripped from the waist up, revealing milk-white skin free of wounds. His beard, although clotted in scarlet, was perfectly cut and curled, as was his hair. His hands bore the traces of jewelry; purpled bands circled each finger indicating the many rings that had been pried from him and the flesh of his ears still dripped blood, torn by men scavenging clasped earrings.

"By the size of him I'd guess he be their captain." declared Nikandros. The hoplite merely nodded. Theron edged out from his file and peered at the corpse; he stared long at it, having never seen a man killed in battle before. Flies began to swarm the cart.

"I have to move along," said the guard, motioning at the two others to proceed. Again the wheel rumbled around, accompanied by the groan of wood as they moved off. Nikandros followed the modest procession with his eyes until, in the distance, the vast stockade of the Persians filled his view. From there he scanned the far banks of the Asopos and for miles he saw myriads of Persian infantry, fading finally into the haze of the late afternoon. Now he looked down the line to the right and into the ranks of the Spartans; the road was carpeted in scarlet and bronze with helmet crests bobbing as men turned to catch sight of the dead Persian.

From the left, where the skirmish had taken place, he heard the thunder of marching feet. The Spartans sent to assist the Megarians chugged their way towards them. Singing issued from the warriors as they approached: "…climb the hill of virtue soldier—never soften your warrior's heart…" The song faded as they passed.

"Do they always sing?" asked Theron of his father.

"Yes, second only to feats of valor they believe music to be most pleasing to the gods," answered Nikandros.

Darkness soon stretched out its cool hands over the face of the army. Orders were given to stand down. Light infantry jogged out onto the knolls and hummocks between the Persians and the Hellenes; these men would secure their front. Behind, in every pass and mountain road, Helot light infantry stood sentinel. Now the heavy infantry could eat. Nikandros and his platoon moved up slope away from the road to a spot designated by Chileos. They staked their spears and piled their shields by platoon and company.

"This is the last of the wine," warned Selagos as he poured it into the pitcher. As always when on campaign these warriors would carry with them a bit of wine to adjust their bellies to water gradually; sadly they watched as the servant squeezed the last trickle of it from the goat-skin flagon. He filled their crude cups while Medios plucked a grape-leaf wrapper from a basket and handed it to his father. Carefully Nikandros unfolded the leaf then pinched a few pebbles of the cheese that hid within. He smiled, delighting in the familiar taste and passed the cheese on to Theron. Across the plain he watched the earth sparkle with the light from ten thousand campfires, more it seemed than stars in the sky. It had been two weeks since he left Tegea, his father and his youngest Alketes. The cheese reminded him of home.

"Oil," he ordered. The boy pulled a flask from the basket and handed it to his father. Nikandros unstoppered the small bottle then trickled some into his bowl. Medios took back the flask, and now that the men were eating he sat himself down to his bowl of goat cheese and flatbread.

Crickets filled the air with song. In accompaniment it seemed, a flute player from the Spartan camp began to pipe in. The melody was pleasant. Without thinking Medios felt for the cord of his flute, then quickly withdrew his hand, hoping no one had noticed. "I am sorry, mother," he whispered. Every so often the musician stopped his music and there could be heard a burst of laughter from the Spartans. Now the music commenced again, this time accompanied by singing.

To the left of the Tegeans, Nikandros looked briefly to the Korinthians; they, like his men, were burdened by fatigue and apprehensive of battle, barely moving about. In contrast the boisterousness of the Spartans increased.

Suddenly one of them burst from the camp, a rag in his hand, he being chased by a naked warrior. A mock cheer rose up from their ranks when the pursuer got hold of him, wrestling the garment free after dousing his face with a cupful of liquid. He slipped the chiton over his head, pulled it snug and them walked back to the throng of men. Another cheer. The other man bent over in laughter. Nikandros stared at the earth between his feet now, measuring his own fear against the lightheartedness of his Spartan allies.

# CHAPTER 10

▼

The ride from Thebes to the Asopos River began at first light for Eurydamos and his father. By mid morning, even keeping to their somewhat leisurely pace, the pair trotted into view of the stockade, and upon the road south came to a checkpoint manned by Thessalian cavalry but officered by a Persian noble. They were quickly recognized and allowed to pass, where again, at the gate to the stockade guards quizzed them before allowing them access. Within the enclosure they heard wailing; someone had died for women bawled lamentations.

"What has happened?" asked Timagenides of a Macedonian horseman.

"Masistios is dead," he answered. "Slain yesterday. They have been parading his body up and down their lines." He pointed south, to the unseen enemy hidden by the timbered walls of the stockade.

Every horse they sighted had its mane and tail close-cropped—a sign of mourning. Even the few helmetless men that walked about had shorn their hair in respect. The two Thebans were unsettled by it all. Timagenides sighed, then nodded to the Macedonian.

He looked about the sprawl of tents and milling men when suddenly the flash of gold caught his eye; straight ahead, in front of a large pavilion he spotted Artabazus as he mounted his bejeweled war-steed. Apart from Mardonios' horse he had never seen such finery apparelling an animal before: rich purple blankets covered its back topped by a leopard skin caparison: its bridle and harness gleamed golden in the sunlight of morning. Artabazus, looked up, training his eyes upon the approaching Thebans.

"Greetings, Artabazus," said Timagenides. "I have just learned of the unfortunate event of yesterday."

"Masistios' death is indeed unfortunate," Artabazus admitted. "The army mourns him." The elder Persian's glance now moved to Euryda-mos. "I see you have come to join your countrymen in the battle line." He stroked his pointed beard with pride. "Take your time. The Greeks will not attack today."

"How many?" asked Eurydamos. His horse now pranced a bit, made nervous by the tromp of a passing sabatam of archers.

"Let us all ride out together and count them," he said smiling.

Several wide streets spanned the stockade's interior feeding the nar-row paths between tents and along one of these Artabazus led the pair deeper into the camp. They watched as hundreds of servants hurried about toting yokes of basketed grain while some pulled small carts laden with stacks of dried fish. Still others scurried after abbreviated herds of goats. Timagenides calculated quickly. "Ten days, no more," he mumbled to himself.

Finally, after weaving around and through the camp they exited through a double-hung gate. Across the river, not far from village of Erythrai, they spotted the army of the Greeks; its stretched less than half the span of the Persian army, but the sight of it caused them to pause and draw a breath. A solitary rider galloped down the mild slope, crossed the bridge and continued on toward them, reining in before Artabazus.

"Lord," he said dipping his head in obeisance, "the Greeks are mov-ing." The horseman drew a line in the air with his lance, tracing the road at the base of Mount Kithairon. "Toward Plataia," he added.

They all sat and watched. True enough. The Greeks were on the move, leaving their unassailable position at the roots of the mountains;

they were marching west toward the Persian right. There between the town of Plataia and the Asopos river sprouted a long ridge and upon it, amongst a stand of trees beamed the bright shrine of Androkrates. It was here that their enemy commenced to reassemble.

"Ah, Timagenides, they move to face your men. And away from our stockade." Artabazus realized that with this move both his wings still overlapped the Greek lines, although now it placed the enemy in even more difficult cavalry terrain.

"For water" said Timagenides. "Why else would they leave the foothills?"

Artabazus studied the Greeks, watching them spill forward upon the ridge. He enjoyed the spectacle, this grand parade of the enemy, and to him it reinforced his assessment—Pausanias would not attack.

"Timagenides, I must join with Mardonios in council. I suggest you see to your countrymen." With a turn of his glance he indicated the far right flank of the army and the assembled northern Greeks—allies of the Great King—and their position above the river. He spun his horse 'round and galloped off. Eurydamos' attention remained with the enemy.

"Timagenides." Bouncing along upon a horse the color of pure alabaster rode the Macedonian King Alexandros, alone and without attendants. "My friend, I have been looking for you."

Timagenides stared in silence; Alexandros was far from a good friend for he had met him only once at a banquet of allies arranged by Xerxes one year past. "King Alexandros," he said touching his brow.

"What do you think of all this?" said the Macedonian, spreading his arms wide in a mock embrace of the landscape.

"I do not understand."

"Why this whole arrangement," he said with a bit of exasperation. "Neither will attack. And if this continues the Persians will feed here all summer on your grain and then, in winter, empty my granaries."

"King Alexandros, if the Persians ride north again the enemy across the plain will be dining in Thebes. I too wish Mardonios to fight. But I fear my city has a much greater stake in his victory—or defeat."

Eurydamos sat atop his horse watching the far ridge while listening to his father. He stabbed at the air with his slender finger, tapping the images of the far off hoplites. "I say thirty thousand infantry, father," he suddenly blurted out.

"Thirty-five thousand," quickly countered Alexandros. "I know this because I know which cities mustered troops. The Lakedaimonians have sent ten thousand hoplites, five thousand of which are Spartiates. See there. They crowd the end of the ridge near those trees." He whipped his hat off and pointed with it. "Eight thousand Athenians face your countrymen." Next he thrust his finger to the tall hill that loomed over the river far off to the right, while still gripping his head-gear. "Would you like to know the numbers of the infantry between the two?" Crafty Alexandros was a friend to all and enemy to none. Paid agents gathered his knowledge for him. He was a welcome guest in most any city, save Sparta and through cunning investment in the right men, knew more about both armies than anyone. He would not allow himself to back the loser, but most of all he wanted his country free of the Persians.

"Mardonios had sent a Carian named Mys to visit several oracles, offer sacrifice and inquire as to the fortunes of his army. At the cave of Trophonios he petitioned, then passed the night as a supplicant at the temple of Amphiaraos in my city. Several other oracles and seers did he make inquires to; they all were clear in their forecasts—stay north of the Asopos and make victory a welcome guest—venture south and destruction will be your companion." Timagenides, assured that he imparted first hand information, was somewhat shaken by Alexandros' response.

"I knew of these oracles before Mardonios did. Impious as this might sound to you friend, rich men rarely receive dire predictions; only the poor and fools hear the truth." Alexandros touched his hat in salute then yanked hard on the reins of his horse. "I must deliver my condolences. Farewell Timagenides."

*          *          *          *

"Go!" yelled Kallikrates. Off sped Bull and Amnestos across the open plain below the ridge, kicking up rooster-tails of dirt as they sprinted.

"My wager stands on the boy," shouted Amompharetos from his perch on the ridge.

Bull's muscular frame did nothing to propel him faster; wiry Amnestos pulled ahead, quickly closing the interval between him and Polydoros, who marked the finish. Bull, in a desperate lunge to gain the victory, went tumbling; a roar went up from the others in exercise about.

The summer heat had forced every creature to shade, for even the lizards that had basked upon the rocks earlier scampered off to cool burrows. Across the allied line, warriors hid beneath propped shields and slung cloaks—all except the Spartans. Half of them strutted below the ridge, naked in exercise, while the remainder worked upon their weapons; thousands of short swords sparkled in the sun as they leaned hard on them with stone, working a lethal edge to the iron. A few combed their long hair.

Behind them, in awesome array, stood shield upon shield, upright with their blazons staring defiantly toward the Persian line. Amompharetos casually walked amongst the men, and in him all around saw the perfect warrior; his hair had been braided, falling long upon thick shoulders; a neat beard added fierceness to his often smiling face; his gait was one of physical power, but recalling the bounce of youth. Behind him trailed his hupaspites, or armor bearer, Prokles.

"Will they attack again?" said Deinokrates, a hoplite from Kallikrates platoon.

Amompharetos grinned a bit. "Not today. The Persian still wipes the blood from his face." He looked out into the potholed interval between the two armies at the cart that carried dead Masistios back to his countrymen. Pausanias had ordered the body of the noble to be cleansed and anointed, then returned to Mardonios; he would soon be amongst his comrades.

A head now bobbed above the hillcrest. "He is faster than he appears," admitted Bull as he strode into view.

"It is a very good thing indeed that swift feet do not win battles," said Amompharetos. "But a strong arm might," he added, looking out at Amnestos; the young man stood in the plain, studying several stones that he held, until at last he discarded all but one. Cat-like, he now crouched and began creeping further out, away from the ridge and toward the unrecovered corpse of a Persian that fed a gaggle of carrion crows. A few of the wary birds flapped their wings and tumbled away from their meal, leaving one still pecking at flesh. Slowly Amnestos rose from his crouch, then fired the stone. Struck, but still living, the bird twitched in agony on the earth, twirling an uninjured wing in a desperate maneuver to flee. Amnestos' eye flitted here and there. Then suddenly he lunged to the ground, snatched a fist-sized rock and launched it. The missile struck, rebounding high into the air; the crow moved no more.

"You are out of practice," shouted Amompharetos. "Two throws to kill it?"

Amnestos looked back and grinned. "He wore the sturdy armor," he said grinning triumphantly, "of a full belly." He trotted up the slope to join them.

Bull, worn from the race, fell to the ground while Amnestos jogged up beside him. "Campaign agrees with you," said Amompharetos approvingly.

"War seems like a holiday," answered the youth, "when measured against our training. Why do our allies sulk and lounge about?" He pointed toward the men of Tegea and Korinth. Men who hid from the sun and napped. Men who had scarcely uttered any sounds but groans of discomfort since the army disembarked from the mountains the day previous.

"Take note boy that the Persians do not cower from the heat. Activity in their camp slows not a bit. Like us their occupation is war, and they delight in it." Amompharetos looked to the stretch of fields that nudged the river near the bridge and there a score or more Persian horsemen whirled about on their mounts in some sort of game, mimicking the turns and sprints of the leader.

"Play is done for your company," he said. "Let the others commence gymnastics." He had estimated the daylight remaining and apportioned the remainder to the pair of companies in his regiment, that had up until now, worked upon their gear and weapons—five-hundred stood ready while five-hundred exercised.

"Polemarch." Amompharetos turned to find Euryanax, commander of the Konosouran regiment, ambling toward him, naked and glistening with sweat from exercise. Euryanax always addressed him initially by rank, as though his name eluded his memory. "How are the men this afternoon?" he asked. A Helot chased after him carrying a kothon of water that he promptly grabbed then emptied without pause.

"They are in very good spirits today," he answered.

"Have you exercised? I seek some challenge today in wrestling."

"Bull will oblige you. I have taken my turn. Besides, he is in sore need of a victory today." Bull had never been vanquished in a match, not since they first entered the Agoge. At seven he had shoulders thicker than anyone in his troop.

"On a day such as this I would challenge even Herakles. Where is the brute?" Euryanax laughed.

"Come and join me in a drink, my friend. I have a trace of wine remaining to flavor the water. Let us finish it together." Amompharetos led him from the crest of the ridge to the cool shade of the stand of trees that embraced the springs of Gargaphia. They sat atop a pair of stools that flanked a small table, waiting for Prokles to return with a pitcher.

"We are in better steads than the Athenians," observed Euryanax. "They have to draw water from the river, dodging Persian arrows in the process."

"Yes, the springs are near," agreed Amompharetos. He shaded his eyes as he gazed into the bright sky. Helios stared back powerfully. He picked up the kothon and sipped slowly, fighting the impulse to drain it in a gulp. "Look behind," he said pointing to the span of level ground between the ridge the mountains. "We sit stranded upon this island of high ground."

"We dare not thin our front to guard it, and no matter, for the Persian cannot see behind this ridge. To him it may be filled with infantry." Euryanax continued to stare at the gaping interval. In silence they both pondered it, sipping the water-cut wine.

✳    ✳    ✳    ✳

Asfandiar tilted the square of Egyptian paper to catch the light of the sputtering oil lamp. He had reread the last letter from his wife Lalagul several times this day, his mind forming her soft voice with every word, and in this he found solace. But every so often during his reading he would recall his brother Tooraj and his commander Masistios, and weep a bit. A servant entered the sleeping apartment of his tent, pausing at the draped opening, shuffling, trying not to offend with his intrusion.

Enter," he commanded, glancing up from the letter. One woman slept soundly, pillowed upon his bare chest while another, in partial slumber, stroked his arm. "Tell her to go," she whispered, her hands tracing his arm, chest, then loins. The smell of stale wine upon her breath smothered the jasmine in her hair. He turned away.

"Lord Asfandiar, the Greeks have released the body of Lord Masistios," he announced.

Now his eyes cleared. He sat up. "When?" he asked.

"Lord, it has been brought through the gates and is at the pavilion of Lord Mardonios." The man, finished with his message, bowed, then backed out of the apartment.

"Out!" He shoved them both onto the carpeted floor. They scurried on all fours, clutching loose bedding to cover their naked bodies. Asfandiar snatched his purple tunic and sword, hurrying from his tent into the bright afternoon. He paused, slipped his tunic on, then warily peeked through eyelids that had been forced shut by the bright sun. In moments he saw well enough to walk on, and fell into a stream of soldiers all making for the pavilion of his general; it was not far.

Several guards fenced off the swelling crowd, but upon recognizing him they parted, allowing him to pass to the courtyard within. There astride a rough-hewn cart stood Mardonios. Asfandiar approached, knowing the contents and trying to form in his mind the sight of his commander, but when he came near and looked into the short bed of the cart, its passenger was unrecognizable.

For sure, it was a tall man—a man of Masistios' stature—but his cleaved face with its single eye little resembled a man, but seemed the incomplete work of a gruesome sculptor. Asfandiar stared at the body. The Greeks had stripped him bare, replacing his garments with a few myrtle branches that criss-crossed his chest. The sun caused his oiled skin to glisten, but it also amplified the stench of death. Induced by habit, he curled his perfumed beard to his nostrils and drew the scent deeply.

"Come look upon him," ordered Mardonios to the officers around him, "and remember this when it is your time to fight."

They all crowded around the cart, staring grief-bound at their slain countrymen. Now eight slaves stepped forward. One of them tossed aside the branches, and then the others edged around the cart, leaning over, close to the body. Gently, they raised the corpse and carried it away in solemn, gliding steps. Mardonios, accompanied by his staff, withdrew to the pavilion.

The crowd soon melted away into the routine bustle of the camp leaving Asfandiar alone beside the cart. Apart from the world, he peered at the few flies that failed to follow Masistios, they making a meal of clotted blood that stained the wood dark.

"Mardonios has honored you."

He looked up from the desolate cart to see the grinning face of Pharnakes. Pharnakes was a large man in body and in manner, and never seemed to lose his grin, no matter the circumstance. The first time he had seen him, seven years before during the revolt in Egypt, Asfandiar watched him hacked from his horse in battle, then circled by three Egyptians, blood sheeting down his legs from wounds, and all the while the man laughed and fought—and killed.

"Lord Mardonios has included you in his picked hazarabam of a thousand."

This indeed was a great honor, for only the most valorous of warriors were selected. He would ride now at the vanguard of the Great King's army, accompanying Mardonios, Xerxes' cousin. His father would hear of this appointment with pride.

"But will there be a battle?" he asked Pharnakes.

"Certainly, but it seems neither will initiate it. We might poke and prod them with our cavalry, for they seem too content upon their ridge." Now his eyes fell into the yawning bed of the cart. "A very sad day. There is a hole in the heart of the army."

Asfandiar nodded but said nothing. The walk back to his tent was swift, for he lingered nowhere and avoided talk, anxious to retreat to the comfort of his letters until inevitably, the battle-horn sounded.

\*        \*        \*        \*

"Be thankful we do not have to play the fox to drink our water," said Nikandros. He stood upon a boulder and gazed off to his left toward the setting sun and the Athenians. Those unfortunate souls being almost two miles from the Gargaphian Springs had to draw water from the river, and when they did Mardonios dispatched mounted archers to greet them. The Persians killed few, but harassed the water bearers, making it more than a chore for the Athenians to replenish their flagons.

Theron watched too. Then suddenly he turned back toward the mountains and searched for the trees that marked the springs. Not much more than tall shadows now, his eyes fell upon them and he smiled. "The heat today was extraordinary," commented Theron. "They must be dust dry," he added, looking back to the Athenians.

A soft breeze swept down from the mountains behind them, imparting the first movement to the air that had hung still all day. At dusk they relaxed not only in body but also in mind, for they knew another day passed without battle. The cool night approached and they would sup peacefully.

"Theron, sit. I wish to speak with you," said Nikandros, crouching upon the boulder. Now he swirled a corner of bread through the oil in the bowl then shoved it into his mouth. "When I was at the Isthmos just how were the olives picked?"

Theron looked to his younger brother, pleading with his eyes for guidance. This dilemma, which he had expected to arise some eight months previous, surprised him now; he must choose between his father's question and a promise.

Nikandros, still waiting for an answer, dropped the last piece of bread into his bowl and looked to Theron, following the boy's glance to his brother. "Do you both know the answer to this?" he said with a glower. "Or must you deliberate first?"

Theron's eyes begged painfully for deliverance from his predicament, but Medios returned a blank stare. Meanwhile Selagos arrived with bowls for them both, handed it to them and walked off, hoping to slip away. Medios spoke. "Selagos, father wants to know about the harvest." Selagos continued his escape, feigning deafness and oblivious to his name.

"Stop," commanded Nikandros in his war voice. Selagos froze in his tracks, but would not turn. "Join us. I would have words with you." He sat, but back from the others until urged closer by Nikandros. "Now tell us, for these two seem to have lost their memories," he said flicking him a sideways glance. "Just how was the harvest taken in last year?" Nikandros placed his empty bowl on the ground beside him and slid down the face of the boulder to the earth. He leaned back while looking skyward, then sighed.

"Master Nikandros, as your father told you, a dozen slaves were hired from the estate of Dioxippos for harvest."

"Undoubtedly man, but who hired them?" Nikandros demanded. Medios straightened up and stepped away, as if to clean his bowl. "You stay!" commanded his father. "Until I have my answer."

Selagos, not a particularly obeisant man, hardly looked away when spoken to, but now he played the part of inferior to its fullest, averting his eyes and muffling his speech, so much so that Nikandros could hear nothing of sense.

Finally, in a burst of courage, or foolhardiness, Medios stood up and faced his father. "Aunt Niobe hired them," he announced, cowering a bit as though he expected his father to toss something at him.

"Niobe!" wailed Nikandros, rolling his eyes. "And all of you knew this and said nothing?"

"Father," implored Theron, "we meant no harm, but Aunt Niobe forced us into an oath. Clearly, if she offered you the slaves, you would not accept them, and she also knew that the harvest would sit in the trees, feeding the birds, without them."

Medios opened his mouth, as if to speak, but his father's glare stopped the words in his throat. "And when did you learn of this deception?"

"When we visited her the day after our return," he admitted.

"By the gods," he bellowed. "Did the whole town know but me?"

"No father. No one else knew, except of course grandfather. And the household of Aunt Niobe," he added meekly.

Nikandros burned. His pride stirred and with it his anger. No one looked at him. No one spoke. He sat, knees tucked up to his chest, rocking his head to and fro as though he were in pain. Nikandros inhaled deeply. The rage fled with his expended breath. He turned to the boy, and in the fading light, saw the face of his wife in him. In silence he rose and stepped away, moving off to where tears would be unseen.

# CHAPTER 11

▼

"Come with us Myronides," begged his friend Praxis. "The town is empty and offers us more shade than our lean-tos."

Myronides scanned the hill and its southern slopes where the Athenian soldiers rested beneath the shade of sagging canopies patched together from cloaks and blankets, desperate to hide from another bright day. He looked away from the Persian line toward the deserted town of Plataia. The promise of shade urged him, and the men who called this surreptitious meeting would not leave without him in their company.

Plataia, a small town nestled at the base of Kithairon and embraced by a wall of stone capped in mud brick, had been abandoned since the invasion of a year ago. When the Persians entered the town they burned what would burn and haphazardly demolished buildings. Enough still stood to make the place recognizable. It was not without some residents; the few Plataians serving with the Athenians managed to slink into the town in small numbers, visit their homes and sneak back to their position on the hill. Pausanias had ordered cavalry patrols to ride there as part of their rounds, and a squad of light infantry stood guard at the main gate.

In less than half an hour they had crossed the Oeroe stream and keeping to the road which sliced the level interval, made quick time of the remainder of the distance. At the gate, and in conversation with several of the Plataian spearmen they came to find Aischines, a member of Myronides dining club. He joked with the guards, and so casually that you would think them long acquainted, but in fact he had never seen them before this afternoon.

"Ah, my friends," he said, catching sight of Myronides, Praxis, Skiron and the rest. He stepped forward and embraced Skiron. Next he greeted Myronides, then nodded to the others. "We have a house," he whispered to Myronides.

The group of men hustled through the narrow, mostly empty alleyways; anything and everything that was not made of stone or brick had been carted off by the Persians. Before them, from a corner house they saw a man peer out an open doorway at them then quickly withdraw, and in several moments three men stepped out. One waved them over. "There it is." Aischines pointed the way.

The darkness blinded them as each one slid from the street into the cool, shadowed town house; eleven men in all crowded into the andros of the house, while one remained outside keeping watch. Friends exchanged greetings while strangers were introduced.

"Gentlemen," began Aischines, "we are here because, if I have judged you rightly, we all love our city and see the perilous road it now travels." The last muffled conversations died away. Now all attended his words. "You were all men of wealth until this war began. You Praxis, and you Myronides, and you Skiron. You and your families built Athens, cultivated the lands of Attika and defended our polis since the times of Theseus. And what now do you have to show for it?"

"I have lost no more or no less than anyone," countered Praxis.

"Have you?" Aischines posed the question and waited for an answer that would not follow. "Would you say the mob that now rules Athens forfeited as much as you? Why they owned little more than the piece of ground each stood upon and this they would gladly part with for a pebble of cheese and a deep cup of akratos wine." He paused and scanned the room and saw more than most nod in agreement.

"Their champion Themistokles robbed us. To pay the fleet for our defense says he, but of all men this year past he grew richest while the Persians completed your ruin."

Again Praxis interjected, "This fleet that you scorn delivered victory."

"Did it? Then why do we fight here? His victory benefitted Sparta and left us cowering in Troizen and on Salamis." Aischines again halted to gather his thoughts; he stroked his beard, sighed then nodded as if to agree. "Friends, do not misunderstand me. Our Spartan brothers in many ways are dearer to me than any rowdy oarsman from our city. The Spartans respect the nobility of the ancient families, and rightfully despise both the tyrant and mob. They know, as you and I do, that only men with a stake in the land can rule."

"You call us here to harangue us with your politics while we stare across at the invader?" Praxis alone challenged Aischines. Myronides stood silent.

For an hour more Aischines detailed a catalog of every item lost to the men in that room, the two years' income from lost crops, the rubble that was once their homes and the desecrated temples and shrines that their families had built and funded through their liturgies. By the end of this hour even Praxis ceased to challenge his words, but listened. Aischines, once he felt the weight of argument had brought a certain suppleness to his audience, moved his talk from the past to the present.

"I submit gentlemen, that you have suffered by far the most. You have lost nearly all while others grow in wealth and power. And whom do they call on to save Athens now? Why you!"

Most unexpectedly, Myronides stepped forward. "Aischines. If all you say is true, and I hear little that I do not agree with, what recourse is open to us?"

"We have an option that has been before us since last winter." Aischines breathed, filling his chest while looking about the room. "Make peace with Xerxes."

The room exploded with groans. Men shook their heads in disagreement, while others merely stared. Praxis turned to Myronides and whispered, "This is madness." Then he raised his arms and shouted, trying to be heard above the growling discontent. "If we are so noble and this so noble a deed, then why do we hide here? Would it not be better to discuss this with Aristides?"

"Aristides?" snorted Aischines contemptuously. "Aristides the Just?" He laughed; others in the room joined him. "The rule of law is his god, and he worships it devoutly."

"Is it the law that you scoff at, or the truth?" countered Praxis.

"Truth is a heady wine my friends and must be thinned. Aristides serves it up full strength to men who cannot handle it." Some in the room laughed, while Praxis and Myronides glared at him. He told them of the agent sent from Mardonios. All they need do is withdraw. Simply march back over the mountains to their beloved Athens, recall their fleet and stand off. Athens would once again belong to noble men of the land.

"And how will we accomplish this?" asked Skiron.

"Three taxiarchoi will follow. The other five generals require but a nudge to fall in with us."

A dark sky greeted them as they spilled from the confines of the town house and into the even more confining alleyway. A man in the lead—a Plataian—guided them quickly to a postern and out of the town. The moon had not yet risen, and few stars could be seen, making for a slow trek back to their encampment upon the hill. Myronides and Praxis straggled behind the others, until they had crossed the Oeroe whereupon they could no longer see or hear their companions. Twice sentries stopped them and luckily the watchword had not been changed during their absence. Once clear of the last guard Myronides slowed.

"Praxis, I hate the mob as much as any of them," he said, "but this!"

Praxis needed no convincing that the plan was folly. "Remember our friend Lykidas. He mentioned peace with the Great King and was beaten dead for it."

They continued on bearing left from the easy grade of the road to begin the climb up the steep slope, threading through the sprawl of the camp until they crested the ridge in amongst the men of their taxi. Myronides strolled forward and found a spot not far from the peak of the hill that the men had come to call the Porch, for from here the view of the Persian lines was unimpeded; stretching across the wide plain sputtered the flames of ten thousand enemy campfires. The sight puzzled him. "Why does Mardonios still offer peace when an army of that size is poised against us?" he said to himself.

✳    ✳    ✳    ✳

"Welcome Lord Artabazus," said Timagenides. He was the last of his guests to arrive for the banquet, and indeed was the one of greatest import. Eurydamos stepped forward and greeted the Persian also, then guided him to a couch nearby. "The hunt today yielded several deer," added Timagenides as he sat upon his couch. "And Eurydamos here brought down the largest."

Artabazus leaned upon the cushion and stretched out an empty hand, which a servant quickly filled with a rhyton of wine. "Undoubtedly your day yielded more profit than mine, for I wasted yet another watching Spartan gymnastics," he laughed then scanned the faces present, letting his grin slowly fade to seriousness. "Is their martial prowess some sort of Greek fable, for they seem to avoid battle?"

"Lord Artabazus, they deal in war as a potter works clay or a joiner shapes wood; it is their nature and they excel at it," said Timagenides. He plucked a steamy slab of meat from a platter and dropped it in his bowl, being careful to use only his right hand, which proper manners dictated; his left hand he reserved exclusively for his own bread.

"Then why do they not fight?" He knifed a slab of venison from the platter, then sliced free a morsel, which he chewed slowly. "Very good," he admitted, "You must show me where you came across such delicious game, Eurydamos." The Persian smiled at him while he fingered his earring. Eurydamos nodded in return. Then his glance moved to the very same servant boy who had attended him in banquets past, his eyes groping at a distance what his hands could not.

Eurydamos hate grew ever stronger. His father befriended the Persians, and in respect to this he treated them with cordiality, but few in the room missed his coolness, above all Artabazus. The Persian would jab him with a question, testing his sympathies and upsetting his thoughts, but Eurydamos persevered. After what seemed to him an unbearable interval, he excused himself from the company and stepped out into the courtyard.

Several Persian eunuchs hovered about there, betrayed by their high-pitched voices and wispy beards, but they paid him little heed as he walked to the far end seeking a bench. He looked skyward, and stared; suddenly a star flared bright and raced across the heavens. Then just as suddenly it flickered and vanished. His stomach sank. His heart pounded. He had only seen such a sight once before in his life, although many others had spoken of them. It recalled the death of Lykomedes; he saw such an evil star, *a disaster*, the last evening of his brother's life. Nervously he mumbled a prayer to Zeus-Protector, hoping to avert any evil conjured by the sighting. Still he trembled, and this chased him from his seat and back to the banquet.

"Ah Eurydamos," said Artabazus as he re-entered. "Good news. Your father has appointed you scout for an important mission."

He quickly forgot the ill omen of the star and looked to his father. Timagenides, wordless, let his son know that this was not his decision, but the Persian's.

Eurydamos walked to his couch, one that he shared with the Persian noble Pharnakes and sat, pretending to receive this information with poise. Finally, once seated he turned to Artabazus and spoke. "And what service can I render to you sir?"

Artabazus grinned. He played with the curls in his beard for a bit, not answering straightaway. Neither did Timagenides offer any words. After a long sip from his rhyton, Artabazus spoke. "Your father counsels us to attack the Greek convoys as they descend from the pass. He says you can lead us 'round their lines." Now he leaned back stretching his arms overhead and yawned, setting his jewels to tinkling. "I must relate this scheme of yours to Mardonios. Our supplies run low. Why should our adversaries enjoy such bounty?" Artabazus rose, and with him the other Persian nobles in attendance. "Thank you Timagenides, for your hospitality, your stratagem, and the lad." The servant boy, his eyes widened by trepidation, reluctantly shuffled to the Persian's side.

Timagenides walked from the andros conversing with Artabazus as he departed. It did not take very long. Soon he returned to the half empty room, in which Thebans only remained, and recovered a seat beside his son. "I told them of Oak Heads Road."

"But why me father? Why must I lead them?"

"I offered any guide. Artabazus chose you."

＊　　　＊　　　＊　　　＊

For seven days the two armies clung to their respective side of the river, reluctant to cross, for the omens and forecasts predicted victory for whomever stood fast, but with each passing day the men grew in discomfort. The sun had been unrelenting, delivering dizzying heat, while the refuse of man and animal, now piled high, choked the breath of every warrior; soon one commander must act.

Nikandros trudged up the rear slope of the ridge toward his enomotai of thirty-two men, mostly kin, and settled upon the earth next to his brother Athamos.

"Chileos, I think, will insist on gymnastics today. The type the Spartans perform. We have been idle too long," said Athamos, rubbing the scar on his thigh. "At the Gates Leonidas required all the allies to exercise. That is until the fighting commenced. Then he enforced sleep upon the men when they were not in the battle line."

"What was it like that last morning?" asked Nikandros.

"What?" Athamos lifted his eyes from the figures he scrawled in the dirt between his legs with a twig.

"The last morning at Thermopylai. What was it like?"

"Strange morning, brother. Very strange." Athamos flicked the twig away, then ground his hands together." I dare say when Leonidas dismissed us, we felt gladdened. Outwardly each man presented a mask of disappointment, but in here," he pounded his chest with a fist, "our hearts flew. Oh yes, we had held back the Persian multitudes for two days, but in truth we all knew they would overcome us."

"In such a narrow place and against armored men?"

"Yes brother. Xerxes numbers were far greater than what you see out there." Athamos pointed out across the shimmering plain, and traced the Persian lines with his finger. "Even without finding the path over Kallidromos, eventually Xerxes' hordes would have prevailed."

"But everyone speaks as it could have been held well into winter." Nikandros recounted the story that all of Hellas told—the pass had been lost because of the treachery of a Malian. Led by the Spartans, the allies would have never failed to hold the pass if not for this.

"Brother, look out there," instructed Athamos. "Count them all if you can, and then multiply it ten fold and that is the number we faced at the Gates."

Nikandros stared out at the enemy and tried to form in his mind the numbers Athamos spoke of. He could not. No Hellene could. The scope was incomprehensible to men from cities that counted their citizens in the hundreds.

"The enemy across the plain is no less formidable," said Chileos as he walked into their conversation. "Like you Nikandros with your olives, Mardonios has squeezed the water free of the oil and keeps only the best with him now."

"Then why does he not attack?" questioned Athamos. "If his lack of numbers do not dissuade him, then what?"

"Precisely because these are his king's best troops, he will not spend their lives freely as Xerxes did at the pass." Chileos paused, hands on hips and looked down at the two men seated upon the earth. "And he is no fool and will not repeat the mistakes of Datis at Marathon. No, he will not charge headlong into our shields."

"Then what do we do?" Nikandros rubbed his beard and bobbed his shoulders in puzzlement. "This land grows tired of us and the heat makes us drink much and often. It must be the same for Mardonios. Neither army can remain here much longer."

"Who will move first? Pausanias has tempted them by edging closer, but still Mardonios clings to the river," said Chileos. His eyes left the distant Persian lines and now gazed out at the Spartans in exercise. "Is time we mimicked our allies. Get your men to their gymnastics. These few days of lounging have softened their legs—and their hearts."

Nikandros rose. "I look forward to their complaints," he said grinning. Chileos hurried away now, leaving Nikandros to the task of informing his platoon of the order. Theron sprang to his feet and quickly pulled his chiton overhead. Athamos slowly moved, kneading his scarred thigh. He hardly displayed his nephew's enthusiasm. And so it was throughout the ranks of the Tegeans; the younger ones welcomed the diversion of exercise, while the older men, shackled by inertia, surrendered their leisure reluctantly.

Now Nikandros paired up with his son, and the two stalked each other in a bout of wrestling. The father benefitted from superior strength, and maneuvered to grab hold of the boy, but Theron dipped his head, swayed to the left and out of reach. Again Nikandros moved for a hold, more intently now, for this circling began to wear on him. But just when he came to grips with his son, Theron's agility left him reaching for air.

"How can I instruct you if you will not remain still?" complained Nikandros.

A rumbling filled the air, causing both father and son to pause. Nikandros peered up into the cloudless sky searching for the storm but saw nothing. "Maybe it is from the mountains," he said knowing that on occasion storms get trapped in the peaks. About the plain men scanned both sky and earth. Suddenly a voice cried out, "Persians! They are charging!"

Nikandros faced north, squinting through the glare to spot a rolling cloud of dust. The sight launched him up the slope of the ridge, toward the stacked weapons of his platoon. The rest scrambled up from the plain to the crest like men racing to high ground during an advancing flood, all wearing wide-eyed faces and many barking senseless words, but hoping elevation would deliver them.

After fumbling with his thorax armor, he finally tossed it aside and snatched up his helmet, spear and shield, then walked about his panicked men, hustling them along while at the same time working to maintain order. From within this chaos he looked to the right, to the Spartans and the other Lakedaimonians. There was no movement. There was no sound. Five thousand bronze shields rested upon five thousand shoulders, each nestled upon a swath of scarlet. Like wheat upon a breezeless day, their spears wavered not a bit. The Tegeans and the other allies whirled about, grabbing weapons and jostling hurriedly into formation. Throughout the other contingents, lines were ultimately formed and ranks dressed, although not the impeccable wall of bronze that the Spartans presented.

Chileos paced the front rank, exhorting the men to straighten their files and face front. Now he scanned the plain, estimating the number of Persian horse that barreled toward them. Several thousand at least but not a full attack, for their infantry still hugged the Asopos. Suddenly when they came within a stade of the ridge, the Persian charge split in two; one column peeled off to the right away from the ridge while another continued straight until within bow range they reined up.

"Shields up! Slope spears!" barked Chileos. The clamor of bronze, wood and iron rang loud as the Tegeans complied with the order. All at once the air hissed, torn by thick clouds of arrows. The missiles rattled in amongst the tilted spears and angled shields. A man dropped, and then another as misfortune and good aim took its toll.

A squadron of Persian cavalry advanced further now, covered by this hail of missiles. They charged to the foot of the ridge then swerved parallel to the front lines of the allies, flinging arrows into them at close range. Like hornets buzzing a great beast, they darted one way, then the next, swarming to the attack then fleeing out of reach at the merest swat of retaliation. This maneuver they kept to for sometime until, after firing a volley of arrows, several of the riders were unhorsed, their mounts stumbling in a boulder field. This tempered their enthusiasm; they watched stationery at the far stretches of bow range.

Movement that until this time had been absent from the Lakedaimonians, rippled through their ranks; Helot light infantry spilled from the shield wall, down the ridge slope in pursuit of the now cautious Persian horse. Shocked at first to a hasty withdrawal, for they had been lulled to complacency by the inaction of the Hellenes, the Persians wheeled from their retreat, fired bolts then galloped off rearwards once more.

Nikandros looked about him now, taking stock of his platoon; a few bent, cradling wounded limbs, and he saw one among them who had fallen to the earth leaning upon an arm and moving a bit. The Helots, after setting their game to flight, jogged back up the slope and melted into the files of the Spartans. It seemed for now the enemy cavalry would keep their distance and offer them a respite. Far off to the east, past the Spartan right, another storm of riders thundered away. They rode out from behind the ridge, spilling out from the level interval between the ridge and the town of Plataia and this unsettled Nikandros. "They have gotten behind us," he whispered within his helmet.

\*     \*     \*     \*

Eurydamos yelled at the Persians to step up the pace. "Kill the slow ones." He whirled about on his horse nervously, impatient at the sluggishness of the captured Greeks and their ox-drawn wagons.

"Impossible!" countered Asfandiar. "We need them to lead the wagons." His three squadrons of cavalry hovered around the captured supply carts of the Greeks—carts snatched from the road as they rambled out from the cover of the foothills.

"Do you not think it strange that this convoy of food was unguarded?" asked Eurydamos warily. "I fear a trap commander." Glad to have this task behind him he was anxious to move on to the north side of the Asopos and safety. To his left he saw the second contingent of cavalry—the one sent to effect a diversion—retiring from the level ground before the ridge of the Greek hoplites. His own column withdrew with excruciating lethargy.

"Move quickly, or by my god *I* will kill you," he screamed at an old man tending the oxen team. The man cowered in fear at his words and flung an arm up over his head to protect him from a blow that never came.

"There is no trap here," stated Asfandiar coolly. "Only Greek carelessness." He stopped and held position, allowing the stream of captives to continue on while he waited upon the rearguard. Shadows stretched long in the late afternoon and the hollows in the mountains to his rear were now dark with night. His smile grew with each passing wagon—several hundred of them and full of provender—grain, pickled fish and salted meat. Enough to sustain the army of the Greeks for many more days, now in the hands of Persia.

✳     ✳     ✳     ✳

Amompharetos dismissed the regiment. The Persians had retired and surely would not attack before dark. He could see from their slow pace northward they were finished for this day.

Kallikrates shouted to him. "Pausanias summons a council of the generals."

Amompharetos motioned to his attendant Prokles; the man hustled forward to relieve him of his shield and spear. The helmet he yanked free and tucked it under his arm, moving along with his master to the damosia skene—the command tent. From behind, Prokles plucked the sweat-drenched felt skullcap from Amompharetos' head, just before he ducked into the fluttering canopy. Skamandridas stepped to greet him. He had not talked much with him since they marched over the mountains, for the Skiritai—the battalion that his friend commanded—anchored the far end of the Lakedaimonian formation. Skamandridas was one of his few foreign acquaintances. They huddled together within the wide canopy, and saw the other commanders in discourse surrounding Pausanias while servants hustled about distributing kothons of water. The chatter subsided when the war leaders sipped, and resumed with empty cups.

"Eight days," said Pausanias, shaking his head. "He looked around at the score or more of commanders assembled; he by far was the youngest, but his age detracted not a bit from the authority he wielded. They stilled their voices when he spoke. "He pokes and prods us, failing to come to grips."

"Tonight the Persians feast on our provender. What will our men eat for the coming days?" Skamandridas was never a man to hold his words—or his thoughts in check. Like the rugged highlands he hailed from his speech was stark and pointed. "I see no other wagons wending down the Oaks Head Pass to feed us."

Pausanias did not answer straightaway but coolly gazed at each man present, this silent retort demanding attention. Once satisfied he had their ears, he spoke again. "Trust me fellows. You will not go hungry. But Mardonios must think it so." Pausanias spread his arms out, as though offering an embrace to the Persians.

"Our king Leotychidas and the allied fleet are sailing east. This news I am sure has already reached Mardonios, and it will induce him to act soon enough." True, with the Persian fleet occupied, Mardonios could expect no sea-borne assistance, either in men or supplies, and his welcome would wear thin in Boiotia; the vast Persian army depleted local foodstuffs with alacrity, while each day Pausanias' forces swelled. Time was indeed playing against the invader. "Gentlemen, I ask that you exhibit more patience than the barbarian, and be ready to act when called upon."

"Patience is a fugacious commodity, especially in the ranks of farmers and such. Unlike you," Skamandridas said looking at the crimson-clad Spartan officers, "we must work our own land. Planting season approaches."

"Our planting season also nears," Pausanias said, his eyes unsmiling. "Be patient and we shall show you how to plant Persians." Laughter erupted from the allies; the Spartan stood grim-faced.

"We have noticed that during the high heat of day activity ceases amongst your men. Emulate us. Embrace Helios and exercise. Keep your men from idleness. If you were at home in your fields you would not shirk toil, so why do you avoid it here? Minds and bodies must be alert." He turned first to Aristides, then ended by addressing them all. "Keep track of your men. Do not let them stray from the camp."

He walked away, having said what needed saying, leaving them to discuss his words. His attention now must be placed upon Mardonios. Euryanax and Amompharetos shadowed him, and when they had arrived at the cluster of trees near the shrine of Androkrates, the three men sat, knees tucked to their chests, gazing out. From their repose upon the knoll, the trio observed with patience the dispersement of the allied commanders

"Of them all the Athenians worry me," commented Pausanias.

"Aristides' men? Why is that?" questioned Amompharetos.

"They are an impatient breed. And impetuous too."

# CHAPTER 12

▼

"Excellent," exclaimed Mardonios. His mouth curved into a broad smile as he greeted Asfandiar and Eurydamos. He surveyed the procession of wagons as it rumbled through the southern gate of the great stockade. "You lost no men?"

"None, Lord Mardonios," answered Asfandiar, "but I do not know if that is true of the other squadrons." He thought of the men who swept up the front lines of the Greeks, keeping the enemy in formation while he and his cavalry raided the supply convoys. Certainly, they would have sustained casualties. Luckily every man that rode with him returned to the camp.

"Eurydamos, you must be commended. It was through your guidance that Asfandiar made quick work of it all." Mardonios approved. He approved of the results of so daring a raid and he knew it was due, in no small part, to Eurydamos and the advice of Timagenides. "Dine with us. And extend my invitation to your father. Both you and he have done us great service this day."

Eurydamos nodded then reined his horse toward the Thebes Road and free of the shadow of the stockade. He hardly wanted to dine with the Persians, but was compelled to deliver Mardonios' invitation to his father. Activity along the road dwindled, ensuring that his trip back to the city was of little consequence, so he slowed his pace to indulge in this fleeting bit of solitude.

The long, warm evening seduced him to stop and sleep in it's embrace, for the day's work left him fatigued, but he continued on until, as the sun began to slip behind the trees and stars flickered low in the east, he trotted amongst the familiar meadows surrounding Thebes. Evenings he savored at this time of year; gentle breezes whisked away the stale heat of day, coaxing sweet fragrance from the few hardy blossoms that endured the summer.

Black against the dark eastern sky, the high walls of his city loomed ahead. Shortly he drifted through the gates, on the road to his family's townhouse. To his surprise no servant greeted him at the front gate, so he rode straight down the mews to the stable and there, strolling its gated yard, he came upon his father.

"Eurydamos," he announced. "You had me in worries all day long." He looked his son up and down, then his eyes settled on his face and he readily saw the tiredness upon it. "Did you find their wagons?"

Eurydamos chuckled a bit. "Father we brought them back with us, although if it were up to me I would have burned them all and fled. Oddly, the Spartans and the others left it all unguarded, and never attempted to recover a single one of them."

"They dare not venture out into the plain." He now reached up to his son, offering him a hand to dismount. Eurydamos slid off the horse, embracing its neck in his fatigue. "Come inside."

"Mardonios has invited us to dine with him tonight," he said stepping through the doorway.

"I doubt you could carry yourself to bed. A night ride back to the Persian camp would be ill advised." He wrapped an arm around his son and guided him to a couch and a waiting table of food. Exhausted, Eurydamos fell into it, rolling onto his back. His father motioned for an attendant to serve the food and pour a bit of wine while he sat upon an adjacent couch sipping placidly from a kylix. Seeing Eurydamos relaxed and eating, he commenced to talk of the raid.

"When you rode behind the ridge today, did you notice the springs?"

"Gargaphia? Why yes we came quite near them actually."

"Were they guarded?"

Eurydamos looked up, not at anything in particular, but his eyes seemed to study the ceiling. "Why no father. We saw a few men drawing water, but no guards."

"Rest. I shall attend the banquet. This Mardonios must know of." Timagenides slipped the empty kylix onto the table and rose. A servant hustled to his side bearing his chalmys cloak, and wriggled it upon his shoulders. "Sleep well," he said stepping from the andros. "I shall pass the night at the Persian camp." Timagenides slipped from the room. In a moment Eurydamos heard only the sharp snort of a horse followed by fading hoof-beats.

*     *     *     *

Myronides sat amongst his dinner-club friends, most being members of his taxi, nibbling on the campaign fare with a bit of disdain. Couriers had delivered some letters this day, coming over the Oak Heads pass with the food wagons, fortunately escaping the Persian interception. Most every note received dealt with the rebuilding of houses and farms, the superintending of these projects left to servant foremen or wives of the hoplites. Myronides wife Thyia managed to detail the progress to his home so far; the foundation had been set and the masons were laying in the walls. He stared at the modest note, so carefully written by his wife and realized that like the city itself each man would find a way to rebuild home, family, and livelihood. He smiled at the thought.

"Good evening, Myronides," someone hailed, causing him to glance up from the letter. Aischines approached, flanked by two servants. One of them lugged a small chair and a wine pitcher, the other a bowl of victuals and a cup. "May I join you?" he asked. He did not wait for answer, but motioned for the attendant to place the chair, and for the other to present the food and cup to him after he sat. Nervously the man with the pitcher tilted it, careful to fill the cup quickly and with neat precision.

"Have some, will you?" Now he turned to his servant. "Leave the pitcher. Get out of here and make yourself useful somehow. Bring more wine."

Myronides studied the wine pitcher for a moment. "No thank you," he replied then looked back to his letter. It had been several days since his wine ration ran dry, and wondered how Aischines managed to have a vessel brimming with it.

"Well," inquired Aischines, "have you pondered my words long enough?"

Eyes still upon the letter, he delayed a reply. He thought of his city and the people that toiled within its patched walls as he sat here. He formed in his mind the long columns of men that climbed the high passes to descend to this very plain and stand eye to eye with the invader. He thought of his son Autolykos. "What do the others say?"

"Twenty men of the noblest families in Athens would join us in this," replied Aischines confidently. "In a day or two all the taxiarchoi will be with us."

"Then what does my opinion matter? The deed, it seems, is all but done."

"You, Myronides hold great sway with the others who have not yet committed to us." Aischines again offered wine and again Myronides refused.

"I am not so convinced, as you are, that we must follow this course." He refolded the note from his wife and looked at Aischines boldly. "I despise the mob as much as any man, but this is not the mob here upon this hill with me, nor is that a mob upon the ridge." He pointed to the twinkling campfires of the Spartans to the east.

"You will have little time to contemplate the matter further, so choose your course carefully." Aischines stood. His servant snatched the chair, trailing his master as he faded into the darkness.

Men had gathered, as they did every night, in a small hollow at the crest of the hill to gamble. He had grown used to the taunting hoots, and brief squalls of shouts, but tonight a familiar voice drew him to investigate.

"You gamble like a woman." The archer snapped up the knuckle-bones with one hand and his winnings with the other, his gaze fixed upon Krios again.

"What's this all about!" Myronides shouldered through the ring of wagerers to stand over his servant.

The archer smiled. "Ah, a sponsor for our unlucky friend."

Myronides stepped into the middle of it. "Why does he need a sponsor?" Krios continued to kneel, refusing to look up to either his master or the archer.

"He tried to pass off a purse of gravel for one of coin. Smart, though, for he had topped it off with a couple of obols."

"How much?" Myronides asked.

"Six drachmas."

"Why he is hardly worth that sum himself. But I'll make it good, and even double it, if you'll take the bet?"

The archer grinned, revealing two yellow teeth and the white of his eyes. He counted out the bet onto the stack of coins, then began to roll the bones in his hand.

"A moment." Myronides opened his hand. "Try these."

The blood drained from he archer's face. He dredged up some false courage and chuckled. "No matter, we need a fresh set." He tossed the four bones, tracking them as they tumbled toward the pile of loot. "Three eyes! You won't beat that."

He handed the bones to Myronides, who began rattling them within his cupped hands, then let them fly. Two dropped right at his feet while the other rolled up to the stacks of coin. Cheers exploded from the onlookers. "Four crowns up, my friend."

The archer fired his empty purse into the ground, then stalked off, trailed by his two cronies. Krios quickly swept up the coins into a fold in his chiton.

"In the purse." He loomed over Krios, while he fumbled with the winnings. "Now give it here."

He tucked it into his belt. "Why would you be wagering what little money you have?"

The slave's cower left him. He moved to stand eye to eye with his master. "To buy my freedom."

"What! Haven't I treated you well enough. By Zeus, if I treated my own son any better, no one could say." Myronides raised his hand, ready to cuff the slave and spend his anger.

"Krios, unblinking, stared at him. "I cannot remain with a traitor."

Myronides clubbed him with his fist. Krios did not flinch but continued staring through eyes that began to tear. A line of blood streaked from his lip where Myronides' ring cut him.

"Go!"

Krios departed, leaving Myronides clutching a full purse and an empty heart. The wrong man struck, and he knew it. Now he wandered away from what remained of the bettors, seemingly without purpose or destination, avoiding men when he noticed them, looking ahead as he walked, but seeing nothing. On a quiet section of the hill, on its far northwestern spur, he stared out into the darkness searching; the crunch of feet upon the dry soil had broken the silence. Ghost-like, a figure formed as it grew closer until the man's gait and silhouette revealed his identity.

"Aristides?"

"Yes. And is that you Myronides, hiding in the darkness?"

"Not hiding," he answered. "The chatter of dinner compelled me to seek a bit of solitude."

"I too crave thoughtful silence, and often walk here at night." Aristides tugged on his arm, guiding Myronides to follow. "Let us find a suitable rock, sit and talk awhile. I have not seen much of you these past few days."

They maundered through the deepening night until, upon the fringe of light from a campfire they spotted a knot of boulders and sat. Voices—far off and indistinct—wafted from beyond. The faint glow of firelight struck Aristides, deepening the hard-etched features of his face; his eyes glistened. He turned, squeezed his chin between his thumb and forefinger, looking to Myronides. "So my friend, you shun your dining-club mates tonight?"

Myronides, still held by the previous moments of silence did not answer straightaway. He thought. He thought carefully, then spoke. "Their talk of late has been tedious."

Aristides laughed. "And have you seen much of Aischines?"

Suddenly his heart pounded. His mouth ran dry of spit and his voice hid deep in his throat. He worked to wet his tongue. "Why yes." He coughed the words out. "I saw him this evening, while we ate."

"And has he arranged any more symposions in Plataia?"

Surely Myronides heart would tear through his chest, for the pounding surpassed all other sounds. Aristides certainly knew. He knew of the plot and he knew, it would seem, of the plotters. Now he could not form a single word, but stared wide-eyed at the man sitting across from him.

"Yes, I know of this scheme," said Aristides assuredly. "And I also know you take no part in it. But by the gods, why did *you* not tell me?"

"It would be a hard thing to betray my friends, even though I do not follow them in this. And in truth, I would never think them capable of it—not when the time would come to act. They talk much and do little."

"Words deal death as does the spear. When passed in dark houses, away from the light and the truth, they are a corrosive thing." Aristides looked out at the fires of the allies. "What would they think of Athens if this plot be known?"

"No city would trust another. We would lose the battle before it begins." Myronides gazed upon the fires too while he spoke, and reformed in his mind the images of men that camped upon the ridge: Megarians, Korinthians, Tegeans, Orchomenians, Plataians and the rest—and of course the warriors of Sparta.

"And what of the oath we all took at Eleusis? Do we dispense with a pact sworn to the gods for measly profit?" Aristides asked calmly, as a teacher would to a struggling student.

"They fear losing Athens. This is their motivation. Their impiety is not by design," Myronides answered.

"Which Athens do they strive to save—theirs or ours?"

"Are they not one in the same?" countered Myronides.

"Are they? Or is their Athens an exclusive one? Exclusive of thought, enterprise and law, for without these things it is not Athens."

"They fear the demos and its fickleness. As do I. As does any reasonable man." Myronides' voice became fired with emotion now. "What is the mob's stake in all of this?"

"They are now part and parcel of Athens. If you have a rash younger brother that wrongs you, do you forsake him? Or do you reconcile with him for the good of your family overall and work to impart some guidance to him? We must look upon the demos as a wayward sibling. And we must never abandon them, or the law, for profit."

Myronides thought upon this awhile in silence then, quite unexpectedly blurted out, "How did you uncover this treachery?"

"Praxis came to me the day after the meeting. But I also learned of it from the Spartans, although they knew not what was said. They recounted each and every one of you that went into Plataia that day. I also know that without Aischines and his companion Aigesias, this subterfuge would have never taken shape."

"But what can be done? If word of this reaches the other allies we are doomed."

"I will give this pair of conspirators a choice, and this choice will insure their silence.

*       *       *       *

Before the first strokes of light dappled the eastern sky Asfandiar rode the outposts along the river, rousing men from their slumber with pounding hoof beats. With each succeeding day sleep extended further into morning; the men of both armies were lulled to complacency in the caress of inaction. Here and there, bleary eyes looked up as he passed, but most curled back beneath blankets or cloaks, clinging to sleep.

As he traced the front battle line he glanced out to the south, across the gauze-like mist that hung over the interval between him and the Greeks on the ridge—a swirl of motion in the fog caught his eye and from this disturbance emerged the figures of men. Carian light infantry—posted forward as pickets—man-handled two prisoners toward the Persian lines.

"Greek deserters," announced one of the Carians as he sighted Asfandiar. The man whacked the most talkative of the captives with the long shaft of his spear to both silence and move him along.

Asfandiar lifted his hand, commanding the party to halt. He paused a bit, reformulating his thoughts into the words of the Greeks. "Where are you from, Greek?"

"Athens," offered the captive. "My name is Aischines. I have information for Mardonios."

Upon hearing this Asfandiar slid from his horse, drew his akinakes sword and pressed it to the Greek's neck. "He is a very busy man, so this information you speak of best not be trifling." He glared into the eyes of the prisoner and saw nothing but desperation reflected back. The man, although filthy from being dragged across the fields, looked to be a man of means—for a Greek.

"Put them over there," commanded Asfandiar. He pointed to a shiny white stone that poked from the earth, one barely large enough to accommodate a single man, but both prisoners accepted this resting spot with relief. He snagged the bridle of his horse and led it forward until he stood over the two Greeks. "You. Take these." One of the Carians grudgingly snatched the reins.

Aigisias had uttered not a solitary word since his capture. Aischines, as was his nature, could hardly keep silent, even when prodded by spear point. Both men sat upon the stone, sheepish faces staring at Asfandiar, waiting for him to interrogate them. Long fingers of sunlight slipped over the hills to the east and struck Asfandiar, illuminating the gold trim on his helmet as he stalked about the two men. The Carians stood by impatiently.

"Who is your commander," questioned Asfandiar.

Aigisias looked to Aischines. Aischines spoke first. "Aristides commands the Athenians," he stammered. "But Pausanias the Spartan commands all the allies."

This Asfandiar knew, and he would test them further. "Tell me of the other allies in your camp."

Aischines began his answer before Asfandiar had ended the question; he listed each contingent, its commander and its position upon the ridge and hill to the south. He detailed the terrain between the Greek army and the supply road over the pass of Mount Kithairon—something that Asfandiar had seen first hand—and it meshed perfectly with his recollection of it.

"Now tell me something that Lord Mardonios does not know." He pulled the strands of his whip through the palm of his hand as he waited for an answer. His dislike for these uncivilized and mendacious Greeks grew with each acquaintance of them, no matter how brief or detached.

Aischines searched his memory for a morsel of information that would save them both, for he sensed the impatience had shifted from the Carians to this Persian commander, who held their lives in his hand. "Water. They have but little. Even their viands dwindle low because of your raid." Aischines paused now searching, not his memory but the face of his captor for any assurance that his words met with favor. Asfandiar betrayed nothing. "They have but one spring and it is lightly guarded," Aischines blurted out in desperation.

"And where is this spring?"

"Your cavalry rode close to it when they captured the wagons. The Springs of Gargaphia lie on the south side of the ridge in a stand of trees and well away from the front lines of the Spartans. There are but a few Helot guards." The man plucked a twig from between his feet and scrawled out a crude diagram of the Greek position ahead, and the springs.

Asfandiar thoughts flew wild with the prospects these words revealed. Away from their ridge the Greeks would become so vulnerable to the multitudes of Persian horse; they huddled, safe for now on this island of high ground, but departing it would leave them exposed. Asfandiar also realized his men must be poised to strike quickly when this opportunity afforded itself.

Now the sun slipped clear of the hills pouring bright and warm over them all. Above him a hawk circled the broad plain, eyeing something in the grass it seemed, for its lazy glide transformed into a tight spiral; it plunged earthward, skimmed the ground and soared high again, struggling with a twisting serpent in its talons. It faded far to the south well past the lines of the Greeks. He was surely not a Magi, one of the priestly class that could so easily interpret this omen, but to him this fatidic vision was clear: the Persian bird of prey would fall upon the fleeing Greeks. This was a portent of victory.

$$*    *    *    *$$

"Timagenides relates the very same condition," bellowed Mardonios gleefully. "Without this spring the Greeks must move, and then we will have Pausanias and his mighty Spartans under the hooves of our cavalry."

Eurydamos and his father Timagenides sat together upon a single couch, very near Mardonios, while Asfandiar recounted the story of the Athenian captives once again. A scribe unfurled a papyrus map of Boiotia. Carefully inked upon it were the positions of the Greek contingents, the Gargaphian Springs and the Oak Heads road that supplied the Greek army.

Artabazus—wily old Artabazus—frowned as he heard this information. "Does this not seem a bit convenient for us?" he asked. The age-hardened man swaggered in front of the map, then struck quickly, pounding the rendering of the Greek position with a fist. "Pausanias may be a youngster, but he is a Spartan youngster. In peace the Spartans are the most forthright of the Greeks, but in war deceit and perfidy are their stock in trade. Remember the oracles, for they warn not to cross the Asopos."

Mardonios rose slowly from his divan and stepped to Artabazus, gripped his arm firmly, then looked down at the map. "You know of course that these oracles are all Greek," he laughed. "And who would know these Greeks better than Timagenides? What say you to this?"

The Theban sipped from his rhyton and then answered, "I truly think these Spartans act with arrogance. Look at how easily you snatched their food from right under their noses. I fear no trap. But if it is my opinion on the conduct of the war you seek, then I say this. Gold can easily accomplish what your army to this point has failed to do. Postpone your risky venture and retire to my city. Wait there while your coin does its work. These two noble Athenians that deserted will soon be followed by many others. Gold will obviate this battle and deliver victory."

His words brought a smile to Artabazus, but Mardonios did not share this reaction. He stood, hands on hips and face in a scowl. "Unfortunately the single commodity I no longer possess is time. The Great King has sent word for me to end this affair quickly." He moved back to his couch and sat, reaching for his horned-cup of honeyed wine. He sipped modestly.

*    *    *    *

"Sir, a rider has come through the lines and wishes to meet with Aristides," puffed the archer, almost breathless from his sprint of the steep hillside.

"Where?" asked Myronides curtly, sipping his water slowly as good manners demanded.

"Being held below the Porch sir, by my men. We dare not bring him deeper into the camp. He may be a Persian spy." The man beamed as he spoke, hoping his prudence would be appreciated.

Somewhat dismayed that this information would now require him to leave his meal, for he was the officer of the watch, Myronides reluctantly stood. "Lead me to him."

The two men threaded their way amongst the dining warriors and glowing braziers, soon coming to the Porch, then skidded warily down the slope. Below them and about half way up the slope, clustered four men around a horse—three of them armed—in conversation, and to Myronides surprise they were laughing and smiling. Upon seeing him approach the three guards went silent. So very quickly they lost their grins. Their prisoner turned, studying Myronides as he approached.

"Your name sir?" quizzed Myronides firmly.

"My name is of no importance, but the information I bring is indeed crucial. I must speak with Aristides."

Myronides took an accounting of this short and stocky man: his hat, a causia type, was Macedonian, as was his purple chalmys cloak. Expensive bobbles adorned him, indicating wealth and status, but darkness hid his features. He stepped to within a hand's breadth of the man, staring all the while. Then suddenly his face attached to an event—an event that Myronides had witnessed the prior winter. A Persian agent or a friend to Athens? Myronides stepped to him, guarding his words. "King Alexandros," he whispered, bringing a grin to the prisoner, "if you wish to speak with Aristides, you must tell me why, or you will advance no further."

"And who are you sir, that I trust my life and the lives of all the Hellenes to?" hissed King Alexandros.

"I am Myronides of Phyle."

"Well Myronides of Phyle, step away from your guards and I will tell you."

The two men moved off, being eyed by the archers all the while, and halted when Myronides was sure their words would remain only with them. Alexandros lifted his wide-brimmed hat, wiped his brow, and then looked around a bit nervously, as a rabbit would at the edge of its burrow before scampering out for forage.

"Only the god and I can hear you now," assured Myronides.

The Macedonian faced forward while his eyes darted furtively. "Mardonios means to attack you tomorrow," he whispered.

"And how do you know this?"

Alexandros bobbed his head with impatience. "I have heard from Mardonios himself, for he had talked openly at his banquet this very night."

"And why do you warn us? Did you not work to convince us just a short time ago to join your Persian master?"

"I spoke true to your assembly then, keeping the best interest of Athens close to heart. But now I must admit that I warn you, not out of love for your great country, but out of concern for mine. You must rid us of these barbarians before they empty both my country and yours of everything of value."

Myronides pondered this. Alexandros never offered a word without weighing its benefit to himself. Would he chance deceiving Mardonios or Aristides? "I will take you to him now."

He whisked him through the camp on the high hill, past huddles of dining warriors, to the tent of Aristides. Alexandros and the Athenian commander talked long inside, inviting no one to partake of their discourse. Myronides lingered outside, along with a trio of officers that waited to speak with their strategos. Almost an hour passed, when at last the two emerged from the tent.

"Myronides, escort our guest to his horse," instructed Aristides. Then he leaned to him and added in a whisper, "I must tell Pausanias of this at once."

# CHAPTER 13

▼

"They attack!" shouted Theron as he tugged his helmet down. The earth trembled, hammered by thousands of hooves as the Persian cavalry crashed across the plain; like boiling clouds clinging to the earth, they rolled forward, finally reining up within bow range. The war-metal of their blades flashed through the dust. Their horses snorted and spun. Finally, with the multiplied rustle of wood on leather they swung their loaded bows upward.

"Shields up. Slope spears," shouted Nikandros to his platoon, initiating a clamor of bronze as the Tegeans complied with the order; shield overlapped shield while every spear point leaned forward toward the Persians. As though launched from a single bow and at the command of a single hand, arrows shredded the hot air of mid morning, plunging into the aspides of the front ranks. Instinctively the entire mass of hoplites crouched lower, shrinking their bodies to fit within the bowl-like protection of their shields. Another barrage of arrows rained down upon them, some working their way through the hedge of spears, dropping unlucky men deep in the files. Nikandros legs quivered now under the strain of this exaggerated crouch, the sweltering morning and the storm of missiles.

The Persians hovered out on the plain, loosing their arrows, calling the Greeks women for hiding and not doing battle; they fired their quivers empty, retired and were replaced by fresh horsemen, for they commanded seemingly infinite numbers of mounted troops, and used these to torment the Greeks till well past midday.

By early afternoon the attack ceased and Nikandros called for water. Chileos had ordered all to stay in formation, and spell their weary bodies in file. Water bearers rushed forward to refresh the hoplites; their personal rations, carried in earthenware flasks strung over shoulders, had long been depleted.

"Father, how long will the Persians keep this up?" pleaded Theron. He flung his helmet to the earth in disgust; its felt liner doubled the weight of it, being soaked with sweat, and the imposing crest that bobbed high upon it fought Theron from keeping his head straight. It felt good to rid himself of it.

"Put that on!" Nikandros had merely pushed his helmet up, clearing his face, balancing it high on his head.

"They are gone," countered Theron. "My head cooks. It suffocates me." He rubbed the sweat-slicked hair from his forehead while tapping the last trickle from his flask. "Where is our water?"

"The helmet son. Or you will not taste a drop," growled Nikandros. "Put it on now or I will tie it to your head."

The helmet, fired day long in the sun, scorched his fingers when he reluctantly snatched it up. He pressed out what sweat he could from the liner with his palm, then dropped it on his head. It wobbled. In disgust he yanked the helmet off once again, snapped the unwieldy wood and horsehair crest off and flung it away. It bounced off the hard earth, tumbling down the ridge face. He refitted it to his head. Nikandros smiled.

Like a far off storm, the rumble began faintly at first. They watched the ribbon of dust grow along with the noise until like an ominous shadow, the Persian horse darkened the plain before them. Again Nikandros barked out the order to form, raise shields and slope spears, but so very differently than earlier in the day, the men now moved languidly, made incautious by heat and fatigue. Nikandros yelled again, extolling them to rise swiftly and form up.

"Look to the Spartans," he bellowed. "They stand under the same sun and fend off the same enemy, but they do not wilt." Helmets and armor rustled as many of the Tegeans bobbed their heads to peer down the battle line to the right where they gazed at a motionless wall.

Before them on the plain the horde of Persians galloped hard, then split their forces in two, whereupon the larger contingent rumbled along their front lobbing arrows into the Tegeans and Spartans. The second smaller band veered off to the right, as on the day the wagons were captured, disappearing behind the ridge.

"They are after the wagons again," observed Theron.

"And they will find none today," assured his father.

*      *      *      *

Myronides licked the spout of his flask, trying to coax the very last dribble of water into his parched mouth. He had watched the Persians ride the front of the army firing volleys into the withering ranks of his taxi, denying them access to the river and the source of water on the far left of the battle line. Aristides had ordered teams of bearers to draw from the Gargaphian Springs near the Spartans, but that was over two miles away and at best they would not return until evening. The Persians, on the other hand, tormented them by splashing their horses through the waters of the Asopos, taunting the Athenians to come drink.

He and the other Athenians had been in rank and file since early morning, fully armored, roasting under a brilliant summer sun. He prayed to Zeus and Aiolos to loose some clouds and a bit of breeze, but the sky glared blue-bright without a wisp of white to blemish it, or a zephyr to chase away the heat.

Aristides prowled in front of the men, heedless to their cries to retire from the deluge of missiles. His triple crested helmet made for an inviting target, but still the Persian archers could not hit their mark. As he passed a man would fall stricken, or another would wince as a bolt clanged off a shield, but he moved obliviously to it all, shouting encouragements, glancing at the Persians defiantly, then shouting again. It was as if the shield of Athena Protectress flicked away the arrows, keeping him safe.

"Men," he shouted. "Hold fast. Grip your shields and endure." Now he strutted, swinging his round bronze hoplon as he paced the front ranks. "They taunt you to drink, calling you women for refusing to do battle. But do they attack? They toss arrows. What the Spartans call spindles. A woman's weapon. Then flee when you merely stomp a foot." An arrow clanged off his hoplon; he looked to its facing to assess the damage and seeing but a scratch upon it resumed. "Athenians," he said holding his shield high for all to see. "Their arrows are no test of our bronze. But it is not bronze they mean to test, but the hearts that beat behind it."

Myronides felt his thighs burning, not from the sun but from the exertion of standing at station for an entire day. Pain stabbed at his shoulder; the twenty pound shield pulled hard upon every muscle. Thirst sucked away his courage. The day wore on, as did the surges of Persian attacks. He longed for the safety of darkness. He prayed by name to each and every god and hero that his memory could summon for water, beginning with Poseidon and ending with Androkrates, as he caught sight of the hero's shrine to the south of the ridge.

Behind him he heard the thud of a man hitting the earth, and turning noticed several felled either by arrows or the heat. Suddenly he felt something wet upon his leg. He tipped back his helmet to peer down and saw a flap of skin curled oddly on his thigh. Dark blood coursed from the wound, bathing his leg in scarlet.

Aristides walked toward him at first while looking out to the Persians then back at his men until he came upon Myronides. "Go my friend and have the iatros tend to it," he commanded, and then without pausing for a response sauntered on.

Formed in open order as the Athenians now were, the one-meter space between the rows of hoplites allowed Myronides easy access to the rear; he had merely to turn sideways and shuffle back through the eight-man deep ranks. Once clear of them Krios came running to meet him and liberated him of shield, helmet and spear.

Only a few trees topped this section of the hill and here Myronides hobbled to find the iatros. A score or more men sat upon the shaded ground, most with wounds to the neck and shoulder; one fellow cinched his jaw with linen while another worked on a wound that had tripled the span of his smile. Myronides lowered himself to the ground, whereupon an iatros—a physician—yelled at a slave to attend to him.

The slave bent over Myronides and lifted the flap of skin, measuring the depth of the wound with a trained eye. He muttered something unintelligible then scrambled off. In moments he returned with a bowlful of moss, a long bronze needle, some dried strands of sinew and a roll of clean linen. He tossed some wine into the bowl, pressing the dry moss in the dark liquid then squeezed out a handful; with this he daubed Myronides bleeding thigh. With out a word he looked to Krios as he reached for the needle and sinew. The slave nodded then clamped his hands upon his master's shoulders.

Myronides winced with the first pass of the needle, but only when it tugged his flesh. Upon each stitch the servant tied off the sinew, then sewed again until he had laced the wound shut with twenty or more passes. He mopped the wound again with the moss, then tapped out a brown powder from a small vial in his hand.

Myronides covered his thigh with a free hand. "I'll not let you dirty it with that!"

The attendant unfurled his fingers and presented the substance. "It is iskai, and required as a cautery."

"He is right master," assured Krios.

Carefully he instilled the wound with the oak fungus then deftly bound it tight with linen.

"Have you no water?" Myronides asked, hoping that during this respite he might also appropriate a drink.

"None. Not since midday," he responded, then sped off to tend to the master iatros.

Krios stood silently by, taking little notice of the battered men that sprawled about in the shadows, but Myronides saw them all. *This is what Hades' hall must be like*, he thought. Pain-induced groans substituted for talk, while the more grievously wounded, slipping away, gasped the names of mothers, wives or lovers. He could not see them, but was sure the air was thick with Keres, these winged daimons that hovered about, ready to snatch the souls of the dying.

"Help me up," he commanded. Krios bent his work-ravaged back, stretching arms to assist his master. He remained beside him while they walked, shuffling along with a shoulder tucked under Myronides' arm in support. Slowly the two limped back to the battle-line. Neither rested. Krios fetched shield, spear and helmet; Myronides reluctantly accepted these, then item by item, donned his panoply before slipping back into place.

"Why are you still here?"

Krios looked up from his knees after knotting the thorax cord under Myronides' arm. "I belong to Myronides of Phyle. I am here at his side, as servant and slave."

"At a traitor's side?"

Krios raised up and looked him in the eye while straightening his helmet. "No traitors upon this hill."

\*       \*       \*       \*

The troop of horsemen under Asfandiar's command worked feverishly to roll stones, tree branches, bodies—any item available—to stop up the springs that they had captured but a short while ago. Upon the ridge, the Greek heavy infantry wavered in formation, bludgeoned by hours of missile attacks, unable to defend the springs. But a few servants and Spartan slaves—Helots—guarded the water and they now lay slain in the dry dust and sun-parched grass behind the ridge.

Asfandiar gazed at the circular shrine of some Greek hero—Androkrates, as he was told by the Thebans—studying it. "Topple the columns. Block the springs with them," he shouted, pointing to the gleaming marble structure. Several of his troopers galloped off and surrounded the small shrine—for it was not much larger than an officer's sleeping apartment within a campaign tent, and then after studying it briefly, they slung ropes around a man-thick column and distributed the ends to others still mounted. In unison they struck their horses, pulling the lines taut. Some on foot piled 'round the stone cylinder, heaving shoulders to hurry its collapse. Announced by a groan, the seams of the column yawned open ruining the illusion of a single, tall pillar.

"Again," yelled Asfandiar at the men shouldering the stone; the riders whipped their mounts sending the horses into violent estrapades while the shifting column moaned as if in pain, seemingly paused its movement, then crumbled. Quickly they swarmed around a single column drum and rolled it down the hill slope towards the pools of clear, cool water.

"Gut them," ordered Asfandiar, his gaze directed at the murdered defenders of the spring.

Most stepped reluctantly to the Greek bodies, for they wished not to rile the gods and summon the spirit dead. One warrior—a Bactrian—trotted gleefully to the corpse of a dead Greek, dragged it by the ankles to the edge of the spring, then plunged his twin-edged battle ax deep in the chest, ripping its blade downward to the groin, as a hunter would dress new game, severing the muscles of the abdomen wide. He wiggled the hefty blade, producing a sickening gurgle, withdrew it slowly, then booted the corpse into the water. Soon a score or more bodies crammed the springs: their stomachs gaped wide; black blood swirled in the water.

The shadows of late afternoon stretched long as the last Persian vaulted to his horse and galloped from the springs. Asfandiar hung back. He stared at the stone rubble and human debris that clogged the once pristine water, wondering why these Greeks so easily relinquished such a resource.

From the foothills to the south, and across the interval that separated the Greeks on the ridge from their mountain-embraced roads, he watched a swelling shadow of men form; seems they now meant to reestablish their claim to these springs. So very calmly he eyed the advancing swarm of light-infantry—for the bronze armored men of Greece still clung to the ridge adjacent to him—calculating the distance they covered and the span of ground remaining. He need hurry not.

Again he turned his gaze to the spoiled pools, regarding his handiwork with disgust. "What a victory," he bellowed at the Greeks on high, then galloped off.

*        *        *        *

With the fading sound of the Persian horse Amompharetos plucked his helmet from his head; he gulped the air as a diver does upon gaining the surface. This day had been long in ending. The sun had squeezed them dry, while the Persians archers kept them crouched behind their shields. As always the Spartans endured. They defied the enemy—and Helios.

"Seventeen," whispered Kallikrates, his ever-present grin diminishing with the light of day. "Seventeen wounded. Three dead." Kallikrates had collected the count from each battalion commander, who in turn received theirs from the company commanders; the enomotarchs, platoon leaders, began it all, rolling the number of casualties up the command chain with a clarion shout. Within a quarter hour of the Persian withdrawal, Amompharetos knew the disposition of his entire regiment.

Around him others now folded to the earth, drained of the lingering bit of energy that combat had dredged up—a godlike but false energy inspired by death's proximity; it kept them to their feet and standing firm while the enemy whirled about on the plain. Now they reverted to mere men. Amompharetos looked upon Kallikrates, staring at the beauty the gods had so rarely bestowed upon a mortal. Kallikrates smiled.

"The gods have something in store for you, my friend," said Amompharetos. "How someone so handsome can go unscathed through this?" Laughing, he pointed to the hundreds of arrows that sprouted from the dusty turf.

"Because when we fight, with our helmets down, the gods cannot discriminate. Even Posidonios is handsome in combat." Kallikrates joked. He was by far the most handsome of a handsome race, for in all of Hellas the Spartans were considered the most attractive. So unlike him, his friend Posidonios possessed a common face upon a very large and uncommon body. But indeed both did display a certain beauty in warfare.

The polemarch left his friends for the command post of Pausanias. He wondered why they had remained motionless again—a target for Persian arrows. "Seventeen is very good indeed," he mumbled, calculating the hours endured and the multitudes of missiles flung their way. "But to what purpose?" Now he saw his commander, solitary at a table with one knee upon a chair, hunched over, reading.

"Lord Pausanias."

The prodikos raised a single finger, hushing him while continuing to read from the table. In a few moments he lowered his hand, turned and greeted Amompharetos with a nod. "Come sit. I have a small bit of water left. Share it with me."

Amompharetos straddled a chair, sitting wrong-ways in it, wrapping his arms around the low backrest. "How long?"

"Do you mean standing to arms?" he asked in return. He slid a half-full kothon of water across the clear side of the table, offering it to his polemarch.

Amompharetos studied the water. Thirst compelled him to lift the cup to his lips. He drank it in two deep gulps. "I have seventeen wounded. I ask myself why? To increase the barbarians' proficiency with the bow? I came here for an answer to my dead and wounded."

"I will tell you why, but you must convey this to no others. Those seventeen, and the scores, possibly hundreds of others of our allies that were struck down today, have helped beyond all measure, our cause." Pausanias lifted a patch of hide, upon which was scribbled a string of letters. "This," he said waving the note, "is from the Skiritai kataskopoi that lurk beyond the river, watching the Persians in their camp. He spoke of advance scouts, who had messaged him with a coded skytale, measured sticks that strips of leather were spiraled around, a message written, then unwound and dispatched by courier, made readable again only by a stick of precise and matching dimensions. "Mardonios will attack soon, for he thinks he has broken us today."

"He is no fool," said Amompharetos. "You must know he will never attack while we hold this ridge. Although without provision we cannot remain."

"Agreed," said Pausanias. Then clenching his fist to his chin he added, "This will be our last night here."

\*        \*        \*        \*

This day, beyond all others, had tested the resolve of the Tegeans, for they stood beside their Spartan allies in the long shadows of evening, weary-worn, tumbled down in heaps where they had once stood defying the Persian assaults. Athamos kneaded his leg, violently rubbing upon the year-old scar in an attempt to overwhelm and exchange the throbbing with a self-induced pain. Nikandros fought to stay kneeling, using his planted spear crutch-like to support him, but his head hung from his shoulders as though the muscles in his neck had turned to clay, melted by the daylong heat. Near him, face up on the ground, lie Theron.

"Father, when do we fight?" he gasped, looking skyward; now a few wispy clouds scooted overhead. Entranced, he continued to follow them with his eyes.

Nikandros did not answer presently, but expelled several puffs of breath, as a sprinter would after a hard run race. Reaching to the crest, he yanked his helmet clear of his head and let it drop unceremoniously to the earth. "I will ask Chileos. Perhaps he understands the plans of our generals better than I."

Around him and throughout the ranks of the Tegeans, men wilted to the ground in exhaustion; they had all been dismissed from formation and ordered to eat and draw their miserable ration of water, but hardly any could muster the strength to stand and walk. To their left the Korinthians too sprawled atop the ridge, collapsing to rest, still in pattern of rank and file. Even the Spartans moved slowly to sup, urged on by their platoon commanders. Nikandros, seeing all this, drew his legs up beneath him and rose—but so very slowly, and once to his feet scanned his proximity and the litter of living bodies that surrounded him.

"Up with you, men of my platoon. Without food you will hardly have the strength to survive tomorrow's attack."

They groaned at his words. Some cursed at Nikandros. Others assured him that food was not their concern, but rest was what they needed most. Limping amongst them, he kicked some, and prodded others with the butt-spike of his spear. Theron, seeing that none heeded his father, sprang to his feet, then pulled his uncle Athamos from the ground. Slowly, and by this example, another man rose, followed by another, until within moments most all of his enomotai of thirty-two hoplites were up and moving rearwards to draw their rations. Nikandros, wobbling on his feet now, watched them all pass, until finally his son walked to him on his way to eat; he looked into Theron' empty eyes and thanked him with a glance.

Selagos and Medios both rushed forward to assist father and son with their panoplies. Nikandros offered up his shield and spear quickly. The boy gladly shouldered the hoplon as though he were preparing for battle. Selagos picked the armor from Pankratios like it was the dirty baggage of a way-worn traveler, treating it with hardly the awe the younger boy did. Around them all and stirred to activity by the onset of dark, swarmed clouds of mosquitoes. Selagos, seemingly impervious to them, continued on with his duties, mindful of the needs of Theron. Medios swatted furiously, his attention drawn from his immediate task.

"Son, they are like the Persians," he chuckled. "A nuisance. Now ignore them and bring me my food."

# CHAPTER   14

▼

Night had smothered both sight and sound with its dark, numbing cloak, leaving only the malodor of battle disclosed and somehow magnified. It crept up from the plain below, overwhelming the aroma of the cook-fires, working its way like an unseen mist over the ridge and into the fields before the town of Plataia. Men shivered. Some wrapped themselves in their cloaks, while others, veterans of such warfare, gobbled the meager fare from their bowls without pause. The younger ones vomited.

Amompharetos stood hovering over the lamplit table, gazing at the schema inked upon the hide map. He worked the plan over in his mind, aware of the difficulties of repositioning an entire army quickly and quietly in daylight, but Pausanias proposed to effect this maneuver in the dark of this very night. Now he traced a broad arc with his finger upon the map.

"We hold the right, the Athenians the left, while the men of the center withdraw?" Amompharetos repeated Pausanias' instructions, posing it as a question to his commander, expecting a confirmation.

"Yes. Then the Athenians will slip behind the ridge and withdraw. We move last." He swept his hands toward the south and the shadow of the rise they stood upon.

"When will that be?" asked Euryanax, leaning upon the small table.

"At first light. What is a performance without an audience?" Pausanias placed his clenched fists on the map, a bit apart indicating the Spartan right and the Athenian left, and then drew both towards him, finally smacking them together. "Your Athenians must close on our left," he said, looking to Aristides. "Then the remaining allies," he said looking to the commanders of the Korinthians, Megarians and others, "can strike the Persian flank."

"This is a dangerous maneuver, Pausanias. It will separate our single line into three, and place us for a time on the open land between here and the town," said Chileos. "What if the Persians attack before we reform?"

"I have never seen a Persian fight in the dark, so I do not think we should concern ourselves with that," he answered with reassuring confidence. "But Chileos, you do offer something to consider. There can be no delays. We would indeed be vulnerable out there," he said pointing to the dark fields behind them, "where their horseman would trample us. Where we would have nothing to anchor our asses to but the breeze."

Aristides shouldered through the huddle of commanders to the table's edge, lifted a sputtering lamp, then waved it above the map, eyeing the plan carefully. "And if they do not attack?"

"Then we are back to the safety of the foothills," assured Pausanias. "Closer to water and our supplies."

"No doubt our men will gladly quit this ridge and the torment of Persian arrows. But if we move, we should move together and as one." Aristides said, lamp still in hand. "This will insure our safety."

"Sir, if safety is your aim, you are most certainly in the wrong place," quipped Euryanax. The other Spartans grinned at his remark.

"I propose," said Aristides, "that we put it to a vote, and quickly."

Amompharetos felt the blood rising in his face, for it flushed at this debate. "And how do you Athenians vote? With pebbles, is it not?" He reached to the ground and snatched a helmet-sized stone, lifting it overhead. "Then I cast my vote now." He heaved the stone at the feet of Aristides, causing him to stumble backwards in retreat.

Chileos the Tegean shuffled to stand aside the grounded stone. "Gentlemen, as our Spartan friend here has demonstrated, this is no the time to debate. Follow this plan," he insisted. "Or do you wish to hunker down for days unending under a storm of arrows?"

Pausanias leaned over to whisper in the ear of Aristides, attempting it would seem, to assure him that his concerns were noted. Amompharetos, brimming with impatience, whirled from the gathering, drawing the eyes of all as he departed. Euryanax followed. When distanced from the war council he called to his friend.

"No one cast a single dissenting vote after your ballot," said Euryanax suppressing his glee. "You nearly struck him?"

Amompharetos looked back as he retreated, somewhat puzzled at the remark. "What was that?"

"Your stone-tossing. Did you mean to hit him?" Euryanax grinned now as he caught up to him. "You certainly quieted him."

Amompharetos continued to stalk off. Euryanax trailed behind. Well away from the crowd of generals and in amongst sleeping Spartan warriors—heads pillowed on shields, all wrapped in their cloaks—he stopped and waited. "Someone must stay behind," he blurted out.

Euryanax lost his smile, for he suddenly realized what his friend meant. "Of course," he mumbled. "A rear guard."

✳     ✳     ✳     ✳

"Pausanias is finding his first command a bit difficult," said Mardonios. Gathered about him were the commanders of his army, in conference and preparing for the next day's action. "And thanks to the success of Asfandiar today, he has been deprived of water."

"Asfandiar, you say only a few light infantry guarded the springs?" inquired Artabazus. A tone of doubt laced his words.

Asfandiar stepped forward, approaching the couches of Mardonios and Artabazus. "Yes, but they fought with fury."

"Did they?" Artabazus asked, unconvinced. Artabazus flicked his hand in the direction of a servant, sending the man scurrying with a pitcher of wine. The slave topped a cup then handed it to Artabazus. He sipped slowly, all the while looking above the rim at Asfandiar. "And you find it not odd that they defended their only water in so lackluster a fashion?"

"I think Artabazus gives these Greeks more than their due," interrupted Mardonios. "You suspect some deception?" Mardonios plucked a date from a golden bowl, pinching it between his fingers as he held it in his lips; he nibbled slowly.

"I heed the oracles," answered Artabazus. "We should stay to our side of the Asopos."

Mardonios reached back to a table and lifted a scroll of papyrus from it, unfurled the document, and read from it silently, then paused looking up. "This is information of the Greek fleet, gathered from agents of the King, and it confirms what we already had surmised. They sail east. Because of this we can expect no re-supply by sea. And out there, across the river we face an army that today is weakened by loss of food and water, but tomorrow, who knows? If they retreat back to the foothills, replenishment will grow easy for them, while we must depend on dwindling sources of provender. You watch, as do I, the swelling of their numbers with each passing day. Pausanias waits and grows stronger."

"We cannot attack him while he is on that ridge," said Artabazus.

"Of course not. But let us suppose that they move and we were to know when. Would it not be foolhardy to discard this opportunity?" Mardonios' words sparked a rumble of hushed voices. "Would we not be compelled to accept this gift offered to us?" Now he grinned.

"And do we know when they shall move?" asked Artabazus.

Mardonios nodded to an officer of his guard; the man slipped out of the huge apartment and within moments returned, escorting Alexandros. The Macedonian doffed his wide-brimmed hat, then approached Mardonios.

"Good gentlemen," said Alexandros confidently. "I come from the Greek camp with information that if acted upon, will end this war to your benefit." Now he reached an empty hand toward the wine-servant, fluttering his fingers impatiently until a full cup was slipped into it. "The Greeks will withdraw from that ridge at first light."

"And they revealed this to you?" said Artabazus. "I did not know you were in their confidence." Now laughter burst here and there throughout the assembled officers.

"I need be in the confidence of only a single well-placed Athenian to learn of this plan. Even before you struck at the Springs of Gargaphia, the Greeks were anxious to move back to the foothills. Food is scarce in their camp as is water, and excepting the Spartans, they worry more about the planting season than this war."

"And when will they move? Surely not in the midst of day?" quizzed Artabazus.

"At first light, while your men still sleep," answered Alexandros.

"Then they will be free of their precious high ground and in the fields between the ridge and the foothills," interrupted Mardonios.

Alexandros licked the rim of his wine-cup, grinning. "Once they reach the foothills of Kithairon, their position again becomes formidable."

"And what do you say to this Timagenides?" asked Mardonios. "You know the lay of the land."

"If they march down from the ridge, they must attack us or retreat, and either places them in wide fields, suitable for your cavalry." Timagenides now looked to his son. "Eurydamos, you rode to the far side of the ridge. Do you think the Spartans can cross that open ground quickly?"

"They cannot and maintain their formations," answered Eurydamos succinctly.

"Pausanias, like me, seems to be a gambler," quipped King Alexandros. "He chanced moving to this ridge, hoping to draw you out. This has failed. Now he must pay for that wager by perilously retracing his steps back to Kithairon. But if you attack piecemeal, as you have done these past days, then I think he will succeed in his plan, although at some cost. You must strike with the full weight of the army. Only then can you end this war."

"Asfandiar, you are certain that the springs are of no use to them?" asked Mardonios.

"They can draw no water there. And if they work to clear the springs, why that will take more than a week." Asfandiar went on to assure that if the Greeks did indeed endeavor to reclaim the springs, he and his cavalry would keep them from this task. Gargaphia, for all intents, was lost to the Greeks. Thirst would compel them to move, and his men would be ready to strike when they did.

Artabazus withdrew to silence now, for the fever of battle had been roused in them all and he knew any words of prudence would go unheeded. He sat and listened. He listened to the orders of Mardonios. He listened also to the ready compliance of the other commanders, each anxious to distinguish himself in one final contest. Every man now saw the end of this long campaign. The decision of combat was welcomed. They departed carrying with them their orders: advance at first light. When the Greeks moved, they would be ready. When the Greeks moved, they would strike.

*       *       *       *

Aristides stood amongst his taxiarchoi, relaying the orders from Pausanias. Around him men grumbled, as Athenians were wont to do when ordered to action not of their own design. But in truth they welcomed the prospects of quitting their bone-dry hill for the embrace of Kithairon and its protecting lower slopes. Most here did not expect Mardonios to attack them when they moved, at least with not more than skirmishers and horseman. The redoubtable Theban heavy infantry, which faced them across the plain, would remain on the far side of the river guarding the roads to their own city.

"But beware. We will be separated from our allies, as will the Spartans, and marching on open ground. Keep to formation. When the salphinx sounds halt, dress the files, and bring your arms to bear." He waved his hands, beckoning to come closer and tighten the loose circle that surrounded him. "All will depend on our actions tomorrow, so go now. Have your men rest. Dispense all the water and food. Have the wagons empty and ready to move at my word."

The eight commanders dispersed to their taxies, and soon had the servants and camp attendants swarming over the hill. But in amongst this bustle the hoplites lie, some eating, others sleeping, but all noticeably slowed by fatigue. Myronides wandered about, restless in thought, and by chance came upon Aristides who sat chairless upon the ground, nibbling the last of his salted boarfish. Robbed of speech by a mouthful of food, he gestured for him to sit.

"They are all glad at the prospects of leaving this hill," offered Myronides. "But I think the Persians will not attack us. They will wake up, find us gone and still hug the river."

Aristides pushed the last bit of bread into his grinning mouth, chewed, then swiped his front teeth with his tongue. "They will attack," he said confidently.

"Will they?" asked Myronides, somewhat puzzled at his commander's sure expression.

"Because they know we are withdrawing." Now he tipped his cup dry.

"And how do they know this?" snapped Myronides incredulously. "Do they have spies amongst us?"

"They know this because I have told them."

\*    \*    \*    \*

Nikandros rolled over, awakened by the sound of a propped shield striking the earth. He squeezed his eyes shut then opened them slowly, trying to acquire his surroundings. The men of his platoon slept still, garnering their energies for the withdrawal they would effect at the coming of dawn. To his right he saw the comforting array of Spartan and Skiritai campfires glowing faintly in the thin mist that smothered the ridge. Now he glanced to his left and the sight struck him hard sending his heart plummeting. The Korinthians were gone! So were the others. The men of Tegea sat upon this ridge, their left flank yawning wide and unprotected.

"Must be the plan?" he mumbled, trying to explain away the dread that struck him. "Our turn will come. Before daylight, I hope." Now he sat up, scanning the still dark plain, and to the north where the Persian lines sparkled with campfires. Beside him, wrapped in a cloak, slept his son Theron and close by him lay Medios. A figure here and there shuffled through the night, in amongst the resting men, but most clung dearly to the earth in slumber.

He stretched and then lay down once more, tugging his cloak tightly to him and closed his eyes, but sleep would not come. Softly he whispered a prayer to Morpheos and another to Hypnos to let him sleep and free him from the fear that squeezed his belly now, but his thoughts returned to the empty section of the ridge and the danger that this morning's march would bring. He sat up.

"Master Nikandros," whispered Selagos. "What ails you?"

"Hypnos denies me sleep." He would not admit to his fear, especially when all around slept so deeply and seemingly without care.

"Is it the god or the coming battle that keeps you awake?" Selagos had attended many battles, and seen the restlessness that stirred in warriors beforehand. He also knew the salve of words. "Rest, whether in slumber or wakefulness, is what you need, sir. Would you like some wine?"

Wine had long since departed their drink; it would quell his knotted stomach, and induce more pleasant thoughts. He succumbed to the offer. Selagos stalked away, gliding through the sprawl of men, fading from Myronides' sight, legless in the mist.

Several others moved about. Now he heard whispers, followed by a rustle of a cloak. Then silence. Above him stars streaked the sky in a broad swathe of white. In his mind he formed them into objects familiar to him: the shape of an oil press, a large pointed-bottom amphora, a cooking pot, and a sickle. But soon these pleasant shapes transformed to the long twisting body of a fanged serpent, a winged lion and finally the swirling, snake-haired head of Medusa. He clamped his eyes tight, trying to rid this image, but it clung to his sight within his mind and grew in detail and size; Medusa's eyes burned like coals in her dark sunken face, her twisting strands of serpentine locks gleamed, while her teeth seemed stained black with the blood of her victims.

"Your wine," whispered Selagos.

Nikandros' eyes snapped open to see his servant bent over him with a small bowl. Hesitatingly he groped for the vessel, then lowered it to his lips. He tilted it quite far—only a faint bit of liquid pooled at its bottom. Almost reverently he sipped the wine, wetting his tongue then pausing, then wetting it again, stretching the scant portion. "Where did you—?" he said softly between tastes.

"The iatros is the only one with wine, and it is for the wounded exclusively. I reminded him of your leg." Selagos lowered himself to the earth beside Nikandros crossing his spindly legs. He said nothing more.

Nikandros looked over to the man. He tugged his cloak tightly to him, warding off the chill of the fog and the dark night, watching Selagos. The man wore nothing more than an ancient woolen exomis, draped about him and gathered at the waist by a grass rope. "Are you not cold?" inquired Nikandros.

"Why of course I am, master Nikandros."

"Where is your cloak?"

Presently he turned and glanced down at Theron. "Your son needs it more than I," he replied. "As you needed that wine. Tomorrow you both will dance with cruel Ares, while I only watch."

From beyond the edge of their vision the two heard a group of men moving toward them, talking. Their converse was guarded, but still in the silence of night, muffled words announced their approach. He could see them now—four men, and each with a bobbing crest of a helmet outlined on their heads. They threaded their way through the bodies to but a few feet before Nikandros.

"Nikandros, assemble your men," said a dark form. By the voice he knew it to be Chileos. "We march presently." The four sliced through the camp quietly, stopping to speak with any of the officers they could distinguish. Word spread. Soon, like some grave and ominous crop, thousands of silent warriors sprouted from the earth atop the ridge.

Bleary-eyed, Medios sprang to his feet, then hustled to fetch his father's panoply. Within moments he returned chugging through the assembling warriors with the shield slung over his back, spear in one hand, and a sack with helmet, greaves and cuirass in the other. A scabbard dangled low from his shoulder, its tip scraping the ground as he ran.

"Quiet," cautioned his father on his approach. The orders were firm—keep noise to a minimum. Now he outstretched his arms to receive the bag, then pulled out the greaves. Quickly he snapped them onto his legs while Medios fiddled with the cuirass, unfastening the pins that kept the two halves attached. The boy now held the fitted armor open by its hinges and Nikandros moved between these half-bells of bronze; Medios cinched the front and rear together with the small leather straps that hung from its side, then secured it by inserting the pins. Immediately Nikandros wobbled under the weight; thirty-five pounds of ancient metal wrapped around his body called attention to his fatigue. It was his father's and it fit him loosely.

Most all of his platoon stood geared and in their files, trading whispered talk, looking to the east and beyond the Spartans for signs of the coming day. Again Nikandros stared to the gaping ridge top where the Korinthians once stood.

# CHAPTER 15

▼

Myronides shuffled nervously upon the hill. As he watched the rim of the sky to the east glow faintly, he thought himself like a field mouse, dallying too long at the grain as day breaks, revealed to the searching eyes of an eagle or hawk. The bird would swoop and strike, and he was still far from his burrow on the slopes of Kithairon.

"It grows late," reminded Praxis. "Why do we not move?"

"Perhaps the plan has been changed?" he offered.

His anxiety nurtured little conversation. Every so often he would lean forward to peer down the ranks of the assembled taxi, hoping to see a herald or messenger passing the word to step off; but none came. They rocked in their files, shields upright upon the earth and leaning against their knees, helmets cleared of their faces. Imperceptibly, night began to fade.

Down upon the plain and across the Asopos, Persian campfires still flickered, but much fewer than had been burning when they first stirred to assemble. Far to his right the Athenian line heaved to the downslope, causing a wave of motion to ripple toward him until they too stepped off. *It was good to be moving,* he thought.

Now and again he snapped his head to the rear, checking to see when the last of his men would dip below the crest of the hill on their way back to Kithairon. His heart drummed, not from exertion but from the thought of Persian cavalry rounding the hill behind them; for long stretches he balked at turning, fearing this sight. Instead he locked his eyes ahead, calculating the distance to the safety of the deep shadowed hills. They were moving too slowly. If he were in command they would be at the trot now. Was this pace Aristides' attempt to maintain cohesion? Cover the ground quickly and reform near the Spartans; that is what he would do. Any sensible commander would agree.

✳      ✳      ✳      ✳

"They have just begun to move?" Euryanax stabbed the earth with his spear, burying its butt-spike deep. He twisted it free then plunged it all the harder.

Pausanias stood back from the Athenian herald. "He was concerned about crossing that ground in darkness," said the regent. "His messenger assures us that he will cover the distance doubly fast once his men can see their feet."

Amompharetos' fatigue held his building anger in check. The Athenians moved almost an hour later than agreed to, and would need to sprint to close on the Spartan left flank as instructed. "The Persians? Do they stir?" he asked while measuring the light in the east. Day would soon break above the hills and the Persian scouts would see the empty ridge. They must also see the last of the Spartans departing.

"None yet," answered Euryanax.

"We move as planned," commanded Pausanias. Now he pointed to Polydoros. "Your regiment will stay as rearguard."

"What!" Amompharetos viewed this change of orders as an affront to his men. His was the regiment next in rotation to perform the maneuver. Furthermore, he knew by the code of merit that his men were best prepared. "Is this your command, or my father's?"

"Oh come now Amompharetos, your father is in Sparta," replied Pausanias. "What influence does he wield here?" Even a Spartan king must answer to the ephors—Pausanias, a prodikos, was doubly accountable to them, and to Poliadas in particular. But he dismissed their authority casually.

"More, it seems, than he should," said Amompharetos. "This is my duty. I will not relinquish it."

"Do *you* disobey me?" said Pausanias.

"You have issued two orders. I choose the first," he returned.

"Gentlemen," interrupted Euryanax, "One thing is certain; we cannot all stay." He faced the regent now. "He will not leave, so for all our sakes turn his insubordination into a command and let us go before the Persians decide the issue for us."

Pausanias clamped his lips tightly. "Stay, but execute this next order precisely." The flicker of rage shone in his eyes. "Follow us once you see the Persians forming."

Presently the regent looked at the Athenian herald. "Please convey to Aristides my displeasure at his delay. Tell him also to close quickly on our flank, for if this lure does indeed succeed, by midmorning we will be inundated in a Persian flood." He shook his head at the sight of Amompharetos, turned to the others and said simply and with no emotion, "Now."

The four other polemarchs melted away to their regiments, and Pausanias too walked away. Within moments the bulk of the Spartans paced down the back-slope of the ridge, holding precise order as they withdrew. Amompharetos moved to the agema of his regiment and slipped into place in the front rank beside Kallikrates. "Any movement?" he asked his friend.

"Why no. They sleep. Even their watch-posts seem to be dozing," he said somewhat disappointed as he peered north to the Persian lines.

The black of night slowly turned to gray. Down in the plain the mist transformed to milky white. They watched the Persians in silence. Suddenly in the east, the colorless sky turned golden, struck by the rising of Helios. Shafts of light streamed over the hills illuminating the Spartans upon the ridge crest.

Amompharetos glanced, per chance, at Kallikrates; his handsome face held the soft light of dawn, while his eyes mirrored the rising disc of the sun. Kallikrates returned this look with a smile.

A far off voice cried in panic—not in Greek but in the tongue of a barbarian. Over and over the same incomprehensible words repeated like the clanging of a bell. "Seems they have awakened," said Kallikrates.

Now Amompharetos studied the battle-line of the enemy, scanning it for movement. He spied a man or two scurrying north toward the Persian stockade, but still the bulk of the Persians did not stir. Abruptly trumpets ripped the morning air, while men on horseback thundered through the gates of the enemy fort; they whirled about on their nervous horses, pointing up to the Spartan ridge.

$$*\qquad*\qquad*\qquad*$$

"They are gone!" screamed Mardonios, fighting to hold his horse steady. Infantry poured through the gates behind him, and into formation along the riverbank sending all the horses of the officers into spins.

"No Lord Mardonios," said Asfandiar. "Look upon the ridge." He directed them to the far left of the ridge line where stood a contingent of hoplites, so difficult to see for they moved not a bit, offering little notice to themselves.

"Then the rest cannot be far." Mardonios, with a snap of his hand, called forward a scout from one of the watch-posts. "Did you see anything? Any movement at all?" he bellowed.

The scout dipped his head in deference then spoke softly, peering down at his feet. "Yes Lord Mardonios. Just before dawn we saw the Spartans withdraw."

"And of the others? What of them?" Mardonios asked.

"I do not know, lord. The ridge, and the hill of the Athenians both are empty," answered the scout.

"Then they are all in flight," said Mardonios, his words soaring. "We advance."

More infantry tumbled through the gates—donning tunics and armor as they ran—and out onto the plain, while squadrons of horse reined up near the bridge, ready to strike across the Asopos. Still, it would take time to form up. At the end of an hour and brimming with impatience Mardonios ordered the advance of his archers and infantry; *he* would lead his elite horsemen. He whispered a prayer to Ahura Mazda, his god, then struck his horse hard with his heels.

*     *     *     *

Eurydamos worked to keep his horse in a slow canter, not wanting to outpace his infantry as it crossed the plain, closing on the abandoned Athenian positions. He hated the Persians, but these arrogant Athenians were his true enemy and today he would grapple with them, and if his prayers to Herakles—hero of his city—be heard, would he vanquish them. They rode on ground still dark with the lingering shadows of night for dawn had arrived meekly today. Before him the hilltop gleamed in light. Beyond the peak of Kithairon sparkled. All else was deep in dark.

Puzzled, he looked again to his left, to the lines of the Persians and noticed that they just now seemed stirred to action. How could they not see the ridge before them empty? The Theban scouts, at the onset of dawn, spotted quickly the bare hill of the Athenians and launched their pursuit. The hill bothered him though for it hid from view the location of the Athenians and the others of the enemy that had withdrawn. Were they far to the south, hugging the slopes of the mountains, or were they strolling across the open farm-fields between this hill and Plataia?

Before long they rolled up to the beginnings of the hill-slope. The infantry spilled around the base of the hill, like a stream diverted by a rock or other obstacle, and on toward the road that split the hill and ridge. Impatient, Eurydamos sent his horse into a gallop; the beast fought against the incline, bounding finally to the crest of the hill. Around the ground was littered with the debris of encampment; the smell of sweat from both animal and man clung to the hill. Now he spied the scene, seemingly as a god would from lofty Olympos: the Athenians were not far from them, strolling amidst the harvested fields before the town of Plataia; far off to his left in the east he spotted the Spartans moving southward also, and he knew that the two contingents were separated dangerously, inviting attack. But he saw no others—the warriors who had held the center of the ridge between the Spartans and Athenians. They must already be in the foothills and hidden from view. Or, in their panic he hoped, climbing up the road into the mountains.

"We attack," shouted Asopodoros, from the road far below.

He leaned back hard, straining to keep his balance as the horse skidded down the slope, carrying him from the golden sunlight which bathed the crest onto the gray-shadowed plain below.

Ahead, Asopodoros spun his lance overhead, extolling his men to assemble, and within moments the prancing cavalry of Thebes formed a huge rectangle. Then at his word they burst forward. Around him, in this frenzy of beast and man, Eurydamos rode, struggling to sight the object of their assault but the dust, early morning mist and jostling of the charge obscured all detail from his vision. Several sharp blasts from a salphinx tore through the air, from the Athenians ahead he was sure, for at this signal he now saw the enemy halt, turn and snap their shields forward, overlapping their bronze bowls like the scales of some huge, brazen serpent.

Trapped in the thunderclap of the cavalry's attack, all sound became smothered—even his own heartbeat for it surely hammered at his chest, summoned by fear, exhilaration or both. But he could not hear it. To his right a horse rolled to the earth, hurling its rider forward; the ground here was riddled with potholes and white boulders, and one of these caught the animal's leg. On he charged, taking only quick notice of the unhorsed warrior. They closed on the Athenians, and when he drew near enough to begin to distinguish individual men—faces separate and above the wall of shields—the sun slipped over the hills and doused the entire front line of the enemy in golden light. For a moment he blinked to clear this vision, for it seemed that the Athenians stood in the gods' favor. Now he watched the enemy infantry pull down their helmets, heave their shields up and then all at once spill their spear-points forward to greet them.

# CHAPTER 16

▼

Ahead of them, nestled at the base of Kithairon like a dog at his master's feet, the vacant walls of Plataia swallowed up the gaining light. A single torch marked the tower gate. As they chugged over the level span between the ridges, the grass shivered to life; hundreds of snakes coursed away from the phalanx, disturbed by the thunder of the warriors' march.

"I can hear them," shouted Bull. "They cannot be far behind."

Amompharetos snapped his head back and caught sight of Persian horse rounding the base of the ridge, charging at them. Before them, but less than a stade's distance was the Spartan battle-line, and in it a hollow slot yawning wide—an invitation to his regiment. Quickly his mind whirred in calculation, measuring the distance to be covered and the speed of the approaching Persians. He wished to avoid sprinting, for his men would need every trace of energy today to withstand the onrush of enemy cavalry.

"Should we run?" shouted Bull above the clang of their weapons that played like music to the even steps of the Spartans.

Amompharetos shook his head. "Why no. We have time," he assured. He snatched a glance at Kallikrates, then looked to the boy Amnestos. Both moved along, chatting with each other, exhibiting faint concern for the wave of cavalry that was descending on them.

Next he spotted Euryanax, in the fore of the Spartan battle line, waving them on and pointing to the gaping hole reserved for them. From behind he heard the air rip with a flight of arrows, followed by more. The thud of bronze upon the earth drew his glance away from the Spartans ahead to his left; he saw Amnestos stumble, upsetting the perfect order within the files as Bull and Kallikrates bent to snatch him up.

"Put me down," he yelled, spinning his feet above the ground. His two comrades held aloft by his arms. His helmet slipped down over his face, through the tossing of his body or by the hand of Bull, and this silenced him for the moment.

"Hush, little one," chided Bull. He smacked the boy on the side of his helmet with the rim of his shield—an oft employed prank in training that produced an unpleasant ringing that temporarily deafened.

Around them arrow-shafts began to sprout from the earth, loosed from Persian bows; the deadly crop grew thicker with the enemy's approach. Amompharetos turned one final time and spotted the horseman charging while flinging arrows, furiously attempting to overtake his regiment before it reached the embrace of the phalanx.

"Double pace," he now yelled, sending them into a jog. More arrows rattled amongst them, clanging off helmets and glancing off their back sloped spears. They closed swiftly upon their lines, and as they neared, he heard the order—"Slope spears"—boom from Euryanax. The Spartans spear point flashed forward, with nary a ripple of delay. Now he could see eyes. And grins. He stepped aside and let his men flow into place then bawled the order to turn about. The Persians viewed a seamless wall of bronze.

As in the days before, the Persians pulled up once within bow range and began their missile assault; the air hissed with death. But unlike earlier days, more Persians kept piling forward, adding their bowshot to the storm.

From behind, the pipes issued the signal to kneel, and each Spartan dropped to one knee while bracing his shield against his left shoulder, prepared to accept the hail of arrows. To their right Pausanias had anchored his formation securely to a boulder-laced stream, but his left flank hung dangerously exposed, waiting for the Athenians to close upon it and complete an unturnable front. Unlike days previous he could not stand here securely and prevail against the massing Persians by simply clinging to the ground he now occupied; the incline was slight and their exposed left would be their undoing. Around the regent clustered the polemarchs anxious to hear the order to engage.

"Get word to Aristides," ordered Pausanias. "If they cannot close, they must send us their archers." He shooed the messenger away. "Ask them, kindly," he shouted after as the man sprinted off.

"Does it surprise you that the Athenians are not here?" shouted Amompharetos, his voice growing nasty with contempt.

"They are in combat with the Thebans," answered Pausanias. "But I cannot reckon why they were overtaken so easily."

Behind the gathering of officers bleated a herd of goats, tended by a Helot and the mantis Tisamenos, waiting for Pausanias to perform the sphagia sacrifice. The polemarchs, Amompharetos included, looked nervously to the regent, hoping he would commence the rites that would allow them battle. Pausanias ignored the goats and Tisamenos, looking to the massing Persians.

"Do we attack?" pleaded Amompharetos.

"Yes," quickly answered Pausanias, "but not yet. The signs are not propitious."

Baffled, Amompharetos scanned their proximity looking for the slain goat and its entrails. "And where did you read these signs," he quizzed.

"No sacrifice is required, dear Amompharetos, to reveal that the signs are not fitting," answered Pausanias grinning. "Look to the Persians. They are our oracle today."

"But how long can we withstand their arrows?" said Euryanax. "Many more archers fill the plain today than yesterday. It will be near impossible to hold our men in check. And what of the Tegeans?"

"We will advance," assured Pausanias. "But for now return to your men. Tell them that we move once the signs are inclined for battle."

Amompharetos squeezed through the formation of kneeling Spartans to his place at the fore of the regiment, then hunkered down behind his shield, all the while eyeing the growing Persian force. With a pause in the barrage, he looked to Bull. "Keep watch on him," he said glancing now at Amnestos.

"He has nothing to fear. He fits neatly behind his shield."

Amompharetos grinned, watching the boy hugging the bowl of his hoplon, only the crest of his helmet wavering above its rim. In contrast huge Bull squirmed to tuck his broad shoulders within the shadow of his shield, but when he worked his left shoulder to cover, the right one became exposed. "You, my friend, need a larger shield," said Amompharetos with a wink.

The Persians now inched forward, emboldened by the Spartans' posture, planting their wicker shields like a great fence from behind which they continued to fling their arrows. All along the line fletched shafts bristled, their iron heads buried deep into the Spartan shields; further into the ranks, arcing clouds of arrows poured into the Spartans clanging off bronze helmets and breastplates. The roar of the missiles forced them to shout even when in conversation with men adjacent. Amompharetos scanned the men around him until his eyes, as though directed by a god, fell upon Kallikrates. The man smiled, then opened his mouth as if to form a word when suddenly his head drooped; his helmet smacked the rim of his shield as he slouched to the earth.

Amompharetos slipped sideways, covering him. From the seam of Kallikrates breastplate sprang a deeply imbedded arrow; with every breath, air gurgled from the wound as the shaft seemed to quiver with the beat of his heart. His eyes burned with anger. He swallowed hard, as though his throat could not open. "To die like this is shameful," he sighed. Again he swallowed, then gasped.

Amompharetos knew this wound; life would not tarry. "Yours is not a shameful death, dear Kallikrates. For today we fight for our liberty."

His eyes became transfixed on the arrow, watching the pulsing slow with each passing moment until it moved no longer.

"Oh but it is," he answered in a whisper. "For I have done little to speed this cause, or to help my comrades." His mouth opened in a sigh. Out flew his life.

Amompharetos planted his spear. He slipped the helmet from Kallikrates head, closed his friend's eyes, then gently brushed the hair from his face. "Yours is a kallos thanatos—a good death." Two Helots had come forward for the body, their eyes pleading with him to allow them to complete their task quickly. Without a word, he turned to face the Persian barrage.

$$* \quad * \quad * \quad *$$

He looked to the road that separated the ridge from the hill they had just abandoned, and watched the Theban infantry rumbled along it in haste. Soon they would add their numbers to the cavalry that was already hammering them. Any of his men that straggled behind had been swiftly cut down by the Theban horseman; many died.

The confusing light of dawn had given way to the clarity of midmorning, a clarity that shocked him. Myronides looked around and saw that they had, by chance, halted their march between two branches of a stream some several hundred yards shy of the Spartans. Across the empty fields in front of them Theban hoplites jostled into position, flashing their shields forward, each with a club—the ensign of Herakles—painted upon its bronze facing. They paused. A single figure stepped out before them all, shouting his orders, ending his harangue with a broad sweep of his spear which he seemingly pointed directly at Myronides. The Thebans surged forward.

"Close order," shouted Myronides to his men, who began to break the long files in two, doubling them forward in compact formation. Each man shouldered his hoplon, lowered his helmet, then presented spear to the enemy.

As the interval between the two masses of armored men—Theban and Athenian—shrunk, the dust and clamor spun minds to near madness. "Aleu-aleu," echoed the Theban war cry as they broke into a sprint. Myronides crouched low into his shield, planted his right foot into the earth and stepped forward with his left, bracing for the collision of metal, flesh and bone. He strained to hear commands, to distinguish any words above the rising din, but his hearing became overwhelmed by the drumming of his heart and wild breathing isolated within the bronze of his helmet. Only vision penetrated. He peered above the hoplon's rim, and locked his sight upon a lumbering hoplite who tore straight for him; the man groaned, swinging his spear underhand, trying to slip its razored point below Myronides' shield, but it glanced off the bronze to his right. Now *he* heaved forward, pumping his spear furiously at the Theban's head. So many thrusts slipped to one side and the other, skimming off the polished, high-crested helmet, until by chance his blade caught flesh, sinking deep into the man's nape; he wailed. Helpless now, the Theban discarded his shield to clamp his hands over the spurting wound in his throat, while crumpling to his knees. With a final lunge Myronides finished him, burying his spear-point deep into his back, crackling his spine with the blow. It took several panicked twists to free the weapon. Now he was being shoved forward, smacked in his back by a shield, forward into the line of enemy hoplites. His purchase upon the ground vanished—the earth had been torn and plowed by churning feet and it was slick with blood, and slippery with piss, shit, vomit and the bodies of the slain. Solid earth sank below this swamp of human refuse.

"I must keep my feet," he repeated within his helmet. He knew once upon the ground, death would follow, for he would either be trampled by his advancing men or run be through by the surging Thebans. Again his foot slid, sending him to a knee, and he scrambled to rise up and move forward. He worked to pull his foot and leg from the muck of battle, but it held him tight, sucking the energy from him as he struggled. In desperation he planted the butt-spike of his spear and leaned upon it, using the weapon as a crutch, but still he could not free his foot. He glanced down and saw a corpse pinning his calf in the sanguine ooze. Now in panic he yanked it hard; it released too quickly, stealing his balance, sandal and greave. He stepped on the body with his bare foot and clambered ahead.

With every meter gained, the Thebans countered and retook one in turn. They shoved. Then Myronides and his men, recoiled, stiffened and responded. For the better part of an hour this grinding of flesh and metal wore on, until each side finally paused in exhaustion. Myronides, knees wobbling and the wound in his leg throbbing with every heart beat, stood straight now and scanned the plot of earth visible through the narrow slits in his helmet; men of both cities lay sprawled before him, all trace of color surrendered to the black mud of combat. Even the Theban cavalry drew back, not in retreat, but to spell their horse and assess their work so far. The Athenians had been hammered to edge of extinction, while their opponents—the Thebans, along with the Thessalian, Macedonians and other Medizing Hellenes—lost no ground, and few men.

*       *       *       *

Asfandiar reined up not more than a few paces from Mardonios, loosed an arrow into a straggling Greek then spoke. "Where are the others?" he asked of his commander.

"They have fled," laughed Mardonios, indicating the scene before him empty of all but the Spartans. "Stumbling to Athens by now."

"Do we attack?" he said pointing with his empty bow to the Spartans on the slight rise of ground ahead. Oddly his eyes were drawn to his father's ring now, the one he would always wear in battle—a talisman of luck. It twisted around his gloved finger, two golden snakes, their open jaws clamped around a bright ruby.

"As soon as all our infantry is up," said Mardonios. "For now, content yourself with killing Greeks from afar."

All around the air hummed with the thrum of bowstrings; clouds of arrows hurtled away from them, raining into the Spartan ranks. Looking to the enemy Asfandiar could see—so very rarely—the tip of a spear waver, followed by the form of a Greek warrior crumpling earthward, wounded by one of the missiles; for their thousands of bowshots, only occasionally did one strike.

Now a rider approached from the rear shouting gleefully. "Lord Mardonios, the Athenians are breaking." The messenger, a Theban, was sent by Asopodoros to inform Mardonios of his engagement. By this word and the scene before him, both Asfandiar and Mardonios were sure they had caught the Greeks at their most vulnerable. Neither Spartans nor Athenians advanced: the former because they would not; the latter, having tried and failed, could not. One third of the Greek force had fled, or so they thought, leaving the remainder exposed, separated and supremely vulnerable.

The great Persian general, entrusted by Xerxes to culminate this war with these nettlesome Greeks, sat high upon his horse, surveying the myriads of warriors waiting on his word. He took it all in along with a deep and savoring breath, then whispered thanks to Ahura Mazda, his god, for this victory.

\*     \*     \*     \*

"Wake up," shouted Nikandros.

Theron blinked his eyes open, and unthinking tried to raise his head, having forgotten of his whereabouts. F-i-i-i-t! Another shaft drilled into the earth between the two. All around, uncountable numbers of red and white fletched arrows blossomed like poppies amongst the hunkering warriors, their murderous numbers growing with each volley. Nikandros reached for the newly fallen missile and plucked it from the earth. He studied it, twisting its shaft to spin its barbed-iron warhead, then looked around at the multitudes of its duplicate angled in the soil like wind-bent grain. "They cannot have many more," he shouted at his son above the roar and rattle of the barrage.

"Father," he yelled, his eyes pleading. "When do we advance?"

"When the order is given," he replied simply.

"But father. Why do we sit helpless?"

He too wondered why they and the Spartans did not attack. Out in the plain the Persian archers stood behind their wicker spara shields, launching death, while the Greeks knelt, dying. "Would be better to die out there," he mumbled.

"What father?" shouted the boy.

Nikandros repeated his words, yelling now so Theron could hear. He glanced to his brother Athamos, who sat with his knees tucked up to his chest and his back propping up his hoplon in protection. "Was it like this at the gates?" he shouted.

Athamos lifted his eyes. "No brother. No space there for archers," he answered. "At Thermopylai we fought. Here they kill us with little cost to themselves."

Nikandros peered above his shield and to the right—to the Spartans. The Persians were gathering thick before them and pouring missiles into them without pause. Far off from the river Asopos to the north, more Persian warriors dashed southward, thickening their already heavy lines. Persian horsemen charged forward, emptied their bows then retired, and this they kept to without respite. The Spartans and Tegeans crouched low—nothing more.

Long into this morning the storm of Persian missiles continued; the noise of arrow upon bronze echoed, like an endless summer hail upon a tiled roof. Men rubbed their stiffened limbs; inactivity had robbed them of flexibility. As the morning wore on, well into the high time of trading in the markets, grumbling spread across the army. "No more of this," one shouted at the sky. "Let us go," yelled another. "Let *us* kill some of *them*," added a third. Theron stood, trance-like in the bowshot tempest, and began to walk forward, down the slope and toward the Persian lines. Others rose up from the earth, in tight groups at first, until the fifteen hundred hoplites of Tegea formed up. Chileos, their commander, tried not to halt them but hustled forward to take his place in the first rank.

*          *          *          *

"Look," said Euryanax pointing to his left. He stabbed at the air with his spear, directing the glance of both Pausanias and Amomphare-tos toward their allies. "They advance."

Pausanias looked out to the enemy shaking his head. "Bring up the goat," he commanded to the boy. "The signs, urged on by our allies, favor us."

The animal trotted, being tugged by a garlanded youngster clad in a white chiton. The seer, Tisamenos, hurried along with them; he sprinkled a bit of water on the goat's head. It shook—a good sign. Pausanias unceremoniously pinned its rear legs with a knee, then yanked back on its neck exposing its pulsing throat. His short xiphidion drew deep and soundless through the flesh. The soil at his feet darkened wet with blood.

"Forward!"

Now the earth heaved up scarlet and bronze as each Spartan rose. Shields snapped to shoulders, and all at once and without a ripple of hesitation, five thousand spear-points dipped forward. The army transformed from this sprawl of limp and lackluster men to a single entity, beast-like with hackles raised, dark-death in every eye. The double-reeders piped out their tune to advance, then slowly, and with a solemnity unseen by any other nation in battle, the Spartans *walked* forward, led in song by Pausanias, a song meant to maintain cadence, pace, and cohesion to their formation. Inexorably they marched toward the wicker shield wall of the Persian bowmen. The enemy, seeing this, loosed arrows furiously. In their panic each successive volley climbed higher, until now most sailed overhead of the Spartan front-rankers.

The distance closed. Enemy archers froze, wide-eyed. Some turned and struggled to flee but the compaction of their formation, so patiently anticipated by Pausanias, provided no escape. The front-line Persians were caught between their own surging reinforcements and the advancing formation of Spartans.

The earth trembled, not from the thunder of Persian horse but the synchronized step of the Spartan advance. They did not hurry. Five thousand feet struck at once, then five thousand more, and steadily the wall of bronze bore down upon the panicked bowmen. With a thud multiplied several hundred fold, the shields of the Spartans rammed into the flimsy wicker wall, snapping Persian shields like dry kindling. After this initial impact, Greek spears plunged into the confused ranks of Persians, ripping through cloth-capped heads and tunicked chests. The Persians stumbled. They tussled in panic at their own men, clutching and clawing, vainly attempting flight through the thickening ranks and to safety in the rear. But from behind, like the flood waters of havoc, Mardonios' infantry dashed forward into the frenzied mass, anticipating victory, ignorant of the butchery at the fore.

Amompharetos pumped his spear-hand, plunging the deadly iron downward and into the bare necks and shoulders of the foe. At times he need not aim but strike and strike again, so thick were the enemy before him. He, like the other front-rankers, trampled down the enemy bowmen, stepping over and around them while the middle Spartan ranks dispatched the still living with plunging butt-spikes as they passed over them. The malevolent harvest continued; the enemy fell like sickled wheat.

Unexpectedly the Persian center heaved forward, urged on by Mardonios himself and his elite horsemen. The Spartans slowed; now they fought to hold *their* ground. Momentum, so far a companion to the Spartans, seemed suspended for a moment, then every man felt it ebb, slipping away to the Persians. The Spartan advance seized. Next the front ranks stumbled rearwards, pressed by the onslaught of Mardonios' horsemen and his freshly encouraged infantry.

*Now the Persians advanced!* With each step gained, Spartans fell. Eerily, the formation acquired a will, one separate from the minds of the individuals within; it propelled itself backwards, heedless to any single warrior's attempt to stem its movement. Every Spartan felt the grip of defeat squeezing him.

From the front ranks stepped Aristodemos—the lone survivor of Thermopylai. He knew what evoked this sudden burst of audacity from the enemy and also knew he was within a short distance to strike at this man Mardonios, so he heaved into the thin line of enemy infantry that separated the two, dropping several so swiftly that none of them could respond or defend. But inevitably the Persian horseman shoved forward to surround their commander and in doing so, isolated Aristodemos. Bravely he struck at them while they swarmed over him like ants upon an overturned beetle. He swung and they fell. And on. Finally several grabbed his arms while others jumped upon his back. Persian arms swung high then plunged, driving their flashing blades into him.

Amompharetos felt his spirits soar. With shoulder pressed into his shield he pushed ahead calling on the others to follow. "See what just one brave man has done," he yelled.

Amnestos stepped forward now to fill Aristodemos' place in the line, and in the melee a horse reared up and struck down with its hooves, toppling him. The rider, spotting the helpless Spartan prone upon the ground, cocked his lance. Seeing this, Amompharetos sidestepped, pulled his shield even tighter to his shoulder and rammed into the horse, sending the beast into a whirl. Then he lifted his spear hand. At that moment several Persian infantrymen lunged at him, slipping their iron blades beneath his breastplate, burying them deep. Under the blows he crumpled forward, dropping his shield and spear.

Bull exploded forward from his slot in the file, plowing aside Persian infantrymen with his hoplon until he arrived beside his friend. He knelt, sheltering him with the left edge of his shield.

"Help him up," he screamed at Amnestos.

The boy rushed to Amompharetos' still unguarded side, then with his empty spear hand, tried to lift him. In bursts of five or six, and emboldened by the sight of a wounded Spartiate, the enemy rushed at the trio.

"To his feet," screamed Bull through the narrow slit of his helmet. "We must get him to his feet."

The pair strained to haul up their comrade; they dare not forfeit their shields, but retaining these monstrous bowls hindered movement. Finally Amompharetos, propped on either side by his friends, wavered to his feet. The Spartan line fought to advance and engulf them within the protection of the shield wall, but with equal vigor the Persians pressed upon them.

Bull—he being the only one still wielding a spear—pumped and lunged at the closing enemy, driving them back with his furious accuracy. They rushed at him, at first full of courage, but as he stabbed and struck, this courage transformed to numbing caution.

It snapped! His weapon splintered mid-haft, driven into the face of white-scarved bowman. The other Persian archers seeing the huge Spartan disarmed, charged at him, slashing. Iron blades rebounded, clanging off the bronze of his breastplate, but a single strike sent his helmet flying, and it was now that they finished him. They hacked at his bare head, while he fought to fend of the blows with his arm, until a wild swing sliced his neck wide.

"No!" cried Amnestos, seeing his comrade fold to the earth. Rage overtook him, but he knelt without spear in hand, holding Amompharetos. Finally the Spartan wall swallowed them, and a man from the middle ranks, Parmenon, stepped to hold the wounded polemarch. Amnestos looked up, and saw but a few meters away the great Mardonios upon his prancing white steed, waving his sword, ordering the Persians onward.

*I would kill him*, he thought, but then squeezed his empty spear hand tight. Now he reached across his chest with his right hand, clamped it upon the hilt of his sword and began to draw the blade clear of its scabbard. He paused. For a single moment all around him faded to silence; nothing moved. His eyes rested on a fist-sized rock at the feet of Amompharetos. The boy dipped low and snatched the stone, reared back, and with every ounce of strength still remaining within him, let it fly. It hurtled true over the chaos, clanging hard off an iron helmet. Mardonios, stunned, leaned left and then right upon his horse tipping almost to horizontal when suddenly he slipped then dissolved into the churning mass around him.

"Mardonios!" shouted a voice within the Spartan ranks. "Mardonios is down!"

At these words even the Persians began to spin their heads, looking for their commander. They spied an empty, tossing warhorse. A roar went up from the body of the Spartans as they redoubled their efforts.

Now the Spartan battle-line rolled forward regaining then surpassing its former momentum; it slamming murderously into the confused Persians, then as though it were of a single mind and body shuddered in a great pause before rumbling onward.

The enemy continued to struggle with valor, throwing their bodies forward, stabbing at the armored hoplites, grabbing at shield and spear, clawing, biting, kicking. The manslaughter raged, uncountable. So many Persians met death bravely—but so many died, struck in their backs as they clambered rearward, sealed off from flight by the continuing press of their own rear-rankers.

Amnestos surged forward with his comrades, unable to pause and consider the fate of his dear friends. The battle raged on and carried him deeper into the body of dying Persian infantry and horse. He felt it clearly now—the Persians would break. One final push, one deadly heave forward and the enemy would crumble. He crouched into his shield, spread his feet wide apart and shoved. Peeking above its rim he saw the hind most ranks of Persians tossing away bow and quiver, wicker spara and lance, any impediment to flight, and scramble across the river toward the safety of the stockade.

More of the enemy fell, but as the Spartans advanced fewer Persians stood their ground, until only scattered clusters hung together, men too tired to run. These flung away their swords and reached out to the Spartans, hands bare in surrender. This sign meant nothing. The wall collided with them, driving them under.

Even with the rout undoubtedly manifested, the Spartans did not increase their pace, as other less disciplined warriors were want to do, to overtake and dispatch their fleeing, vanquished foe. No, they continued on with their measured pace, keeping in step and time with the tune still piped by the flute-players. Amnestos at the front rank in place of his comrade, looked left and saw their allies the Tegeans roll forward with them. Beyond them he heard the voices of thousands—men singing the paean to Kastor, the hymn of battle. Pouring forward and coming into view were the Korinthians. They had advanced at the double, from near the shrine of Hera, and now covered the vulnerable left. This sight re-energized him, as it did the others around him.

With each step they closed upon the river and the Persian fort that desecrated its far bank. He looked around. Gone was the gleam of polished bronze that had marked the army that morning. Blood, muck, and dust clung thick to everything. Men bled as they marched. Some dropped, succumbing to wounds ignored. The rest trudged on, across the low waters of the Asopos toward the timbered wall of Mardonios' camp.

✳     ✳     ✳     ✳

"Withdraw!" The word sliced through the din of combat like the single shrill note of an ill-tuned flute. Eurydamos' heart dropped in his chest. They were winning and he knew it. With the fired gaze of incredulity he looked back and saw Asopodoros wave at him with his spear. "Withdraw," he repeated.

Eurydamos yanked hard on the reins, spinning the horse about, then sent the beast into a gallop. "We are winning," he exclaimed, drawing up to his commander.

He fought to keep his horse steady, but the clamor unsettled it and kept it tossing and weaving nervously. The Theban cavalry broke free of the Athenians, not in flight but to reform and strike again, allowing their infantry to retreat with order. More officers poured around Asopodoros, puzzled by the new command.

"Look," he shouted at them. "The Megarians have advanced to help the Athenians. And a messenger has just ridden from the Persian left in panic. Our allies are routed, running for their lives before the Spartan phalanx." He studied the battle before him. His infantry would now try to disengage—a difficult and deadly maneuver, and the cavalry must screen them. "Form up," he shouted. "And ride hard into them."

Squadrons coalesced, taking their places along the line of attack. Then with a yell Asopodoros launched them into the Athenians once more. They thundered down upon the enemy hoplites and just before colliding with their shield wall veered sharply, skimming the front ranks, picking off Athenians that stepped clear of the formation. Eurydamos, hemmed in the inner ranks of his cavalry, followed the swerving wave forward. Upon turning along the front, the squadron lost cohesion and his section thundered forward, failing to peel away.

Before him he spied the object of their charge; a body of Athenian hoplites, eager for victory, had broken from their phalanx, trying to run down the retreating Theban infantry. The enemy took no notice of the swooping horseman until they were within a few meters, and then the Athenians, dumbstruck it seemed by this most unexpected sight, turned their heads to stare at Eurydamos and his men.

One stood apart and Eurydamos keen eyes spotted him; he steered his horse toward the solitary figure, rearing back his spear arm in underhanded fashion, ready to strike. His thrust was true, but the Athenian flicked it aside with a parry of his shield then spun slashing wildly at him with his kopis sword.

His ankle burned. Eurydamos peered down to snatch a quick glance; blood sheeted from a gash above the anklebone, splattering upon the flank of the horse as he rode. He flipped his spear in the air, only inches from his grasp, reversing his grip to overhand, then circled his horse and bore down upon the man once more. He closed on him. The Athenian angled his shield, brandishing his thick pointed sword overhead, ready to strike again. Eurydamos heaved his spear hand forward as he passed, but again the man ducked away and swung his blade; it sliced the horse on its rear flank. The beast felt nothing, and galloped on.

Eurydamos' chest convulsed for breath as he reined up, staring at the determined Athenian. He took no notice of the battle around him, but set his eyes upon this foe only. Then he spurred forward, bellowing his war cry to encourage both him and his charger. Across the diminishing span of the battlefield he watched the Athenian tuck his shield tight to his shoulder then brandish his sword overhead, preparing to defend. Oddly Eurydamos focused at the dark helmet slits that hid the man's eyes from his as he closed. Without eyes he seemed not human, but like some wildly animated statue, bereft of expression. The interval between them compressed. Eurydamos again wielded his spear overhead, leaning forward but at the same time reaching back with his loaded arm, summoning all his strength to deliver the blow. Just before striking he deftly re-gripped the shaft to underhand and slipped its iron blade beneath the Athenian's high-held shield, burying it deep into the man's groin. He reeled with the strike, carrying Eurydamos' spear with him to the ground. Suddenly weaponless, Eurydamos groped for his sword, and swiftly drew its blade free of the scabbard.

From behind he heard a shout. "Reform!"

# CHAPTER 17

▼

Dust rose from the plain, dark and thick, marking the fleeing Persians, like smoke above a dying fire. But a few meters from him now the Spartans lumbered onward, machine-like in their unremitting march towards the river. Asfandiar snapped a glance back over his shoulder towards the stockade. Panicked men jammed the gates in flight, seeking the safety of its timbered walls. Next he scanned the plain toward the center of the battlefield, and the position where he expected to find Artabazus, his Medes, Bactrians and Indians—a full one third of the army. But there he saw an empty plain.

Giving no thought to his safety and the haven of the fortified camp, he galloped across the Asopos, north following the Thebes Road and the plumes of telltale dust. Anger, more demanding than any lash, drove him on. Soon he glimpsed men, some on foot, others on horseback, but all moving in haste northward. Within a quarter hour he blew past the stragglers; they trudged, heads hung low, but none exhibiting the appearance of a battle fought; their spear-points gleamed brightly, unstained. He measured his own blade-ripped tunic against theirs: the rich purple was smeared with the black of blood, his trousers wet with gore. The mass of men choking the road now slowed him; he screamed at them to part, and struck at the ones who did not move with his whip, forcing his way forward.

They scowled at him, dark-eyed, displaying scant regard for his rank and impatience. Before him, on a hillock shadowed by plane trees, he spotted Artabazus and his officers, surveying the withdrawal to Thebes. Asfandiar peeled away from the road and galloped up the easy rise towards them.

"Why?" he snapped, pulling up near Artabazus.

"You mean why aren't we dying out there with Mardonios?" countered the crafty old general, pointing south to the roaring battle. Now Artabazus lifted a single gloved finger. "Before you speak—and this it seems you have attempted to do well before thinking—I will tell you of the battle as a whole, something which you could not have seen."

The stolid old man paused, displaying the same reason and caution in his speech as he did in war. "I rode forward, following the command of Mardonios, but unlike you my men had to advance up the steep slopes of the Asopos Ridge, and with great care, for the Greeks could have been lying in wait, hidden from us in the shadow of it. I reached the ridge crest and my heart sank when my eyes beheld the scene spread out before me. Your men were ensnared in combat, reeling under the Spartan advance, and to my right the Thebans and our other Greek allies struggled with the Athenians. The abandoned center of the Greek army was not so empty, for I saw ten thousand heavy infantry of the Greeks arrayed in the foothills before me."

"And seeing this you did nothing?" ranted Asfandiar.

"I saved for Xerxes, the Great King, many valuable men," retorted Artabazus. "Or do you think otherwise?" At these words the officers straddling Artabazus clamped their hands upon the gilded hilts of their swords. "Be silent," he warned, "and let me save another."

\*     \*     \*     \*

They crashed upon the stockade wall like heavy surf upon a stone breakwater, slamming the timbers, then receding when their efforts failed to move it.

"The gate," yelled Chileos. Within moments the Tegeans roared to the near gateway and began heaving shoulders and shields into the groaning door. They stepped back, then surged forward, repeating this ebb and flow till the draw bolts cracked like kindling wood. The torrent, now loosed, inundated the defenders within. Before a sword or shield could be raised in defense, the storming Tegeans cut them down, multiples of spears finding each Persian chest. Like netted fish, enemy soldiers whirled in panic, surrounded as they were, not knowing from which direction the next blow would come. Nikandros and his platoon stabbed at them until they fell, then plunged their spears deeper while their still living bodies writhed upon the earth.

There was no bare ground—not a speck of soil lie uncovered by an arm, a severed head or a corpse. Nikandros kicked aside the smaller debris when he could and stepped upon the fallen bodies at other times to press forward; beside him fought his son Theron and his brother Athamos. The battle took on the form of a great hunt, the Persians transformed to quarry, bereft of sense and driven by instinct, while the Tegeans' blood burned with the anticipation of the kill. The defenders hardly fought back, stunned to see the Hellenes breach their fort so quickly they collapsed away from the ring of attackers, compressing their numbers like a panicked herd, adding to efficiency of the slaughter.

Suddenly it stopped. Before him, a miserable few Persians stood in terror, hands held out, pleading for quarter. Dust hung thick mingling with the moans of the dying. Nikandros looked down; around him, piled to mid-thigh, were the dead. His feet swam in a quagmire of hot blood. Vomit climbed into his throat. He planted his spear into the earth before him, then slid his helmet up, off his face, and looked around. His brother Athamos leaned upon his spear, head hung low from his shoulders; the man was dyed crimson. Theron also steeped in the bath of combat, but unlike Athamos, had dropped his weapon and lowered his shield. He sobbed. Gore dripped from his helmet, arms, and shield, but Nikandros knew this dreadful mire came from the Persian dead, and not his son's wounds.

Smoke, thick and mephitic, billowed from flaming tents. Sound rushed back in to fill the gaping silence. Women screamed. Dying men wailed. In Nikandros' proximity the hoplites of Tegea merely stood—silent and motionless—stunned by the carnage. More allied warriors continued to pour into the stockade. A salphinx blared. Emerging from the black haze strode three Spartans who were met at once by Chileos. The four chatted, as casually as neighbors meeting at the market. After several moments Chileos nodded, then turned to Nikandros and the other Tegeans. "It is over," he announced. "Withdraw."

With no complaint the empty warriors shuffled out, the fever of battle spent. Flames now raced up the walls of the stockade near the gate, set alight by the rows of blazing tents. As the Tegeans departed, parties of Spartan Helots passed by, entering the encampment coolly and with a predetermined purpose. The trio of Spartans stopped one of the Helots, conversed briefly, then departed with the last of the Tegeans.

Once free of the encampment Nikandros collapsed to the earth, dropping weapon and shield. Theron ran to him; he tossed away his helmet, then bent over his father.

"You look terrible," said Nikandros from his back.

"Father. Are you hurt?"

"No son, I am spent. I have nothing left," he said. He stared up at the flawless blue of the afternoon sky.

His son dipped his face into view. "Is it truly over?" Now he rubbed his face with the back of his hands streaking the mask of grime. Remnants of sobs slipped from his throat.

A shadow covered Nikandros, and within it he found the face of his brother Athamos. "How can you two stand?" he asked, still supine.

Both Athamos and Theron folded to the earth beside him; Athamos fell flat on his belly, while Theron sat, knees drawn-up, watching the Helots as they raced into the stockade. The three Spartans surveyed it all. Past the rush of Helots and through the battered gate a woman emerged, running toward the Spartans. "Lord Pausanias," she cried upon reaching them. "Spare me. I am no Persian, but a captive of Mardonios." Pausanias raised his hand to quiet her, then spoke softly to the woman—so softly that Nikandros could not discern the words.

Through the gates came a gaggle of serving women, each swatting wildly while tugging their arms from the Helot guards that herded them forward like a flock of bleating goats. They halted before Pausanias and the two other Spartan officers. He tipped his open hand, as if to offer them something, and they passed, along with the woman, away from the stockade and toward the allied camp.

"Not a mark on you. Any of you," bellowed Chileos cheerfully as he approached them from the smoke of the torched fortress.

Nikandros propped his head up with a hand, and squinted at his commander. "Is it truly over, Chileos?"

"The battle—yes," he answered. "But the Thebans have fled to their city. Our work is not yet done."

"Have we not killed enough for one day?" Nikandros lay back, arms crossed to cover his face, trying to seal out the sights and sounds.

"Yes, my friend, our spears have had their fill. But the Athenians are pressing this issue. They have already set off north on the road to Thebes, hoping to catch the Medizers before they retire to their walls."

"If they despise them so much, let them go it alone," snapped Athamos. "Twice I have left my home behind to save Athens."

"Father! Father!" From out of the throng of warriors sprinted Medios. He skidded to his knees at Nikandros' side. "You are alive!"

"Why of course your father is alive," said Chileos as he towered over both of them. "And your brother. Your uncle too."

Nikandros tugged his son to him, surrounding him with an arm, then an embrace. The boy clung tight.

"Medios, I have something for you." Chileos reached into the bowl of his shield and pulled out something that flashed bright in the afternoon sun. "Not as good as your mother's but a respectable one just the same." He dropped the joined silver pipes into waiting hands, then strode off toward Plataia. Just before losing sight of them he turned and said, "A gift from the Great King."

✳     ✳     ✳     ✳

Dust choked them as they marched along the road north. They threaded their way around discarded weapons, toppled carts and baskets of provender, all jettisoned by fleeing survivors. Myronides detested the Thebans, but he hated even more this absurd command of pursuit. If they closed upon the rearguard, Theban cavalry would surely fend them off. There was no hope of catching them, but Aristides would not be dissuaded.

At least they had been allowed to pause at the river, drink and fill their flasks, but hunger now kicked in his belly while Helios raged in the sky above. Ahead he spotted a copse of trees, dominated by a thick-trunked plane tree.

"Where are you going," shouted his friend Praxis.

"To sleep," he snapped back at him. "The conquest of Thebes I leave to you," he added.

Praxis tossed his head around, then slipped from the column of hoplites to join Myronides in his languor. Still some distance from the trees, they spotted something upon the ground, mixed in the shadows. Myronides peered back over his shoulder to the Athenians on the road. No one had noticed their departure.

"It is a man," called Praxis. He shaded his eyes and leaned forward to sharpen his view.

Once under the branches both dropped their spears and shields and stepped closer. "He is Persian," observed Myronides. He knelt, studying the face-down body of the man; he could see the slashes in his bloodied corselet made by thick bladed weapons. This man was not slain by an Athenian, for jeweled bands still wrapped his arms, and his sword rested secure in its scabbard. He stared at a hand, the flash of a single golden ring catching his eye. The bobble slid easily from the corpse's finger. He studied it, twisting the ring until the single red gem was revealed to him; it was gripped in the jaws of twin serpents. "Here," he said, flipping the ring to Praxis.

"But why do you stare at his gloves?" asked Praxis, as his out-stretched hand snagged the loot.

"Because I found a pair that could be their twins."

\*        \*        \*        \*

"More water?" asked Amnestos as he bent over his wounded friend. The warrior could not speak now, but nodded to the boy. The lad reached for the flask, unstoppered it, then tilted its narrow spout gently, trickling water past the lips of Amompharetos. "The surgeon will be here soon," he assured. "You will be fine."

Amompharetos smiled at these words for he knew otherwise. The shattered blade buried deep in his ribs plugged the wound; once removed death would rush upon him. "Old Tolmidas proved me wrong," he said, forming a fleeting smile. "He vouched for someone when I would not. Tell him," he paused to swallow. "Tell him he was right." Amompharetos twisted his head painfully to look to the side and spotted the bodies of two Spartiate warriors shrouded in their war-cloaks; Helots worked to unfasten the wooden name tokens from their lifeless arms.

"Yes, it is Bull and Kallikrates," assured Amnestos. The warrior let fall his head to rest upon the pillowed cloak. He winced a bit. His mouth fought to form words, but no sound passed his lips. Amnestos leaned closer. Amompharetos moved his hand to his wound. "Take it out," he whispered to the boy.

"The surgeon will be here soon. He will free the blade and bind the wound."

Amompharetos slipped his blood-wet hand into the boy's and clamped it tightly, then tilted his head to behold Amnestos. "I would join them now."

Amnestos chest heaved in a single spasm of grief, but he fought it back. It tore at him to see this powerful warrior, his comrade, so frail. He stared. His throat tightened. Within the eyes of his friend he no longer saw the fire of youth but the peace of a full life and this frightened him.

"Boy, take it out," he whispered again, "and let me go."

He moved his hand along with the warrior's till it rested upon the ragged iron that protruded from his ribs. He gripped the broken end of the blade as best he could but it was slick with blood and only a small portion of it remained outside of the wound. With fingers clamped he pulled, and to his dismay the shivered spearhead began to withdraw.

Amompharetos smiled a bit. His eyes expanded.

The boy swallowed hard then with a final tug, slid the blade from the wound, releasing a stream of crimson. A mellifluous breath slipped by the lips of his friend; his eyes locked skyward.

*       *       *       *

He peered through the dust searching for pursuers. Eurydamos and his weary squadron paused on a knoll, as rear guard for the heavy infantry that humped its way back to the walled city. *I will die*, he thought, as he measured what remained of his horsemen against the combined armies of Sparta, Athens and the others—Thebes would die also. With every far off dirty cloud that drifted skyward, he felt the grip of fear, until finally as darkness drew down, his depleted emotions could no longer rouse him. Now to him and the others, death was as good as sleep and he invited either to join him.

Presently he quit his horse, smacking its flank, sending it tearing down the road away from the hillock and north to Thebes. "Even at a sprint you will not catch Artabazus," he yelled, laughing. Others in his squadron, whose heads dangled in partial sleep slowly looked up; a few managed smiles. "Join him if you wish," he added, shouting to his comrades.

Apollodoros, the commander, trotted his horse over to Eurydamos. "They are not coming. Too late for that. Maybe tomorrow."

"And I will be the first to greet them," said Eurydamos, his subdued laugh transforming to a cough.

"They will hardly take notice of you, a single haggard Theban. We are going home. Ride with me," he said, slapping the back of his horse.

Eurydamos crumpled to his knees, slipped his sword and scabbard free of his shoulder, then fell back upon the cool grass, staring at the gathering darkness above. He said nothing. Contently he pillowed his head with both hands and crossed his legs, much the way he would when he was a young boy wiling away a lazy summer afternoon. "I prefer this place," he answered. "Either way I am sure we will be in the company of Pausanias and his army soon. Give my regards to my father." He plucked up a naked twig and stuck it between his teeth then grinned.

He blamed his father for this war of the barbarian, a war in which he and his city would pay a dear price. Both his father and Attiginos, the shapers of this nefarious alliance with Persia, sat in apparent safety behind the thick walls of Thebes. He knew also, after today's battle, no walls could stand against the vengeance of Athens and Sparta.

Apollodoros wasted no more time on him. With the typical bawl of a commander he gave the order to withdraw, and within moments all that remained of the Thebans was the lingering smell of horses and the fading rumble of hooves upon the hard limestone road.

Above him whispers of clouds drifted from the north, carried by a fresh wind. It felt cool. The atmosphere of death that had smothered him daylong was quickly a lost memory in this peaceful evening. For the first time in more than a year he thought of other things than war. He recalled his first patrols—these part of the training of eighteen year olds, to accustom them to military duty; Eurydamos thought of them as grand outings, full of adventure with dear friends and comrades. Often these excursions brought him to this very knoll, on many such nights in the month of Ippodromeios. He and the other boys would pester the drillmaster to recount stories of his bravery in battle, but always he would speak of heroes past, of Herakles, and others—never of men still living, and this it seemed, kept battle dressed in the apparel of pleasing myth. Those were the last days he thought of war with anticipation. Those were certainly the very last days he honored the war-god; now every evil that Ares could conjure pressed close upon Thebes. Dire as this fate seemed—and he clearly understood it—its inevitability released him from care. The struggle was over.

Slumber, the twin brother of Death, carried him off. He slept deeply and with nothing but pleasant dreams, delivered to him upon wings by powerful Morpheos. He dreamt he was a boy again, dozing on the hill near his farm—the hill where an oak older than Kadmos shaded him from the hot summer sun. The place where he would always slip away to when he wished to be alone with his thoughts. Below him, on the road to the city he saw the army march along, drilling as they did several times after the harvest, to reiterate the simple craft of hoplite warfare; it took scant time to learn but enormous courage to execute. His father strode along the road, in with the others of his tribe and family, their congregation joyous in this escapade of mock combat. Laughter filled the ranks, imparting an incongruity to his smothered memories of these few, recent days. Unknowingly in sleep he smiled.

He could hear warriors joking now, but not in the broad speech of his land. They spoke in Doric. Lifting a fist, he rubbed his eyes to dispel the vision, but louder these voices became until the harsh light of day struck him.

Spartans! Morning had come and he slept well into it. Below him on the road he spied a seemingly endless column of scarlet and bronze men, tromping with grave celerity toward Thebes. None had seen him. By the look of the sun in the sky, it was easily mid morning. These

Spartans could have been marching for hours by now, and their lead elements may indeed be at the very gates of his city.

Now he slunk low, skidding down the far side of the knoll, away from the road, keeping out of sight of the invaders. If he kept to the dry streambed his journey home would be quick and surreptitious. Only at a few locations did he need to resort to stealth in crossing brief intervals of open ground so the soldiers upon the road would not spot him.

By mid afternoon he had slipped into the groves that brushed the southern wall of the city. Enemy hoplites secured Thebes, to be sure, but they hardly expected that someone would be trying to enter the place. He found the sally port and eased into the shadow of its portal. From here he could see the terminus of an alley, a narrow chasm between lumbering buildings, one of which was the blacksmith's, the shop of his friend Stenthelias. A slit trench that was used to drain wastewater ran beneath the gate from one of the buildings, and at its end he caught sight of the blacksmith's son emptying a crockery.

"Leukides," he whispered.

The boy looked out toward the main street, then seeing no one bobbed his head this way and that, peering at every window that opened out onto the alleyway.

"Leukides," he repeated a bit louder.

"Master Eurydamos," yelped the boy. "What are you doing out there?"

"Get your father to open the gate. He would know how."

Still staring wide-eyed at him, the boy did not move straightaway. Then suddenly he sprinted off.

Behind him stirred men, Hellenes like himself, but speaking with the sharp accent of Lakonians. He pressed further into the portal, squeezing almost flat to the wood and iron of the gate. Now he heard a stream of water splattering the stones, not but a few feet from where he hunkered in the shadows.

"Damn that felt good. I haven't taken a piss all morning." The words were followed by the crunch of feet upon the dry soil. They moved closer to him. Then suddenly he heard the clang of bronze.

"I'll tear the hide from your back, you little—!"

Again the ring of metal echoed. The Spartan backed away from the wall and came into view. He held his shield high, parrying away rocks that careened at him from high atop the wall.

"Master Eurydamos." The smithy unlatched the bolt with a large offset key and carefully pried the gate, just wide enough for Eurydamos to squeeze through edgewise. "Come quickly. Leukides keeps them busy." He followed Stenthelias down the alley and into his open-sided shop. Once within, the smith scooped a cupful of warm wine and handed it to Eurydamos. He sipped it at first, but could not maintain his manners, and without another breath emptied it dry.

"I must see my father."

"Your father is with Spartan officers. They arrived this morning."

*Good. They are talking,* he thought to himself. "I must go to him," he said, handing the blacksmith his cup.

He moved quickly and unnoticed, for the streets proved empty of townsfolk. As he closed upon the agora, the rumble of hundreds of voices dispelled the illusion of vacancy that had walked with him.

The agora stood crammed with men, and on its edges perched in trees youngsters looked on. By the size of the crowd assembled he knew where to find his father. As he approached he could hear the shouts of a few men in argument. Upon reaching the thick of people, he shouldered his way through, producing scowls from the ones he bumped by, until he could see the focus of it all. In the center stood a squad of Spartan infantry formed into a pair of perfectly ordered lines of eight men each, spears pointing skyward, shields gripped but resting on their shoulders. In front of them, helmet tucked under arm, paced an officer no doubt, for all eyes followed his every move. When he spoke, everyone else fell silent.

"I will restate the terms of Pausanias, captain-general of all the Hellenes. Your city will be spared. In return for this gesture, you will remand to my custody your leaders. To this there will be no further negotiation."

"And what is to be our fate, once in your hands? Are our deaths predetermined, or will a trial be afforded us if we agree to these terms?" said Attiginos.

Unexpectedly Timagenides turned. His eyes joined his son's and he acknowledged Eurydamos with a smile. A mask of relief fell upon his brow. He nodded.

With no further words the Spartan wheeled away from the Boiotarchs, leading his detachment toward the citadel. All along the street townsfolk watched, sullen-faced and in deathly silence. Not until the very gates of the Kadmea swung closed after the Spartans did people begin to melt away from the roadside and commence to converse.

"It is so good to see you," said Timagenides, stepping forward to embrace him. "Apollodoros said you would not return with him, and we feared you had been taken by the Spartans."

"Morpheos protected me," he admitted. He told his father of his night of dreams and the vision he awoke to on the knoll, and of his clandestine entry into the city. Suddenly he reached for the forgotten twig, but before he could snatch it his father spoke.

"You have earned that small indulgence." The forgetful grin faded."In a short time I must go," he announced. "The sun will be setting and the Spartans, I am certain, will be punctual."

"But father," he protested, "if you go with them you will surely die."

"Do not be so sure. Pausanias is a noble man, and a just one also."

"But the Athenians. They would press him to execute you all, trial or no."

"In this I am not so sure. But it matters not, for if we fail to accompany them, Thebes would be destroyed. Of that I am certain."

"Then I will go with you," said Eurydamos trying to comfort him.

"And who would be here to attend your mother? And the estate? No, you must remain."

"But who will bear witness for you?" quizzed his son. "I shall go and tell them the words of truth which should be spoken, words others may not speak."

"And whose words are these?" asked his father with a wrinkled brow. "Theban words would sway not a soul amongst them. In fact, such a testimony may endanger its deliverer. You, my son, will remain here." He gripped Eurydamos, one hand each upon the crests of his shoulders, and held his son's eyes in his. "This you will promise me."

They embraced—not the quick and casual embrace that they had so often exchanged with no more thought than a *good day*—but an embrace to savor. Timagenides gently pushed free of his son, then called for Nestorides his servant, who had assembled his master's traveling kit and stood not far off waiting for a summons.

"Pray to Zeus, Dispenser of Justice. With his help I will return in time for the Thargelia," assured Timagenides as he swung up onto his horse. Nestorides slung the double basket over the rear quarters of the mount, then stood back, eyes in the dirt.

Words would not pass by the lips of Eurydamos; he walked beside his father's horse in silence, until they both arrived at the southern dipylon, or double gate. There waited two grim Spartans on horseback. Timagenides, still mounted, moved between them. He did not turn as he departed, but merely raised a hand in a wave to his son. Darkness soon swallowed him.

# CHAPTER 18

▼

In a few short weeks they trudged south to their home in Arkadia, passing the shrine at Eleusis, where they picked up the road to Megara. Half-a-day's ride further they came upon the rocky cliff, skewered with hundreds of arrows, fired in panic when the Persians were ambushed by the Megarians a few weeks prior. Traffic choked the road now, traffic of commerce—not of war. At each and every hamlet, town or city, the inhabitants treated them to the best of food and wine. Nikandros knew of only a handful of men who had ever been lavished with such attentions—the victors of the games at Olympia. He and his band of Tegeans were certainly no *athletes*, but their victory over the Persians had for this brief moment elevated them to these near divine honors.

In Korinth they dined with their brothers-in-arms from that city, and witnessed entertainments of poets and musicians. Even this city's famous hetairas—female companions—spared no affections. The formidable Isthmian Wall, the last bulwark against the invaders, became the haunt of little boys, playing at war and other games of pretense; not a warrior or workman could be seen near it now.

"Father," shouted Medios, his eyes growing with anticipation, "the bridge!" The boy pointed to the new bridge, it's planking still tawny and ungrayed by age. In the golden light of a full afternoon, the stream hardly appeared the ominous obstacle of that wild day. Medios ran down the path, tugging his mule behind. He paused at the foot of the bridge, then tested it with a ginger step. Assured, he bounded across, reaching the far bank in a snap. His heart fluttered as he stroked the syrinx flute that hung by a cord around his neck, then he whipped an arm back and forth above his head. "Much easier this time father."

Nikandros swept his vision from the tame stream ahead to the cloudless sky above, and every tree, rock, blossom, and blade of grass in between. He was truly home.

As they approached the pathway to the farm, the last bit of sun withdrew below the trees; the sky in the west still glowed warm, but everything around was steeped in shadow. Like countless days before, the gate creaked when he swung it, and the same broken shutter winked at him as he shuffled toward the farmhouse door. Now his two sons passed by him, anxious to immerse themselves in the long-sought comfort of their home and the company of their grandfather. The door cracked open a bit; a head bobbed out—just a dark outline in the lost light of dusk—then Pankratios slipped out into the pathway to greet them. The two boys grinned hugely at the sight of him, then rushed ahead. Nikandros slowed a bit at seeing the reunion, to allow this reacquainting to continue undisturbed.

Unexpectedly his eyes were drawn to the gaping doorway of the house, for another head peered out, but only for a moment. The head retreated. He continued on past his boys, where they huddled in a single embrace around their grandfather, smothering him in stories of their adventure. "Where is Selagos?" asked Pankratios as he passed by. Nikandros paused, simply shook his head then continued down the path. He crossed the threshold and into the dim lamplight of the cottage. There just inside the doorway, statue-like, hovered Niobe. He smiled. She looked down at the dirt floor.

"Are you cross that I am here?" she asked in a hushed voice. Still she would not look at him.

"Why no. You are so very dear to the boys," he answered. Beyond her, sleeping upon a pile of fleece near the hearth was his son Alketes.

"And was he trouble to you Niobe?" asked Nikandros, as if he had just returned from a day in the fields.

"Trouble? Certainly not. The boy is precious." Now she lifted her face, it hidden by the wispy fabric of her veil. Her eyes glistened. She convulsed into sobs.

Nikandros gently lifted Niobe's chin, searching out her eyes from behind the veil, then stepped closer, wrapping her in his arms. He felt every shudder of her body. "Why do you cry so?"

She reached up with a hand, trying to brush away the tears that glistened upon her cheeks, but it did little good; her eyes welled up anew. "I cry for you dear Nikandros," she said sniffling. "The gods have delivered you, and answered my prayers.

*        *        *        *

*The boy tilted his head away from the writing table and toward the man sitting in the chair by the hearth. "Is that all, master Herodotus?"*

*"Of this tale—why yes it is," he stated leaning back, as if to view the ceiling of the place, but truly just to gather his thoughts. "Should there be more, Kleandros?"*

*"I should like to hear of Timagenides," he said, reaching for the triple spouted oil lamp that sat upon the shelf over the hearth. Darkness had snuffed out the last light of day; the boy fired the lamps, brightening the room and releasing the fragrance of the heated oil. "And I should like to hear of Myronides the Athenian. But mostly, I am curious as to the fate of the Spartan Amnestos." Now he sat again, eyes locked upon his master.*

*"The tale of the Theban Timagenides I can recount to you, for it is a tale that does indeed end." He paused, rubbed his silver-flecked beard, then continued. "He, along with the other leaders of his city, save the man Attiginos, rode to Korinth to stand before the tribunal of the allies."*

*"What of Attiginos, master Herodotus?"*

*"In a most perfidious fashion the man slipped out his city, avoiding Spartan patrols, and made his way to Asia and his master Xerxes."*

*A bit of wine was what he needed now to coax the words from him. The cup was full and within easy reach. He did not delay long. "Bravely, Timagenides testified. He told of the plight of Thebes, and how impossible it would have been for their city to defy Xerxes. This sensible argument moved not one of the allies. He, with his other countrymen, was executed—choked by a knotted rope."*

*Kleandros hung his head for a moment in thought, then he looked again to Herodotus. "The Athenian. What of him?"*

*"Myronides did not travel on to Korinth with the officers of Athens. He cared not for the trial of the Thebans and others that had been rounded up by the victors. He cared not for the presentation of prizes of valor. He went about rebuilding his home. And when he was done with that, superintended the reconstruction of the High City and its temples. He and his wife led a long life together."*

*"And what of the Spartan youth? What of Amnestos?" As he spoke, they heard the groan of dry dirt beneath sandaled feet. Through the window, the single one that looked out onto the street, he saw the figure of a man pass. The footfalls ceased, followed by a rapping upon the door.*

*"Enter," beckoned Herodotus.*

*The latch rattled a bit. The rough-planked door squealed on its hinge pins. Through the portal stepped a tall man, wrapped in a scarlet triboun—that long, plain cloak so out of favor with young men, hardly seen and even less appreciated. Silver hair fell to his shoulders in braids, matching the color of his close cropped beard. Kleandros ran to the stranger and slipped a chair behind him. He lowered himself into its embrace, motioning for the boy to sit also.*

*"This journey is more difficult each year," sighed the man. "I fear this will be my last."*

*"I too will not return here. In three days time I will sail for Thurii, to settle on the estate of a friend. And to finish my work," said Herodotus. Suddenly he turned to the boy. "Wine Kleandros. Fetch our guest some wine."*

*The boy jumped to his feet, reaching for the mostly empty pitcher that sat on the table, and poured what was left into a waiting cup. The old man smiled and accepted it from Kleandros. He sipped it slowly. He smiled again.*

*"How many years have you come here?" asked Herodotus of his guest.*

*The man slid his empty cup with extraordinary care back to the table. "Forty years. And always at this very season."*

*"Do you visit friends here abouts?" asked the boy.*

*Both the men restrained their smiles at his words. "Yes I do have friends nearby. The dearest a man could hope for."*

*"I might know of them sir," said Kleandros, "for I have lived here in Plataia all my life. May I ask their names?"*

*The visitor turned to Herodotus with a questioning look. He nodded in reply. "These men, penultimate in valor," continued their guest, "I knew by these names: Kallikrates, Posidonios and Amompharetos."*

*These words stole the breath from the boy as his thoughts became reacquainted with their story. He stared at the man.*

*"Well good friend I must beg your leave to be once more with them," he said rising slowly from the chair. He shrugged his shoulders to settle his long cloak upon them, then pulled it tight across his chest. Kleandros stood and unlatched the door, swinging it open for their departing guest. The old man dipped his head to clear the doorframe, then paused mid way out and turned, extending a hand to the boy. "Take good care of my friend." With those words he slipped out into the gathering night.*

*"Who was he, master Herodotus?" asked Kleandros as he slid the bolt across the door.*

*Herodotus smiled.*

# Glossary

*Agoge*—The Spartan system of male education, beginning at age seven and ending at eighteen when military service commenced.

*Aspis*—a shield.

*Akinakes*—Persian short sword or dagger.

*Athletes*—a champion of athletic games.

*Bouleterion*—council house of the city.

*Chiton*—commonly worn tunic comprised of two rectangles of cloth sewn together.

*Ephor*—one of the five magistrates of Sparta elected annually.

*Exomis*—loose fitting tunic commonly worn with one shoulder dropped to free movement

*Gerousia*—Spartan council of twenty-eight, comprised of men over the age of sixty. Each served for life.

*Hazarabam*—Persian regiment of one-thousand.

*Hebontes*—a Spartiate male between twenty and thirty years old.

*Helots*—serfs conquered by Sparta and tied to the land. They were required to turn over a portion of their crops to a Spartan master and could neither be bought nor sold.

*Himation*—long cloak.

*Hoplites*—heavy infantrymen of ancient Greece.

*Hoplon*—bowl-like shield employed by *hoplites*.

*Kopis*—a thick pointed sword with a curved blade.

*Kothon*—a tankard or large cup.

*Kylix*—a shallow cup, usually on a stem, used for drinking wine.

*Lochus*—in the Athenian army a company of one-hundred men. In Sparta a regiment of nearly one thousand men.

*Prodikos*—Spartan regent.

*Spartiate*—a male citizen of Sparta.

*Strategos*—a general. In Athens one of the annually elected ten generals representing each tribe.

Taxi—in the Athenian army a division of up to 3,000 hoplites.

*Triboun*—a Spartan military cloak.

*Trireme*—a warship equipped with a ram and propelled by three banks of oars on each side.